THE JOURNEY

The Journey
by
Paul Anthony

The right of Paul Anthony to be identified as the author of this work has been asserted by him in accordance with the Copyright, Designs and Patents Act of 1988

~

First Published 2022

Copyright © Paul Anthony

All Rights Reserved.

Cover Image © Paul Anthony Associates

Published by

Paul Anthony Associates UK

http://paul-anthony.org/

By the same author

~

In the 'Boyd' Crime Thrillers…

The Fragile Peace

Bushfire

The Legacy of the Ninth

Bell, Book, and Candle

Threat Level One

White Eagle

The Sultan and the Crucifix

Thimbles

The Journey

*

In the 'Davies King' Crime Thrillers…

The Conchenta Conundrum.

Moonlight Shadows

Behead the Serpent

Breakwater

Harbour Lights

~

By the same author

~

In the Thriller and Suspense Thrillers…

Nebulous

Septimus

Sapphire

*

In Autobiography, true crime, and nonfiction…

Authorship Demystified

Strike! Strike! Strike!

Scougal

*

In Poetry and Anthologies…

Sunset

Scribbles with Chocolate

Uncuffed

Coptales

Chiari Warriors

*

In Children's book (with Meg Johnston) …

Monsters, Gnomes and Fairies (In My Garden)

~

To Margaret - Thank you, for never doubting me.
To Paul, Barrie and Vikki - You only get one chance at life. Live it well, live it in peace, and live it with love for one another.
To my special friends - Thank you, you are special.

~

With thanks to Margaret Scougal, Pauline Livingstone and Patricia Henderson for editing and advising on my works over many years.

~

... Paul Anthony

Prologue

~

Dense groves and floating mats of vegetation had fashioned the swamp over the years. Now the bog was comprised of reeds, papyrus, and cattail that dominated the waterlogged terrain. Long tapering leaves from the audacious rhizomes were smooth and velvety to the touch and held no fear of the environment in which they flourished. Their spongy presence merely added to the damp treacherous character of the swamp. But then the wetlands changed as part of their daily routine. Warmer air above the neighbouring lake gradually encountered the cool surface over the land and the mist was born once more.

The ghostlike vision rose from the depths of the swamp and gradually spread its restless blind tentacles to create a silent white blanket. The spirit of the mist wanted no more than to govern the downtrodden everglades in which it had been born. The spectre was a dull grey colour, to begin with, but once the haze was established a silvery-white mist fully emerged from the swamp and concealed the precarious pathways that crisscrossed the savannah.

Crocodiles and hippopotamus that inhabited the waters scuttled to their lagoons and hidden creeks where they watched and waited for the unexpected. Even the elephants abandoned the area and made for the high ground where the earth was solid and firm. It was such a dangerous forbidding place.

Noiseless and bloodless, the phantom of the mist boasted no discernible shape over the field of vision that the men might enjoy. The mist crawled over the disputed land that countless tribes, cultures, religions, nations, and people had fought for over the centuries. Now the land that had witnessed so many squabbles, skirmishes, and wars, was no more than an evil mysterious swamp that encircled the lake that had once been the focal point of life in the area. The lake was dying now, retreating into itself for no apparent reason other than a plethora of explanations offered by the scientific community.

The swamp conspired with the mist. Such a menace presented a daunting experience for the unsuspecting explorer. Rising to the height of a man, the mist firstly crawled, covered, and eventually concealed the secret pathway from the village where the men came from.

They could not be seen as they walked the secret path to ply their evil trade. The mist veiled their presence and screened them from the sight of others. The trail was known only to the men from the swamp. It was why so many of them were unknown, feared, and of notorious infamy. They were neither legend nor myth, just a terrifying reality. The men were the emperors of the wetlands, kings of all they surveyed, and formidable masters of their own making. Yet despite their untold wealth, the enigma of their being, and the pure insolence of their beliefs, they walked through the mirage-like body of mist carrying their weapons of war.

The swamp was their land, their home, their secret headquarters in the land known as Chad.

For Malik, and the men who followed him, there were riches for the taking. Such fearsome warriors did not bestow peace upon their fellow man. They were not givers of love or lovers of women; they were the breath of death and the takers of life.

They moved inland towards Sangaria. The men from the swamp were on the loose once more.

The journey had begun.

~

Chapter One

~

The Schoolyard
Recently

The hoop revolved ahead of the twelve-year-old boy, but it wobbled every which way it wanted. Rolling all over the place in an errant fashion, it surely had a mind of its own. Try as he might, Hassan couldn't control the direction of the hoop with his scolding stick. Kayode, the slightly older youth next to him, was more concentrated. His hoop was upright in its bearing and as straight as a die in its course.

The two youngsters glanced at each other as they chased the hoops around the schoolyard doing their best to beat the other and keep the hoop upright until the finishing line. The faster the scolding, the more upright the hoop. The race was on.

It wasn't just a game. It was comparable to a medieval joust between two of the oldest children at the village school. It was all to play for and neither wanted to lose. The bragging rights were high.

There was laughter when a young girl tried to join in, but her hoop travelled a yard and then collapsed completely when, rather than roll the hoop, she battered it with a stick and sent it off course.

'It's all in the stick, Yetunde,' shouted the teacher who was tall and slender, perhaps in her thirties. 'Push the top of the hoop with the stick and roll it a little faster each time. Don't beat it. Tease it. Watch your brothers Hassan and Kayode. They'll show you how to do it, Yetunde.'

The class were fascinated by the hoop and stick chase and didn't see the first army truck approaching the school. There was just one vehicle, to begin with, but within moments a convoy of old green Leyland army trucks appeared.

The teacher, Joanne, glanced over her shoulder, saw the convoy, and felt a trickle of ice rush down her spine. Her body went cold; her mind was invaded by fear.

Joanne shouted to the class, 'Okay! That's it for now. Inside, everyone. Inside!'

Hassan and Kayode ignored her and chased the hoops each occasionally scolding them with their sticks. The hoops rolled on and the youths chased them around the schoolyard happy in the day, carefree, and loving every moment of their young lives.

Yetunde watched her brothers, tried to follow suit and mimic them, but couldn't get the hang of the hoop and stick.

The headmaster emerged from the ramshackle wooden building that had served the community for the past ten years. In his mid-fifties with a paunch that had stood the test of time, Barnes stood at the entrance and said, 'What's wrong. It's early. They can still play out, Joanne.'

His colleague pointed to the convoy approaching the village school and said, 'Maybe they'll just drive on, Mr Barnes. I suggest we get the children inside just in case.'

'I agree,' came the reply as the headmaster's eyes studied the oncoming cavalcade and shouted, 'Children! Everyone inside now. Quickly now.'

The girls obeyed. The boys began to take notice, but Hassan and Kayode continued to chase their hoops. Some things were more important than the headmaster's words.

'Quickly now!' shouted Joanne. 'You heard the headmaster. Mr Barnes wants everyone inside as quickly as possible.' Joanne espied the army trucks heading towards the school and added, 'Now, please.'

Roy, the only other teacher at the school, emerged from the building and realised what was happening. The youngest of the teaching trio, he engaged his mobile phone and made a call. Whilst waiting for a reply, he announced, 'I told you this would come in handy one day. I'm calling the police.'

'They might even answer if we're lucky,' replied Joanne. 'You're one of the few who has a mobile phone in this Godforsaken country. Tell them to be quick, Roy.'

'If they come this way, I'll deal with them,' explained Barnes. The headmaster looked towards the army convoy and continued, 'It's my job. I'll speak to them. They'll understand me. I'll plead with them if I have to.'

'Will the ground defences hold?'

'I hope so,' voiced the headmaster

'Those fence posts and the wiring are all that stands between them and us. It's all we've got.'

The three teachers looked out across the schoolyard and gazed upon the double-strand fence that encircled the school.

'Fingers crossed,' remarked Barnes. 'Hopefully, it will put them off.'

Amongst the convoy, a handful of anti-aircraft and anti-tank guns stood proud from the rear platforms of some of the present vehicles.

'No! Please, no!' muttered Joanne as she watched the lead vehicle turn from the main road towards the school. 'Not here! No!'

The driver of the leading army wagon exchanged a dark toothy smile with the front seat passenger and then accelerated hard towards the school. There was raucous laughter in the wagon when the vehicle bulldozed its way through the first wire security fence. The padlock and chain exploded with the force of the wagon as it sped through the locked gate and tore the fencing down in the process. Undeterred, the wagon hurtled through the second strand. There was a huge flurry of dust and dirt when the nearest fence pole was uprooted, snagged on the rear bumper, and trailed behind the lead vehicle. A trail of fence posts bounced on the ground in wild abandoned ferocity as the truck sped on.

'Attack! Attack! Attack!' screamed the wild-eyed driver as the Leyland bounced over the uneven ground.

More fence posts were uprooted in the surge forward.

The vehicle pulverised the weak defences and dragged a line of security fencing that bobbed uncontrollably behind the vehicle as if it were a reptilian monster intent on a journey of unforgiving evil. An engine roared and gunshots sounded as the convoy of trucks burst into the schoolyard and headed directly towards the headteacher who stood in front of a dozen schoolchildren.

'Run!' he yelled. 'Run, children! Run as quickly as you can!'

The passenger door of the army truck opened, and a huge muscular man manoeuvred onto the footplate and fired a salvo of shots into the air before jumping onto the ground and pointing the weapon at the teachers.

'Tell the children to stop running,' ordered the gunman. 'Now!'

Another vehicle broke the fence line, destroyed the thin barrier that offered the only protection available, and then came to a standstill next to the first wagon. Within minutes, a fleet of old army wagons and a dozen flat back pickups mounted with machine-gun posts on the rear platforms overwhelmed the area.

Men dressed in full-face shemagh headscarves, khaki trousers, dark singlets, and desert boots jumped from the vehicles and began rounding up the schoolchildren.

Hassan and Kayode dropped their scolding sticks, abandoned their hoops, and ran from the yard chased by a tall lean man armed with a machete. They sprinted towards the lake with the invader lashing out at a hoop with his blade as he screamed at them to stop. Drawing a handgun from his holster, he pulled the trigger and fired.

His bullet flew from the muzzle of the gun and pierced the air between the two boys before slamming into a tree and splitting the low branches.

'Stop!' the shooter yelled.

Frozen to the ground, scared stiff, the boys did as they were told as the blade of the machete smashed another hoop into a dozen pieces.

'Come back here,' yelled the gunman.

It was all over within ten minutes.

The schoolchildren were captured and loaded into the army trucks. Men with machetes, bandoliers, AK47s, sidearms, and knives dominated the schoolyard and herded the children towards the vehicles.

The leader forced the teachers to the ground and smiled when they knelt before him. Opening his headscarf to reveal himself, he said, 'Remember my face.' Then he walked around the trio, bent low and stared menacingly into their eyes and pointed at his face before announcing, 'You are spared! You are only spared because we want thirty million Naira. Do you know what Naira is? Money! That is the ransom you will pay. They will want to know who I am and who we are. I show you my face so that you know who I am and who we are. Do you understand?'

'Yes! Yes!' replied Barnes. 'I know your face from the government television channel. But what is your name, sir? I'm sorry, so sorry, but I don't know your name.'

'Malik!' replied the leader who boasted stubble on his chin and a thick black moustache on his upper lip. 'I am Malik, the leader of Boko Haram!'

'But they are children,' pleaded Joanne. 'You've no right to kidnap them. Let them go.'

Slicing through the air, Malik's machete decapitated her in an instant. Joanne's head fell to the ground, rolled in the dust, and came to a bloody rest at the killer's feet. Malik kicked her head as if it were a football and watched it bounce towards the school entrance.

'Don't tell me what my rights are in my land,' snarled Malik.

There was a noise from Roy: an electronic disturbance that emanated from the breast pocket of his shirt. His phone was ringing. He placed his hand over the phone to kill the noise.

Malik ordered, 'Now! The phone! Hand it over.'

Shaking his head, Roy took a nervous backward step and withdrew the phone from his pocket. He lifted the phone to his mouth to speak.

Withdrawing a handgun from his holster, Malik shot Roy twice in the chest and watched as the teacher's body catapulted harshly into the school building.

Malik turned to a colleague and ordered, 'Bring me the phone.'

Gurgling, Roy twitched and extended a hand towards his phone. His fingers reached the device, but Malik pulled the trigger again and shot the teacher in the head. Blood from the wounds trickled from Roy's body and soiled the dry wooden platform upon which he took his last breath.

The children screamed when they heard the gunshots and realised what had happened. It was a day they would never forget.

A follower handed the phone to Malik who examined it and said, 'The police! Three calls. Looks like he got through in the end. They were ringing him back.' Dropping the phone to the floor, Malik ground his heel into the mobile and muttered, 'Silly man! Infidel!'

Turning to the headteacher, the brutal assassin voiced, 'You are spared. Your female friend is not. Her problem. Not mine. She was not invited to speak. Thirty million Naira cash is the ransom the government will pay. Understood?'

Barnes nodded but screamed when Malik pulled on his hair and forced his neck back. Then he felt the cold steel of the machete gently touch the skin near his throat.

'Understood, Mr Headmaster?' bellowed the killer. 'Yes! I know who you are. Do you understand me, Mr Barnes?'

'Yes! Yes! Don't kill me,' pleaded Barnes.

'How much did I say?'

'Thirty million Naira! Cash!'

'Good!' grinned Malik. 'They will deliver the money in cash to the crossroads near the lake at twilight in three days. That will give them time to gather the cash together. They will know where to drop the money and they will know what will happen if they try any trickery. You live for a reason, Mr Barnes! Don't forget otherwise your precious schoolchildren will get this.' He pointed his machete at the children being loaded into the trucks and repeated, 'And you wouldn't want those children hurt, would you?'

A scream of joy invaded the atmosphere when one of the thugs began shooting wildly into the air from the rear of a desert-ready combat vehicle.

'Burn it!' ordered Malik as he threw Barnes to one side and stepped back. 'Not him. He needs to be able to talk.'

Four men rushed forward, emptied kegs of fuel onto the school's wooden porch, repeated the action inside, and then ignited the liquid with an old cigarette lighter. The flames immediately engulfed the dry wood and rippled through the school.

Within minutes, the building was ablaze.

'Let's go,' ordered Malik. 'The swamps! Take them to the swamps!'

A roar of engines was followed by the sound of gunfire and the cold bitter hollering of a gang who came to conquer, came to kidnap, came to kill, and then vanished into the countryside with their trophies captured and unable to escape. Forming a circle, they drove around the schoolyard, fired into the flaming school, and crushed the remains of two more wooden hoops as they abandoned the area and sped towards the swamps.

In the back of a wagon, children like Hassan, Kayode and Yetunde, huddled together, wept, and worried about the future.

The atmosphere was alive with crackling burning wood, glowing embers climbing into the sky, and the pungent smell of sulphurous cordite. The country was a war zone and a battle had been won and fought by the strong who defeated the weak.

In a city in the north of England, the sky portrayed a dark bundle of clouds as night pushed day into another uncertain frenzy and the atmosphere provided fresh air and a quiet calm that, in comparison to a faraway schoolyard, was the lifeblood of the nation.

It was a balmy relaxed summer's evening in Carlisle, Cumbria. The moonlight reflected on each of the three rivers upon which the city stood. The Petteril and Caldew flowed into the Eden which meandered into the Solway Firth and the Irish Sea. The country enjoyed a topography and a culture that was thousands of miles away from a schoolyard in Africa now littered with dead bodies and the remnants of a burnout village school.

A detective strolled in the shadows of Carlisle Castle near a car park in Devonshire walk. His name was William Miller Boyd, and he was the leader of the nation's Special Crime Unit. He cut a handsome figure who was tall, athletic, and with a broad and a finely-honed body to match. Married to Meg: a Cumbrian nurse, the detective sported a square chin and deep blue eyes and was the father of their two children. He had begun his police career on the streets of Carlisle. Now he was the Commander of the nation's most elite policing unit.

Running adjacent to the pathway, the River Caldew flowed towards its nearby confluence with the River Eden. A moonlit sky cast a myriad of shadows on the water.

Boyd engaged his throat mic and radioed, 'I'm at Bravo turning to Charlie.'

'All secure,' came the reply from Boyd's second in command, Detective Inspector Anthea Adams. Married to Raphael, a senior Portuguese detective, Anthea was more than just Boyd's driver and surveillance partner. She'd kept her maiden name and had proved the lifeblood of the department. A crack shot, Anthea's auburn hair flowed to her shoulders and no further. An intrepid member of the unit, she did not suffer fools gladly and occasionally spoke her mind. Intelligent and extremely competent, Anthea looked forward to a weekend flight to Lisbon whenever she could. Tonight, as it approached midnight, she was half a mile away looking through high-powered night binoculars when she radioed, 'No sign of your man but the road is clear.'

'I have that,' from Boyd.

'Ricky!' radioed Anthea. 'I have car headlights towards you.'

Detective Constable Ricky French was in his late twenties. An ex Flying Squad officer, he had an abundance of informants in London's criminal underworld and was studying for a master's degree in criminology in his spare time. He was also the 'gizmo' man skilled in technological surveillance. Clicking the radio, he reported, 'Ricky has that. Wait one.'

Anthea bit her lip.

Boyd strolled along Devonshire Walk whilst a car rolled quietly into a car park near the tennis courts on Dacre Road. The driver got out of the vehicle, locked the car, and turned the collar of his jacket up to fend off a cold January breeze. Then he placed a baseball cap on his head and checked his mobile phone. Glancing around, he stood for a moment watching the car park entrance before moving off and adopting the footpath that would take him towards Devonshire Walk.

'I have the contact on the plot,' radioed Ricky. 'Wait one. I'm checking for company.'

Ricky watched the traffic journey down the nearby link road, studied the car park entrance and adjacent footpath, and then declared, 'Your man is alone. No followers. All clear.'

'Copied,' from Anthea on the radio net. 'Stand by for drone coverage report.'

Boyd clicked his communication device twice as an acknowledgement.

A thousand feet above the area in question, a drone surveillance device, the size of a crow, beamed a signal to Anthea who confirmed, 'Drone coverage shows no anomalies. Proceed with caution. All clear.'

'I have that,' from Boyd. 'Let the surveillance log show that safety is confirmed. I am making the meet.'

'Timed and entered,' from Anthea. 'Proceed! Caution advised.'

'I have that,' replied Boyd.

Crossing the road, the detective walked towards the contact that was approaching him. On reaching a long avenue of trees, Boyd stopped and leaned against a chestnut tree. The branches were low and the leaves drooped towards the ground to provide extra cover if the men were to be interrupted.

The contact appeared from the darkness and Boyd recognised him immediately having known him from his early days as a detective in the city.

'You are well, my friend?' queried Boyd.

'Aye, and you,' came the reply from Boyd's informant.

'I'm good, Olly,' replied Boyd shaking hands. 'Any problems?'

'They've no idea you're onto them if that's what you mean. I've been careful. Listened like you said, kept my mouth shut, and done as I was told.'

'Is it still going down?' asked Boyd.

'Aye! They're full of it, that's for sure. They've done a cold run three times. They know what to do.'

'Three times? We missed them all. Are you sure?'

'You asked me to tell you the truth. How you handle it is your problem. That's what I heard.'

'Cheers! When will it be?' queried Boyd.

'Soon!' replied Olly. 'I'll tell you more when I know what day. It's close so I reckon it will be this week.'

'Whereabouts?'

'A bank in the middle of Penrith. Near the Monument, whatever that is. I don't know. I've never been to Penrith.'

'Not to worry. I know it. How many of them, Olly?'

'Three in one car.'

'Does that include the driver?'

'One driver and two on the job,' explained Olly. 'The wheels have been used before. I don't know the make of the car or anything about it because it's kept under wraps somewhere in the city. It's only brought out for special occasions.'

'Like birthdays, bank holidays and Christmas,' quipped Boyd.

'Something like that.'

'And a bank robbery is a special occasion,' suggested Boyd.

'Looks like it,' confirmed Olly. 'I think the motor is on false plates. It's nicked from somewhere. That's all I know. Look, boss, it's the team you wanted, isn't it? They've been bang at it for a year or two now. So what about my money? I'm a bit short at the moment. You know how it is.'

'I do,' nodded Boyd. 'Here, take this to be going on with.' He handed Olly a couple of twenty-pound notes and said, 'That's all I've got on me but I won't let you down if it all goes down as you say. You'll get paid properly when the job is done.'

Olly's bundled fist gathered the notes and pocketed them.

'One thing,' continued Boyd. 'You mentioned a couple of weeks ago they'd be armed. Is that still the case?'

'Aye! Sawn-off shotguns like last time.'

'Knowing them,' questioned Boyd. 'Would you reckon they are the type of people who would pull the trigger and kill?'

A set of car headlights appeared at the end of the road and caused the two men to step further behind the large chestnut tree.

'Sudden entry from Caldewgate west,' radioed Anthea. 'Stand by. Unidentified vehicle approaching the area. Caution advised.'

Boyd heard the message and replied with two clicks on his radio transmitter.

Olly watched the headlights disappear in a different direction before replying, 'No doubt in my mind, boss. At the very least the guns will be loaded and they'll fire them. Don't get in the way. That gang know how to shoot. Believe me. They're determined and won't give two hoots for anyone. They just want money like the rest of us. Your problem is they choose to use violence to get it. Look, tell me the truth, boss. Are you sitting on them?'

'What do you mean?'

'Watching them, boss. You know. Surveillance?'

'Why do you ask?'

'Because if you're watching them, you're watching me and I don't want either my name, my photo or anything about me mentioned in those books that you people keep. Logs or whatever.'

'You're safe, Olly. Don't worry.'

'So, you're not watching them then?'

'I didn't say that,' answered Boyd raising his voice slightly. 'I said you're safe. Leave it at that, Olly. Trust me.'

'Do I have a choice?'

'Yes, you do but I read you loud and clear, Olly. You've said from the start you're not involved so I'll take your word for it. Back off, pal. I've looked after you for a long time now. Don't push me on this one. You do what you do, and I'll do what I'll do. Just like in the old times. Okay?'

Olly considered, wondered, and then nodded in agreement.

'Main players?' queried Boyd.

'The three you wanted,' replied Olly. 'Two brickies and a scaffolder who've made more from crime than you'd imagine. No more. I've been here too long. Good luck. I'll ring you on the confidential line if I hear anything more.'

'Stay safe!' replied Boyd.

Olly turned and walked directly to his car as Anthea checked her night binoculars and the drone facility before radioing, 'Natural movements. No assertive threat. Move to the closure of the meeting.'

Boyd stood for a minute or more and watched Olly walk away. Based upon his protocols for secure meetings relevant to the unit he was responsible for, Boyd replied, 'I have that. Withdrawal in progress.'

Strolling back to his car, Boyd contemplated how difficult it was to address operational security amidst the desire to accrue intelligence. I have more questions to ask, he thought, but he's gone because he's frightened of being caught out in the open with me.

Such were the procedures for officers dealing with such people and the criminal gangs they were part of.

~

Chapter Two

~

The Straits of Dover
The South Coast of England
Recently

Zak heaved the oar towards his chest and felt a surge of water rush towards the stern of the vessel from the blade of his paddle. The traveller's bruised and battered knees bent when he reached forward and repeated the performance. Sweat oozed from his scrawny body as he dragged the oar through the water again and convinced himself that it would be over soon. His shoulder muscles bulged, and he knew his legs would ache for eternity. Yet again he pulled the oar, closed his eyes, and felt the broadness of the blade power through the water.

Exhausted, his session done, Zak untied the safety rope from his ankle and resigned his position to the next man before collapsing in the middle of the dinghy. His lungs cried out for oxygen and his hands were swollen from gripping the aluminium oar. He hoisted a thin canvas bag across his shoulders and crawled to the side of the dinghy. Devouring a lungful of oxygen, he clung to a safety rope and ducked as a wild unwanted wave ravaged the air and soaked everyone onboard.

Bucking like an untamed bronco, the vessel rose high towards the sky, reached the pinnacle of its journey, and then plunged into the watery depths with a terrifying splash.

Any thoughts that the stretch of water dividing France and England offered no challenge to the ten adventurers were quickly set aside when their dinghy began to roll up and down with the waves. The further the vessel journeyed across the Channel, the more unruly the Straits of Dover became. Trying to negotiate the waterway that stretched from Brest to

Amsterdam was neither a passage of escape nor a voyage to freedom. It was the biggest test they had ever faced and to contemplate defeat was beyond their understanding of the difficulties that awaited them.

From the bow of the dinghy, the white cliffs of Dover were visible in the distance through the thin mist that hugged the surface of the water. Countless boats and ships carved their way through the Dover Straits. Some travelled the full length of the Channel; others journeyed only the twenty-one miles between Dover and Calais. Wherever these seafaring vessels travelled to or from, they all had one thing in common and that was the wake they caused.

The dinghy began to swell up and down in the water when it was caught in the wake of one of the larger vessels that ploughed northwards through the Straits on its way to the Dutch coast.

'The white cliffs!' yelled Kosso when the mist finally lifted. Pointing at the coast, he shouted 'I see them! Make for the white cliffs, Chad. We're here, Youssef. I see the white cliffs.'

'They're grey,' came the response.

'Maybe! But we're here,' shouted Kosso as his hand worked the tiller of an outboard motor that angled the bow towards Dover. Piloting the vessel, Kosso engaged full speed whilst the oarsmen used every ounce of energy they possessed to paddle as hard as they could. Yet top speed from the weak outboard resulted in a cough and a splutter from an incompetent engine designed for paddle boats, not ocean-going vessels.

Kosso muttered a prayer pleading for Allah to combine body power and horsepower to trounce the storm.

The dinghy bounced over the waves whilst unwelcome spray showered the vessel, plunged to the deck, and sloshed around at their feet. The dinghy began to fill with water. Just a trickle to begin with but as it pitched and rolled the water level gradually rose to their ankles.

Fear spread across the faces of those determined to make Dover as the white cliffs slyly beckoned the adventurers forward.

There were ten men in an inflatable boat made for the comfort and safety of five. Yet the dinghy was lightweight, compact, and easy to assemble and inflate. They'd set off from the French coast near Dunkirk having arranged the journey with Louis Martin: the top man in human trafficking in the region. His organisation had charged each passenger five thousand pounds to cross the Channel. There was no requirement for passports or identity papers. Just hard cash upfront and nothing more.

'From the point you leave France, you are on your own,' he had revealed.

Louis provided the men with an inflatable dinghy, four oars to fit in the rowlocks, a second-hand outboard motor, and instructions that would ensure the vessel adopted a current in the Channel that would naturally take them towards Dover. The plan was to land somewhere in the vicinity of the town and make their way inland.

'Simple,' Louis Martin had said. 'Sit in the dinghy and when the white cliffs come into view paddle towards them. The current will take you there naturally without any need for seamanship.'

It was a different story today when the sea opened its jaws wide and threatened to consume the offering made. Now it was time to negotiate their way through the seafaring traffic that dominated the watercourse. The boating holiday was over. A storm was brewing and a nasty wind emanating from the headland at Cherbourg Peninsula in France had decided to threaten proceedings when it whistled at speed through the Channel.

Made of high-quality materials, the dinghy was sturdy and durable, as well as resistant to saltwater and sunlight. When dry, the inflatable floor boasted a completely even surface which added to its stability on the water and was a boon for the self-appointed Captain Kosso. The four aluminium oars were ergonomically designed with two anchored in locks on the port side and two similarly secured on the starboard side of the vessel. There were four sturdy inflatable seats for the rowers and a fifth for the outboard motor operator. Such a vessel would normally cost the buyer less than three hundred pounds. Louis Martin was making a fortune without breaking a sweat, and that was only one of many services he was the master of. Those not seated in the dinghy sprawled on the deck with their bags and scant belongings. No one had a suitcase or a holdall. Only plastic bags or haversacks were allowed. There was no room for luxuries. The Channel-Crossers carried what they could and no more.

Dressed in casual wear, ranging from shorts to jeans and woolly jumpers to hoodies, those not rowing clung to the double strand of rope that ran the entire length around the interior of the inflatable. A similar strand of rope ran around the exterior of the vessel. It was a lifeline that might represent the difference between life and death when the sea turned rough. To let go of the rope when the stakes were high and the sea was at its most evil meant certain death. To hold onto the rope at the worst of times might save a life. The situation was simple. If you want to live, hold the rope tight. Otherwise, you may drown.

Kosso occupied a seated position at the stern where he governed the outboard motor and oversaw every movement of those before him.

'Harder!' shouted Kosso. 'Paddle faster! There's another one coming our way.'

Chad and Youssef occupied the front rowing area of the dinghy. In their mid-twenties, they took the strain as two others behind them joined in working the oars as if their life depended on it. And it did.

Kosso saw a huge ocean-going oil tanker bearing down on the tiny dinghy. He gripped the tiller tight and glanced at the beast approaching them.

'No!' screamed a passenger on the deck of the dinghy when the oil tanker's bow created a tremendous wave. The dinghy rode the wave, reached the pinnacle, and then crashed into the depths as the tanker closed with the travellers.

Then he was gone.

'Man overboard!' someone screamed.

Kosso glimpsed an arm protruding from the white frothing mass of ocean that the tanker had caused. Then the arm was gone and seen no more.

'Adamas! My brother!' yelled another passenger lying in the centre of the dinghy. The man stood up and reached out to his brother. He let go of the safety rope, took a step forward on the decking, and lost his balance when the wind took him.

The dinghy climbed with the surf, discharged the passenger into the sea, and lunged downwards once more.

'Hold tight!' screamed Kosso. 'Don't let go of the rope.'

Now they were eight.

Zak bundled himself close to the bow. Wearing shorts, a tee-shirt, and trainers, he tied part of the poncho he was wearing to the safety rope. He pulled tight and realised he'd made an unyielding connection. If thrown overboard at least he would have a line connecting him to the dinghy.

The vessel headed skywards again as the oil tanker ploughed through the Channel pushing the wake out, from both the bow and the stern, increasing the danger, completely unaware of the tiny dinghy beneath it.

'Down, Zak!' shouted Kosso. 'Lie down!'

'You lie down, Kosso,' replied Zak. 'Watch out!'

Whether the tanker changed course, or the dinghy lost momentum was hard to tell, but the dinghy bucked skywards and shook out the passengers as if they were peas in a pod.

An oar was dropped, loosened itself from the rowlock, and flew into Kosso's face knocking him into the sea. Chad followed suit as the forces of nature overwhelmed the travellers and claimed Youssef.

At the height of the mayhem, the dinghy emptied itself and then returned to the sea upside down with only a few hands held tight to the exterior of the dinghy. The stern of the tanker caught the aftermath of the dinghy's journey, created a mountain of high-speed bubbling froth in its wake, and rolled the dinghy over.

A plastic bag raced into the air followed by an anorak and someone's bobble hat as the body of the tanker drew away from the scene of slaughter and continued its journey towards Brest.

Only an upside-down dinghy floated quietly on the surface. With the danger passed, it pitched and rolled in the water but there was no crew trying to power the outboard motor and no hands rowing as fast as they could.

They were only young men. There were no women or children amongst them. The white cliffs of Dover stood out proud as the current caught the dinghy and drew it towards the coast. Yet the vessel would never make Dover. The current would take it further south miles away from the planned landing point.

There was no one to save them, no one to see them, no one to hear them in their final moments. They were just travellers who didn't make it.

The empty dinghy floated south away from the main ferry routes and the Brest-Amsterdam traffic. Only an upturned dinghy remained as a marker for their watery grave.

Then a hand appeared from beneath the dinghy and reached across the keel, across the bottom of the overturned vessel.

The tail of a poncho appeared. It was tied to the structure of the dinghy. Beneath the dinghy, there was a gap, a space between the upturned vessel and the surface of the water where a layer of oxygen existed.

'Zak!' screamed the survivor. 'It's me, Zak! Where is everyone?'

Only the wind replied with an evil conspiratorial whisper when it whipped across Zak's face and blew spray into his eyes.

'Kosso! Chad! Youssef!' yelled Zak wiping his face. 'Where are you? It's Zak. I'm here. I'm at the dinghy. Where are you?'

Glancing over his shoulder, he saw the tanker steaming south. A glimpse to the north revealed another huge ship heading his way. Zak untied himself from the safety rope as the gale moved on and began to subside. Gasping for breath, looking around for survivors, he wondered if he were alone in the rolling waters that had defeated his fellow adventurers. He loosened the thin canvas bag he had carried with him from his home in Sangari, watched the current take the dinghy on a journey into the unknown, and swam towards the coast.

Above him, a colony of seagulls braced themselves against the breeze, hovered constantly, and conquered the thermals. It was as if they were watching over proceedings, squawking at the drowned men as they looked down on Zak swimming towards the coast.

The lone traveller wondered if they were vultures waiting for the ice-cold waters to take the latest offering to the depths of the Channel. Would he rise again, bloated and beyond resurrection, ready to be pecked and devoured by a bunch of hungry gulls that would eat anything presented to them on the surface of the water? They would swoop down, peck, taste, and either abandon or gather for a feast. His inner mind shuddered.

Zak struck out, swam strongly to begin with, but soon realised he was making little progress towards the shore. Deliberately, he ducked his head in the sea, shook himself loose, and kicked hard with his legs as he simultaneously switched on those powerful shoulders. The water was cold. It was freezing and he knew that he wasn't going to make it. The temperature was such that he had little time.

His life would be over soon. Zak would freeze to death before he drowned. At least, that's what they had told him at the camp in Calais.

But Louis Martin had said it was just the national media churning out rubbish. The waters were cool, chilled, and calm.

'There was no need to worry,' Louis had advised. 'It was only twenty-one miles on a millpond. Just relax. Don't believe what they tell you. *C'est très simple.*'

'I don't speak French,' Kosso, the leader, had replied.

'English?' queried Louis. 'It's very simple. Maybe Arabic for you. *Iinah sahl!* That's what the main man who sent you said. Okay?'

Kosso had nodded and moved on, inflated the dinghy, added the oars, fitted the outboard, and listened to the advice that had accompanied his actions little knowing they had been conned by a master craftsman of crooked enterprise. They didn't know it, but there was no such man as Louis Martin. It was a false name. A name that fitted many in France but not the man who had taken the cash and sent the men to their deaths.

Zak began to lose control. He flopped onto his back, looked towards the heavens above, and kicked his feet as quickly as he could. It reminded him of his younger days when he had been a child and his father had taught him to float on his back in Lake Chad. He tried to relax and think of his mother and father, but he felt himself sinking. It was as if his parents' arms were gathering him, pulling him downwards, taking him to a place he had never been before. His mind journeyed down a time tunnel of glorious memories that reminded him of the lake and Sangari. Ordinarily, a tear might have formed on his face before it dribbled down his cheek. But he had only a fleeting second or two to think back to his younger days. His time was nearly up. The clock was ticking and about to stop.

Mustering what strength he had left was akin to climbing a never-ending mountain. Yet he found the strength to kick out once more as he prayed for a miracle in the middle of nowhere and thousands of miles from home

Then it happened.

Zak lost control, felt an icy refrigerator encompass his physique, and weakened in the split second that dragged his body below the surface. He was drowning and had no answer to his predicament. He rolled over. Head down, Zak felt himself travelling in a bizarre spiralling fashion that saw his body begin to tumble whilst his mind went numb. He was gone, finished.

When his feet touched the bottom, Zak lifted his head. The miracle he had prayed for had happened. He forced his body upright. He was alive and although he was a hundred yards from the shore, he was upright in the water which was chest high. He took a step. Then another, and then lashed out with his arms thrashing and his legs kicking as he made for the shoreline and the last hundred yards he might ever endure.

At waist height, Zak took another breath. His chest was free. A tee-shirt clung to his frame and shrouded every bulging muscle he possessed. He took another step, and then another, and then began to run to the beach when he saw the water level drop to his thighs, and then his knees. Then he was paddling, and a beach became his target when the water reached his shins but no further.

Falling in the last few yards, Zak regained his feet and powered up the beach with the tide breaking on the sand and a dribble of water tickling his toes. He made the wet sand before meeting the dry sand and collapsing in a heap. His chest heaved up and down and his legs felt like iceboxes. The dry sand clung to his damp skin, matted his dark hair, and covered his lips. Forcing himself upright, he turned, glanced at the Channel, and saw the sun setting somewhere in the distance. Inside himself, he wanted to shout for Kosso, Youssef and Chad but instead, he took only a few steps back into the sea where he scanned the surface of the water. There was no one to be seen. Even the dinghy had disappeared. There was no oar floating on the surface, no canvas bag marking the spot, no clothes, and no drowned bodies floating in demise. He was truly alone.

Hands on hips, he stepped back and laughed before screaming, 'I'm alive. I'm alive.'

Then Zak dropped to his knees and sobbed. Five minutes went by, maybe ten, he neither knew nor cared before he began rubbing his legs and saying, 'But I'm not free. I will never be free unless I do what I have been trained to. And then I will be forever free. I've only one way out, but where are my people?'

Zak stood up and screamed, 'Chad! Youssef! Kosso!'

Far away the sun touched the horizon, and the sky turned rouge causing a billowing pattern of redness on the incoming tide.

Turning, he felt the sand beneath his feet and saw the dunes ahead. He glanced behind, out to sea, and thought briefly about his wife and family in Sangari. Shrugging his shoulders, he took his first step towards the dunes.

Minutes later, a pair of Wellington boots squelched in the final ripple of water that reached the beach. The boots sank into the sand a millimetre or two, left a shallow impression, and then ventured on.

Bernard, the wearer of the boots, shouted, 'Bloody channel crossers again. Where are they?'

Zak heard the words and rushed further into the dunes with the words of Louis Martin ringing in his ears, 'If you want a hotel for the night, interrogation by the Immigration people, and put into secure accommodation, then claim asylum and enjoy the holiday until they decide whether to keep you or send you back. You'll get all the government benefits if they keep you. If you don't want them to know you've arrived then get off the beach as quickly as possible and get out of their way. Run and hide. I just want your money, not your life story and the reason for your journey.'

Run and hide, thought Zak. Run and hide!

On the beach, the wellington boots were still squelching in the wet sand. 'Where did they go?' from one of the searchers.

'How would I know!' replied another voice on the beach. 'Where were they when you first picked them up with the binoculars?'

'Three maybe four hundred yards out!' from a searcher. 'It was misty, but they were incoming on the tide when the tanker ploughed right across them.'

'Right across them?' queried Bernard.

'Well, it looked that way from where I was standing. Difficult to tell but the dinghy overturned and tipped them out.'

'So they swam to the beach?' persuaded Bernard.

'Or drowned in the Channel.'

'Maybe they're still swimming!'

'I doubt it. Mind you, it depends on what they were wearing. If they were wearing wet suits underneath their clothes then yes, they might still be alive. If they wore normal clothes, I'd give them five minutes at the most. It's the water temperature you see. They've no chance in this wintry weather. Probably too cold for most of them, particularly the older ones.'

A torch flashed and skimmed the surface of the English Channel looking for evidence of survivors.

'I think they could have landed further along the coast. Maybe Winchelsea Beach. They might even have made Hastings.'

'Must have drowned,' suggested another searcher.

'Is there anyone in the dunes?'

'I'll take a look,' declared Bernard. 'Wait there.'

A torchlight shone into the dunes. Zak automatically ducked. The torchlight shone over his head and continued as if it were a searchlight scouring a prison camp. The beam scoured the dunes.

'Drowned!' shouted the voice.

'Winchelsea or Hastings,' came the reply from Bernard.

'You got money on that?'

'Never! But it's your round tonight if I remember.'

'You're right,' a voice replied. 'The watchers further on will tell us if they find a dinghy at the weekly meeting. No signs here. No drowned bodies. No dinghy. The tide might bring them in later.'

'Fishbait!' laughed Bernard.

They moved on with their torches flashing randomly out to sea and then into the dunes.

Zak took a deep breath, crouched low, and made inland. He was wet, cold, and freezing as he shivered his way through the dunes. It was too much for him. As he neared the point of exhaustion, he glanced over his shoulder again, saw no one, and hunkered down onto his haunches to get his breath back.

Ahead, the dunes gave way to a stretch of grass, then a tarmac road, and then a larger stretch of grass which grew darker as night approached.

Flattening out, Zak crept forward parting the clumps of grass that obstructed his view. Then he looked both ways and stood up. He felt the grass beneath his feet. Taking a step forward, he glanced both ways again and then darted across the road into the larger stretch of grass that seemed to extend for miles.

A car horn blared but the vehicle carried on at speed.

There was an outhouse close to a building about fifty yards from the road. Zak presumed it was a toilet or a storeroom. The door was ajar. He pushed it open and entered. The building was vacant save for empty cardboard boxes, a couple of tarpaulins, and several plastic bags. He crawled into the corner and grabbed a tarpaulin from the floor. Gathering it tightly around his body, he fell asleep.

Hours later, Zak's nightmare invaded his sleeping mind. His head began to jolt from side to side as the horrendous dream festered inside his brain.

There was a lake and a woman. The woman had three children with her. They were paddling in the shallows, laughing, splashing, and having fun. Then Zak threw a ball into the water and the woman caught it and threw it back. The children were of school age: primary school. They wanted the ball. Zak threw it back and they rushed after the ball, splashing in the water until the woman beat them to it and threw the ball in the air. They were having fun and chased the ball as they splashed in the lake and enjoyed the sunshine.

Then Zak's mind went blank. All his brain could bring to the fore was blackness as a cold swathe of perspiration crept across his body and a group of men surrounded him. He was in a different place. The woman was gone from his mind and there was no thought of the children splashing and enjoying themselves in the lake. They'd been replaced by a brute of a man who was kneeling on his neck with a gun pointed at his head and an overabundance of words that he understood but did not want to hear.

Restless, troubled, Zak turned over violently in his sleep, unwrapped the tarpaulin from his body, and threw it away.

The barrel of the gun bore into his temple as the man gabbled at him and twisted the barrel once more, deeper this time, threatening. Then the evil being removed the weapon and pointed it into the dark. A light shone and a woman and three children appeared. The woman was sobbing relentlessly. The children were screaming.

The brute of a man pulled the trigger. There was no sound of gunfire, but the woman fell to the ground. He pulled the trigger again and the children screamed.

Zak sat upright, wide awake, sweat pouring from his body as tears rolled down his cheek and pooled on his chest.

'No!' he shouted. 'No!'

Banging his head against the wall in desperation, Zak eventually closed his eyes and drifted into an agitated sleep. It had been a nightmare of a day that had ended in a bad dream that he understood but could not tolerate.

In Cumbria's only city, a figure dressed in black walked along the pavement and found himself on the edge of a rundown housing estate. There was row upon row of terraced houses followed by an avenue of semi-detached buildings and a small shopping arcade that boasted no more than a couple of takeaways, a hairdresser, a newsagent, and an array of small family businesses. It had once been a council house estate but over time, it was now the base of a working-class brigade who enjoyed the ability to buy their own homes. Yet the estate felt overwhelmed by the many blights that often infested such neglected locations. The streets were strewn with litter. A burnt-out car had been abandoned in the once picturesque park located in the centre of the estate. The car was surely stolen and vandalised; the park was no longer a place for families to enjoy the flowers and freedom offered.

The man strolled through the shopping arcade, ignored the boarded-up windows and *lease for sale* notices that testified to the social standing of the estate, stepped over a puddle of dirty water, and broke out into the estate once more.

He kept his hands deep in his pockets and the hood of his anorak shrouded over most of his face. The darkly clothed figure walked beneath the lamp standards that cast a dull shadow across his path. On reaching the cut, he turned sharply into the narrow walkway that led him to a row of rental garages lying at the perimeter of the housing estate.

Removing a key from his rear jeans pocket, he unlocked the padlock that secured a garage door, entered, and closed the door behind him. Switching on a light, he removed the sheet of cloth covering a grey saloon car and checked the number plates. Opening the driver's door, he leaned inside, popped the car bonnet, and checked the oil and water levels. Then he fired the car engine and examined the fuel level before checking the tyre pressures. Satisfied, he moved to a cabinet fixed to the garage wall. Sorting through a collection of registration plates, the man selected a pair and the necessary tools. He fixed the plates to the front and rear of the vehicle before unlocking the boot.

Hidden beneath a tartan blanket were two sawn-off shotguns. Handling one at a time, he broke the weapons and inspected the chambers.

Returning to the cabinet on the wall, he removed a box of ammunition and took half a dozen shotgun slugs and placed them beside the shotguns. He covered the weapons with the tartan blanket and took a cloth from a canvas in the boot.

The man spent the next fifteen minutes wiping the number plates, doors, and shotguns with the cloth so that they would be free of fingerprints.

He locked and secured the vehicle.

Outside, he clamped the close link padlock tight, looked both ways, and then retraced his steps pocketing the key on his way.

Ready for the job, he thought. All ready.

~

Chapter Three
~

Twelve hours later.
The following morning
Rye, East Sussex

Zak sat up, yawned, and rubbed his eyes. He removed his tee-shirt before wiping a river of perspiration from his body.

Bizarre, he thought as he replaced his damp top. Twelve hours earlier I nearly froze to death in the English Channel before managing to reach the beach and a building of some kind. Shaking his head, Zak recalled rolling in the sand and rubbing life back into his legs. Where am I, he wondered. I know why I am here. I have nightmares about it. I want to go home but I can't. I promised them I would do what they asked and I will. But where am I? Am I really in Dover or did we land back in France?

It was morning. Zak's troublesome sleep was over until the next time, but it had left him tired and lacking energy. He crept towards the door and pulled it ajar. The brightness of a beautiful day hit him square in the face and he recoiled in fear. A humming noise invaded his ears. His eyes had not yet accustomed to the environment. He rubbed his face again and looked out.

Zak heard traffic from the nearby road before pulling the door open further and studying the immediate surroundings. A man was riding a machine on the grass. Zak decided an odd-shaped box was attached to the rear of the machine.

The immediate area was completely covered with pristine green grass, several sand bunkers, and a post that was embedded in a hole in the ground. The post boasted a numbered flag. The grass seemed to run forever and disappear into the far distance. The man that Zak was watching was cutting the grass which was spewing into the closed collection box attached to the machine.

The rider swung the machine's steering wheel and set off in another direction leaving Zak confused and unsure of where he was.

Perplexed, Zak had never seen such a sight before. He retreated into the building and examined the contents on the floor. Flipping a piece of cardboard over, he read the label on what was an old box once used in postal delivery. It was addressed to Rye Golf Club, Camber Road, Camber Sands, Rye, New Lydd Road, Essex, United Kingdom.

I'm in England, he thought.

A rush of adrenalin surged through his body to complement the relief he felt.

Standing up, Zak studied an old map pinned to the wall. The map drooped from one corner since it was held to the wall by three drawing pins. Of poor quality, it had seen better days. On the map, he could see the blue stretch of water that was the sea, then the dunes, then a road, followed by an expanse of grass and several buildings close to the road. Zak surmised he was in one of those buildings and shook his head in dismay.

This isn't Dover, he thought. They will not pick me up from here. They won't know where I am. I must find Peckham. That's where they are. That's where I must go otherwise it's over.

Zak studied the rest of the wall and read a plastic poster that was pinned in the corner. The poster showed a man playing golf. It was designed to help people improve their game and learn how to play from scratch.

We have one golf club back at home, thought Zak. It is in the capital and there is no grass. Just sand, but we have people using golf clubs and putters as they are in the poster. I'm in a golf club. At home, only rich people play golf. The clubs in N'Djamena are mainly nightclubs, not golf clubs. In

41

nightclubs, you can buy an alcoholic drink if you are in the right company. But I don't drink.

Thinking of his home in Sangari on the edge of Lake Chad, in the country known as Chad, Zak thought of his wife and children and the world he had left behind.

There was one golf club and no more than a handful of alcohol clubs in the whole country, and what there was could only be found in N'Djamena. It was a secular country wherein the religion of Islam was strong in the north and centre of the country but Christianity had a slight hold in the south. Depending on where you lived might determine whether you went to seek alcohol or not for the consumption of alcohol was against the Islamic faith.

I wonder how safe England is, thought Zak. Chad is extremely dangerous but I have been lucky. I can speak English as well as Kanuri, my native tongue. I have my parents to thank for that.

Shaking his head, thinking things through, Zak wished Kosso, Youssef and Chad were still around for advice, but he feared the worse and presumed they had been lost at sea. Should I surrender to the authorities, he pondered? No! That is not the way. I have been trained by Malik to kill and kill I must for that is the way to succeed in the life that I have chosen to lead. I gave them my word and to turn back from my task now will mean an end to everything that I desire. I must find Peckham.

More determined than ever, the man from Sangari set off on his quest.

Zak opened the door and walked into the golf course. Except there was no one there other than the grasscutter who was half a mile away on the fairway close to a couple of males who were teeing off on the third.

Strolling towards the nearest building, Zak pushed open the door and saw that it was a changing room. There was row upon row of metal cabinets, shoes on the floor, and a couple of jackets hanging on pegs. He began to rifle the contents.

Within minutes Zak found a wallet with banknotes neatly folded inside the leather compartments. He threw the wallet away but pocketed the cash. Then he pinched socks, shoes, and a pair of jeans as well as a hooded top. Finally, he found an anorak in another cabinet. There was more money to find and he took it. He tried the anorak on and realised it was a great fit. Moving around the room, Zak noticed his reflection in a full-length mirror next to a drink dispensing machine. He posed, turned his head, swung his body, and decided he looked good in his new anorak. Finally, he tilted the drinks machine forward and banged it on the side with a clenched fist. A can fell into the dispenser tray. He flipped the ring top and took a long satisfying drink before dumping the empty in a nearby bin.

Examining his surroundings, Zak read a list of the club members on a notice board and details of a forthcoming competition. Next to this notice was a map that denoted a motorway system and an arrow pointing to Rye. The words *You are Here* were visible. Studying the map, he realised he was standing where the arrow was situated. He was in Rye Golf Club. Zak ran his fingers across the map from Rye to Dover then up to London and realised that to reach Dover he had to keep the sea on his right-hand side and the land on his left-hand side.

If I keep the sea on my right I will eventually find signs for London, thought Zak. Then I must go left and north until I find the big river: the one they call the River Thames. When I find the big river I must keep the river on my right. It will get narrower as it moves from the sea inland. I will find London that way. Kosso had a map and Youssef had a spare, but everything is at the bottom of the Channel now. I am not stupid but I will find the River Thames and my way to Peckham even if it takes me a week or more. I wonder how far I must travel. I hope I have enough time to get there.

There was a sudden noise when the door burst open and a cold wintry breeze invaded the room. Zak ducked down and between the rows of cabinets. Two men entered and began to undress. Changing into checked trousers and coloured tops, they removed bags of golf clubs from a metal cabinet. One of the golfers locked the cabinet and pocketed the key.

Blatant, cheeky, Zak stood up and strolled nonchalantly between the two men. Nodding to them both, he offered, 'Good luck!' and walked on.

'Thank you! How did your round go?'

'Good! Yes, good!' replied Zak as he left them behind. 'I enjoyed it very much.'

The door closed behind Zak as the two golfers glanced at each other, shrugged their shoulders, and prepared for their session.

Neither suspected me, Zak thought as he made the main car park. Determined, undeterred, he held his course. Brazen! I must be bold and barefaced, he decided. Just like home! Now I remember why Malik picked me when there were so many others he could have selected.

It was tempting to glance over his shoulder but Zak concentrated on the way ahead and saw a scooter parked in one corner of the parking area.

England, he thought. I can speak English well. But now I must find Peckham.

Pausing, Zak knelt and pretended to tie a shoelace. He studied the scooter in front of him. It was a small-sized Honda with a few thousand miles on the clock and a couple of years' wear on the tyres. Signs of rust crept around the metal footboard. He moved to the front of the machine and unclipped the engine cowling, withdrew an ignition wire from the plastic holding, bent it in two, and then reinserted it into the ignition system returning one end to its original housing. He threw his leg over the side, sat on the narrow driver's seat, and pressed the starter switch on the handlebars. The engine coughed twice before bursting into life. He rode across the car park, bounced over the grass, and landed on the tarmac.

Zak twisted the accelerator and changed gear. He set off with the sea on his left, realised his mistake, turned around, and headed in the direction of Dover.

A voice hurled abuse across the void causing Zak to glance at the golf club and see a woman sprinting from the changing rooms towards the road. She was young, fit and agile, and darted across the car park holding a golf club in her hand.

The woman leapt into Zak's pathway.

'Get off my scooter,' she yelled wielding the golf club in a threatening manner.

Ducking beneath the golf club, Zak ramped up onto the offside pavement before regaining the roadway. A vehicle horn sounded and he saw a single-decker bus headed straight for him. Zak remained cool and swerved.

The front offside wing of the bus clipped the rear end of the scooter. The scooter wobbled when its rear tyre scorched the highway. The rubber dragged across the tarmac and lost alignment with the front wheel.

'Ring the police!' screamed the woman with the golf club.

Undaunted, Zak dropped his head and roared down the road with the woman losing ground as she ran after him and a bus driver standing in the middle of the highway shaking his fist.

The bus driver rang 999.

'Emergency! Which service please?'

'I want to report a road accident. A scooter just collided with my bus, and I want to report a stolen vehicle too. Some crazy kid is going to kill someone if you don't stop him soon.'

'Connecting you to the police. Stand by.'

On the highway, Zak wrestled with the scooter and found it impossible to reach high speed, but five minutes later he left Camber Road and found himself on the outskirts of Rye. The rear of the scooter seemed to be constantly pushing the vehicle to the nearside whilst Zak steered it towards the offside. The chassis was fractured because the collision had broken the scooter and it was unmanageable.

A police car crossed Zak's bow when he made the main road at Rye. The police driver hit the brakes, reversed into a vacant space, and waited for the scooter to arrive.

Is it the army or the police who are after me, thought Zak as he roared along the road with the exhaust pipe now loose and rattling loudly from a broken chassis?

A blue light on the police car roof rotated when the headlights came on and the motor sauntered into the road broadside to Zak. PC John Sanderson, the driver, was out of the vehicle with his hand held high signalling Zak to pull in.

He's going nowhere, thought Sanderson. The scooter is dying.

In the seconds that followed, PC Sanderson activated the body-worn video camera on his chest and began to record proceedings.

'Stop!' ordered the policeman. 'Stop right there!'

Zak threw the scooter to his nearside, selected a lower gear, and twisted the accelerator. The vehicle coughed and spluttered. The chassis fractured a little more and Sanderson jumped out of the way as Zak powered his fragile escape and the scooter shook its rear number plate off.

There was a clank on the tarmac when the number plate slapped onto the ground and an errant nut and bolt embraced the gradient and rolled to the nearside of the road.

Running to his patrol car, John Sanderson jumped into the driver's seat and radioed his controllers before firing the engine and giving chase.

Zak made the main highway to Dover, twisted the accelerator, and found no response. Glancing over his shoulder, he saw the police car chasing him, saw the blue light flashing, saw the headlights on full beam, and heard the slow and steady wail of the siren. He swivelled around to face the road ahead and realised he was on the wrong side of the road.

A thirty-two-ton articulated wagon headed straight for him.

Zak swung the handlebars. There was no response. The chassis snapped in two. The rear wheel area departed the body first and at speed. The front of the vehicle collapsed onto the roadway.

Heading towards the tarmac, Zak glimpsed the bumper of the artic closing with him. He hit the ground and rolled to one side. The wagon crushed what remained of the scooter beneath its colossal wheels and carried on with its horn blaring and Zak's heart racing.

The scooter exploded into a score of metallic shards that showered the tarmac.

Zak rolled down the embankment at the side of the road, stood up, glanced back, and then climbed the fence that separated the highway from the railway.

PC Sanderson was out of the car chasing on foot hollering at his target, screaming for him to stop, and ordering him to surrender.

Zak was over the fence running alongside the main Southampton to London train line when a slow-moving goods train crept past him at a speed slightly faster than his. Timing his actions, Zak neared the train and reached out but the nearest goods carriage was a container and there was nowhere suitable to grip.

The train began to overtake Zak with Sanderson still in the chase and hot on the heels of his target. The goods train was ahead of Zak who was ahead of Sanderson.

Glancing over his shoulder, Zak spied an empty flat back carriage on the goods train. The stanchions were fitted on all four corners but there were two more in the middle on either side and the flat back was empty. The only other thing in sight was a dark blue uniform bearing down on him at speed.

John Sanderson was gaining ground.

Striding out closer to the railway line, Zak reached out and grabbed an upright stanchion as the goods train began to gather speed on a slight descent.

'Gotcha!' yelled Sanderson as he gripped Zak's hood.

Zak wrenched himself free, gripped tight the stanchion, and felt the speed of the train drag his legs along the ground. He finally heaved himself onto the footplate. Glancing back, he saw that Sanderson had caught hold of the rear corner stanchion and was copying his every movement.

Taking a deep breath, the man from Chad yanked himself up and flung his legs from the footplate onto the flat back. He wobbled, slid, caught hold of another stanchion and held tight as the train's speed increased and Sanderson manoeuvred his body in a similar style onto the flat back.

Unexpected movements caused a ripple in the train. The carriages realigned with the extra weight and ruses of the two human bodies who had climbed aboard. Jolting, the flat back carriage threw Zak towards the front of the carriage whilst simultaneously unbalancing Sanderson who lost his footing.

PC Sanderson screamed when he toppled backwards, hit his head on the corner stanchion, and fell from the train.

There was another lurch forward when the carriages realigned and left the policeman fighting for his life as the iron wheels of the goods train rumbled inches past his skull. He bounced and bobbed along the ground at the side of the train when he realised the trouser of his left leg was entangled with the stanchion.

Sanderson looked up at the flat back carriage. He was trapped, snagged by his trousers, and helpless. He could neither release himself nor climb back onto the carriage. The policeman was a prisoner of the moving goods train as it sped effortlessly along the railway line with the traveller from Chad still free and the policeman close to death.

Yard by yard, the train carried Sanderson along as both the stanchion and the trouser cloth held firm.

Zak scrambled to the rear of the flat back, reached out for the policeman, grabbed his outstretched hand, and pulled.

The body-worn video camera on Sanderson's chest captured Zak's image full on. The two men were only a foot apart.

A curve in the railway line came into play and threw Zak to the opposite side of the carriage leaving Sanderson to fend for himself.

Undeterred, crawling across the flat back carriage, Zak grasped Sanderson's trousers and pulled them away from the upright stanchion.

The cloth ripped. Sanderson was free.

Closing his eyes, the policeman scrunched up his face when his body bucked and tumbled as the full force of gravity slung its unwelcome attack on Sanderson's back. He hit the ground, had the presence of mind to roll away from the wheels, and slammed into the fence at the foot of the embankment.

The goods train continued with Zak standing upright holding onto the stanchion with one hand whilst extending the other towards Sanderson who was losing consciousness at the side of the track.

Glancing beyond, Zak heard the faint sound of the siren on Sanderson's police car as a blue light rotated from the roof and the goods train made its way towards Ashford International railway station.

Sanderson drifted into darkness, his patrol car a few hundred yards away, a vacant track now boasting cold steel, and a couple of car drivers on the main road wondering what on earth was going on.

The driver's door of Sanderson's patrol car was open and the siren still blaring when the first curious driver ventured towards the empty police car. He peeped inside, saw no one, and picked up the radiotelephone cradled in its holster.
'Hello!' said the curious driver. 'Is anyone there?'
'This is Bravo Control! State your Callsign,' came the reply.
The man was momentarily shocked, unsure of what to do, and still somewhat confused when he tentatively radioed, 'Hello! This is a Mr Yates from Rye. I've found an empty police car. Do you know where the driver is?'
The airwaves were unusually silent for a while before a voice replied, 'Mr Yates! This is police control. What is your precise location?'

A mile or so away, Zak stood forlorn on the flat back carriage with his mouth open and his arm still outstretched offering a hand to a man no longer there. Confused, and shocked, his mind was in turmoil as he bent over the side of the carriage to try and see if the policeman was alright. But Sanderson was out of sight and the train was now headed in a north-easterly direction.
Shaking his head, wiping a tear from the corner of his eye, Zak took a deep breath before gradually exhaling a long burst of air.
Focus, he reminded himself. I must focus. There will be many lives lost soon. Don't concern yourself with this one. It's the job. It's what I must do. It's what Malik said I must do.
Zak was on his way to London and right now, that was all that mattered to the man from Chad.

Miles away, in Peckham, nimble fingers worked a pair of metal levers into a thin keyhole inside a wooden door. There was a push down with one lever and an exploratory twist with another.

An armful of leverage and a sudden wrench caused the tumblers to react and fall into place. The door opened and the man entered.

Standing perfectly still, the intruder waited for both his hearing and his eyesight to become accustomed to their new surroundings.

'Red Alpha Three is on target,' he radioed using a throat mic.

'I have that. All clear here!' came the reply.

Red Alpha Three removed a pair of slip-on covers from a leather bum bag on his trouser belt. He placed them over the soles of his shoes before exploring the house.

'Red Alpha Three is progressing,' he radioed.

'I have that. The subjects are static in the café. No change.'

'Understood,' from Red Alpha Three. 'Phase One deployment taking place.'

'I have that. No change.'

The trespasser moved gradually through the downstairs of the terraced house pausing only to lay down and fix covert listening devices in each room. Then he ventured upstairs where he deployed further devices. Every room in the house was now fitted with a well-hidden listening device. Finally, thirty minutes later, he returned to the hallway of the house and removed a camera from the bag on his belt. He began fitting the camera to the wall above the front door.

'Phase One complete. Phase Two taking place,' he radioed.

'I have that,' came the reply. 'No change.'

The camera the intruder fitted was similar in size to that of a drawing pin yet it was fitted with a high-tech wide-angled lens that captured the full extent of the hall, the bottom of the staircase, and entrances into the kitchen and the lounge.

There was a thin almost invisible wire that was no more than an inch long.

With gloved fingers, Red Alpha Three connected the wire to a box that was already fitted above the doorway and powered the front doorbell of the premises concerned.

Upon completion, he stood back and radioed, 'Phase Two completed. Phase Three Test, please!'

In a Surveillance Observations Centre, an operative turned to a computer screen and typed a command on the keyboard. The product of the camera appeared on the screen and a positive response from the listening devices followed.

The operative radioed, 'Product is Ten Ten and we're up and running.'

'Understood! Sitrep, please,' from Red Alpha Three.

'All clear!' from the radio. 'Subjects are still in the café. No change.'

'Leaving target now. Safety check,' radioed Red Alpha Three.

A watcher peered through the window of a high rise building and replied, 'From Red Alpha Four, the street is clear. Come!'

'I have that,' came the reply.

'Red Alpha Two is moving to the plot,' radioed another voice.

'I have that,' from Red Alpha Three.

Red Alpha Three removed the slip-on covers from his shoes and returned them to his bum bag. He listened, heard a car engine, and then opened the door. Red Alpha Three stepped out into the street. A car drew up at the edge of the pavement and the intruder took three steps, opened the passenger door, and sat back as the car drove away.

'Red Alpha Two and Red Alpha Three are clear,' across the radio waves as the car cruised gradually away from the target premises and blended naturally into the local traffic scene.

'I have that. No change. Subjects are still in the café. Confirm total closure.'

'Red Alpha Three confirms operation completed. Closure confirmed.'

'Red Alpha Four, you have control.'

In a high-rise building, a hand removed the top from a vacuum flask, poured a hot coffee into a plastic mug, and replied, 'I have that. Red Alpha Four has control. Closure confirmed. No change!'

On the rail tracks, Zak was through Ashford International and Maidstone without a stop and Rye was the best part of a hundred miles behind him. He was headed towards London without a care in the world. The man from Chad was an intruder asleep on the flat back wagon of a goods train carrying freight out of Southampton Port into Sussex and beyond.

The travelling, the excitement, the state of his troubled mind and the apparent death of a policeman he could not save, all added to Zak's mental problems. He was both physically and mentally drained.

A severe bend on the track jolted Zak wide awake. Sitting up, he orientated his mind to the flat back carriage, glanced at the goods wagons ahead of him, and then turned around to view the rest of the train snaking its way through the countryside behind him. He was safe. In celebration, Zak rubbed his hands across his face and invigorated the skin.

Yawning, Zak saw the big river he had been told of. It was called the Thames if he remembered correctly. Or was it something else? The Times? He couldn't remember. All he could remember was an address in Peckham. It was ingrained in his mind, all he needed to know. Kneeling, he looked across the railway lines and saw the river on his offside.

I must keep the river on my right until I lose view of it, he thought. I must stay this side of the river and find Peckham.

The word 'DARTFORD' appeared on a sign along the route. Zak held tight and remained low as the train hurtled along the track and through a railway station. People were standing on platforms on both sides of the track, but no one seemed interested in the goods train. They were waiting for the next passenger train.

As Zak kept watch he felt the train reduce speed as a red signal showed on the line ahead. The track was no longer in the countryside. Now it was surrounded on both sides by embankments that bordered housing estates and industrial complexes. It was time to go. The river was gradually disappearing from view and all that lay ahead were enormous buildings that stretched towards the sky.

Zak steadied himself on a corner stanchion, saw the gravel path running alongside the train and waited. The train slowed but the signal changed to green and Zak felt a slight acceleration beneath his feet. He jumped to the ground and rolled onto the grassy embankment.

Waiting for the train to pass him, Zak crossed the tracks and climbed the opposing embankment. At the top, there was a narrow path often used by maintenance staff from the railway. Zak strolled along the path until there was a break in the wire fence. Perhaps the fence had been deliberately broken by children or vandals in the area. He did not know as he stepped from the railway system through the gap into a housing estate.

Walking through the estate, Zak marvelled at the two-storey orange brick houses and the gardens. There was no such thing in Chad as a council house or a community development of this magnitude. The people who lived here were wealthy, he surmised. There were no mud huts by the side of a lake. They were all brick with glass windows and thick plastic or wooden doors. There were cars parked in front of the houses and children playing on bicycles. They were rich. He was poor in comparison.

Zak kept his head down and dug his hands into the pockets of his jeans. Inside one pocket, his fingers wrapped around the banknotes that he'd stolen from Rye Golf Club. He had plenty of money in his possession.

On arriving at the main road, Zak recognised a taxi when he saw one. He signalled the vehicle to stop, got into the rear passenger area, and said to the driver, 'Peckham! I want to go to Peckham.'

'Whereabouts?'

Days of being told where to go and what to do when he arrived in London came to the fore when Zak's memory kickstarted his voice and he blurted out the address.

The taxi driver looked Zak up and down in a suspicious manner and then said, 'You got the cash?'

'How much?' replied Zak holding his notes for inspection.

'Oh! Right! Forty quid!' declared the smiling taxi driver.

'How long before we get there?' asked Zak.

'Forty minutes! Depends on traffic.'

'You want money now?' queried Zak.

'When we get there, pal. No rush.'

Zak wondered how he and the driver were suddenly friends. Pals, the driver had said. Why is this so? I have no pals here. They are floating somewhere deep inside the English Channel.

The driver fired the engine and they set off leaving Dartford in the rear-view mirror as they routed south of the River Thames to the Borough of Southwark. They were headed for Peckham, an area long inhabited by the nation's largest British-Nigerian population.

'We are still south of the river?' inquired Zak. 'I'm a little lost at the moment. It is my first time in Dartford, pal.'

'Oh yes,' chuckled the taxi driver. 'You don't want to be in the north, pal. That's for sure.'

Zak settled back into his seat confident that he was travelling in the right direction. As instructed by his newfound pal, he was south of the river. Not north.

~

Chapter Four

~

In the North,
Penrith, Cumbria
That Day

Boyd looked out onto Penrith's distinctive clock tower standing in the Market Square. The Monument was erected in 1861 as a tribute from the town to Sir George and Lady Musgrave of nearby Eden Hall, in memory of their eldest son. Musgrave Monument dominated the town centre and was the focal point for virtually every event that took place in the Cumbrian market town.

Situated in a second-floor storeroom above a local grocery shop, the detective sat on an overturned wooden box and espied not only the clock tower but also the broad expanse of retail shops and buildings before him. These included the long lane that connected the part of town known as Burrowgate with St Andrew's Church before it emerged into Market Square at Barclay's Bank and its junction with King Street and Devonshire Street. It was the bank that was the focus of Boyd's attention. His problem was that the bank he was watching wasn't the only bank in the area. There were three banks of interest to his surveillance team and they were all within a thirty seconds walk of each other: The HSBC, the NatWest Bank and Barclays. In addition, there were two building societies close by, namely the Penrith Building Society and the Newcastle Building Society. The plot was complicated by the location of both the Cumberland Building Society and the Skipton Building Society. Neither appeared on Boyd's immediate radar but he was aware of how close these premises were.

Perm one from seven, he puzzled as he watched the people in the streets below. Three banks and four building societies. But which one? That was the question.

Boyd's other problem related to three well-known Carlisle criminals that Olly, his informant, had indicated were planning to raid a bank in Penrith. As a result of regular phone calls received from Olly since their last meeting, Boyd knew the raid would take place on this day, but he didn't know its whereabouts. He had received what was known in the unit as 'raw intelligence'. Normally, such information was 'hot off the press' and came verbally and directly from a covert source to the handler. The handler, or receiver of the intelligence, would then frame the information into a formal intelligence report and submit it via their supervisor to the Intelligence Bureau for assessment. The whole process was restricted to some degree in that only people with approved access levels could read such reports. The Bureau would assess its veracity, consider the credibility of the source, any background material that might be relevant to either the source, the handler, or the case in question, and then recommend what steps ought to be taken in respect of that report. A security access level was also awarded to each report. The Bureau would then record the report in the computerised intelligence system where others could gain access to the report provided they enjoyed an appropriate level of security. Such levels began with everyone at the bottom level and ended with only a few at the top level. The document containing that intelligence, and the decisions relevant to it, would be considered by various methodologies and opinions in the Intelligence Bureau. The argument existed that 'analysed intelligence' could be acted upon with minimised risk. But such things took time. Sometimes, too much time. Yet Boyd was a proven expert in the covert acquisition of 'raw intelligence'. He would use it without analysis when he considered that the source was reliable, had a record of delivering the goods, and the situation was such that immediate action was required without waiting for the experts in the Bureau to respond.

Often 'raw intelligence' indicated that something was happening very soon. Perhaps within the hour, the day, or the week. Since it hadn't been assessed by the Bureau, it was often regarded as 'risky' for some and accordingly should be placed on the back burner until more information became apparent. Boyd had no backburner and accepted the risk that the intelligence might not be completely accurate. This had been mentioned in the briefing earlier that morning in the hope that it would be a bank that would be raided, not a building society, and that the intelligence was otherwise correct and likely to happen on this date.

Boyd had designated the Carlisle criminal suspects by their surnames Crawford, Donaldson and Edwards and had instructed a relaxed attitude on the net.

Which bank, thought Boyd? Or will it be one of the two building societies? If Olly is correct the raid will be today, and it will be a bank, not a building society. I've no reason to doubt his information. I've known him so long and he's never let me down, but which bank? I hope it's a bank because if it isn't there will be those who will not hesitate to criticise me for taking a risk when the operation had not been assessed by the appropriate people. Such was the inner politics of the police service. Life in the police was sometimes akin to working in a bureaucracy that often dismissed reality as an unnecessary truth.

It was midmorning and the crew had been out on the streets since eight o'clock. Boyd's second in command, Anthea, sat in the driver's seat of a gunmetal grey series 5 BMW which had been borrowed for the day. It was usually driven by DS Janice Burns: a feisty Scottish detective from Greenock who was an expert driver and surveillance officer with a fearless reputation.

Engaging her throat mic, Anthea radioed, 'We're in position at Burrowgate, close to the plot. Guvnor! Sitrep, please.'

'No change here,' reported Boyd. 'All quiet. How about you, Martin?'

Martin Duffy sat in the bay window of the dining area of the George Hotel drinking his coffee and reading a newspaper. Glancing through the window, he engaged a device that replicated a mobile phone and radioed, 'No change. How about you, Terry? Are you still awake, my friend?'

Detective Sergeant Terry Anwhari was driving a top of the range silver-coloured SAAB motor car around the town centre. He found a parking space opposite the Monument and reported, 'I have sight of all three banks but no car cover. I'm standing out like a sore thumb so I'm going on foot in the vicinity. Understood?'

'I have that,' replied Anthea. 'Come in, Janice. You okay?'

'Aye!' replied Janice glancing at a posse of armed plainclothes detectives with her and added, 'Raring to go. Just say the word.'

'Okay! All units in position. Stay awake,' radioed Anthea.

'Mind ma car,' replied Janice. 'Nae a scratch on it, ye ken.'

'It will be washed, polished and hoovered before I return it to you,' radioed Anthea. 'By the way, thanks for leaving a can of Coke and a bag of sweets in the glove department. Just what I needed.'

'Mmm… My mistake,' muttered Janice. 'Dinnae go drinking that coke and leave ma sweets alone.'

There was no reply from the net and Boyd chuckled to himself as he listened to the small talk and banter whilst watching the traffic trickle through the streets. He knew they were unloading stress from the ongoing operation and remained silent.

Boyd cast his eyes in the direction of a charity shop knowing that's where Janice and a team of armed officers were in hiding. The location was in the lane near St Andrew's Church and they were waiting for the word as the hands of the clock on the Monument moved on.

Half an hour went by before Martin radioed, 'Guvnor! Third time around for that grey Mercedes.' He added the registration number and continued, 'Three male occupants. Ricky! Can you make the number, please?'

'I see it,' replied Boyd. 'Wait one! Ricky, can you assist?'

The Mercedes had driven along Middlegate through the Narrows and was now in Devonshire Street. The vehicle swung right at the Musgrave Monument and climbed the slight hill towards Penrith railway station. In so doing, the vehicle drove past all three banks and all four building societies at such a casual speed that the driver had time to glance at each one.

Ricky French was the team's technical operator. In a van parked north of Penrith near the Pennyhill estate, he studied the product of a drone stationary in flight above the town centre and reported, 'I have it, Guvnor. I'll get back to you shortly.'

'Understood,' from Boyd.

'The Mercedes is coming around again,' reported Ricky.

'I have that,' replied Boyd.

Sliding his chair along the van floor, Ricky engaged another computer screen and tapped the registration number of the Mercedes into the search panel.

There was a beep from the drone control panel and Ricky swung back to the other side of the van. Watching his computer screen, Ricky took in the route of the Mercedes before radioing, 'Cloud cover is disrupting the view slightly but the Mercedes is held at the lights in the Narrows close to all three banks. Stand by for movement.'

Acknowledgements on the net followed before Ricky reported, 'The Mercedes is stopping near the Monument. One passenger out. The Mercedes is moving off. Up the hill towards the station. Coverage is widening. I'm following the Mercedes with the drone. You have the plot.'

'I have that,' from Boyd. 'All units, I can identify Crawford as the subject who has left the Mercedes and is now standing on the footpath near the Monument. Stand by all units.'

'Guvnor! Permission!' from Ricky on the net from the confines of a van two miles away near Pennyhill estate.

'Go ahead,' replied Boyd.

'The Police National Computer indicates the plates on the grey Mercedes relate to a red Mercedes that was stolen from Workington twelve months ago. Something is not right with that vehicle. I suspect the Mercedes may be stolen. Over!'

'I have that,' replied Boyd. 'All units acknowledge.'

More acknowledgements rippled through the net before Boyd's target strolled casually along the street and approached each bank separately. He faltered, peered inside the front door of the HSBC, and then took a step into a shop doorway.

'Loss of eyeball,' radioed Boyd. 'Do you have him, Martin?'

'Yes! Yes!' replied Martin from his seat in the George Hotel. 'He's just watching the street by the looks of it. Crawford is making a phone call from his mobile. Hold your positions.'

Ricky chipped in with, 'Drone coverage shows driver has a mobile phone in his right hand. He's holding it to his ear whilst driving. Intermittent cloud. Lost him.'

Crawford stepped out of the doorway and began walking back along the street. This time he paused at the rear of a grey builder's van that was parked on double yellow lines outside one of the banks. He peered inside the windows of the rear doors before moving further down the street and stopping again. The Carlisle criminal took a pace backwards into another shop doorway and ran his eyes along a row of parked cars. Taking in Terry's empty Saab, he then leisurely glanced at the second and third-floor windows of the shops opposite the Musgrave Monument.

Ever ready, Boyd stepped back from his observation post and felt his back hard against the storeroom door.

'The Mercedes is coming around again,' radioed Ricky. 'He's through the lights that are on green, moving to the nearside, dropping another male off on the footpath. A male passenger is out and approaching Crawford. The car is off up the hill again. I have one car and one driver. You should have two males near the George Hotel.'

'Confirmed,' from Boyd. 'The second subject is Donaldson.'

'Donaldson joining Crawford, understood,' voiced Anthea.

'Funny old world!' ventured Boyd on the net. 'Why are they both wearing long raincoats when it's not raining?'

'I think we know why,' suggested Anthea. 'All units, exercise caution. These two may be armed.'

'Thank you, Anthea,' voiced Boyd.

The Carlisle crooks stood on the footpath close to the Monument. From their position, all three banks were visible as well as two building societies, and they had a good view of the street topography around them. They seemed more interested in the banks than the building societies. Casually, they looked over each other's shoulders as they chatted but it was obvious to the watchers that the two suspects were checking to see if the area was safe for them to operate in.

Boyd radioed, 'I'm leaving my perch and moving to street level. Take control, Martin. All units take closer order as discussed.'

Another ripple of acknowledgements filled the net.

Meanwhile, the two suspects crossed the road and sauntered to the entrance of the George Hotel.

Detective Constable Martin Duffy poured more coffee from a silver pot on the table in front of him and then glanced out of the hotel's bay window from his leather-bound armchair. Studying the two men who were chatting to each other no more than a few feet from his location, he realised only the glass window separated the would-be raiders from himself and Cumbria's most wanted when he quietly replied, 'I have that. I have control. I have the eyeball. I'm only a yard away from them both.'

Janice opened the rear door of the charity shop and said, 'Did you hear that? The suspects are standing in front of the George Hotel. It's an opportunity not to be missed.' She ushered her team out into the lane and whispered, 'You know what to do. Close order nice and easy. Take up your positions and hang in there. Dennis! Stay here with me.'

Plain clothed, the armed detectives slid quickly and quietly into the St Andrew area and made for their close order positions.

The heavily built Crawford scanned the immediate vicinity of the George Hotel. There were several shoppers in the area, a few families, a postman, and various people moving around the streets. Yes, there were a few individuals on their own. But they were acting naturally and did nothing to raise the eyebrows of the suspects. Crawford's eyes suddenly caught movement in the bay window and he remarked, 'Tourist?'

'Yeah! Coffee and cake time!' replied the curly-haired Donaldson. 'No sweat.'

Calmly, Martin shook the broadsheet newspaper, turned a page, and concentrated on the printed word.

Outside, Crawford and Donaldson nodded to each other and moved on towards the NatWest bank.

'Subjects moving towards the NatWest,' radioed Martin.

Making for the rear entrance of the shop, Boyd nodded to the shopkeeper who winked at him and said, 'Thank you, Mr Boyd. How long do you think it will take to decorate that room?'

'An hour or two, I'd say,' replied Boyd. 'I'll be back with a quote for you shortly if that's alright?'

'Of course, Mr Boyd. Whenever.'

Boyd left the building as the shopkeeper smiled at a customer and said, 'Just getting the flat decorated upstairs. Anything else before you go?'

Pointing to a tray, the customer replied, 'Half a dozen loose carrots and a cauliflower, please, Mike.'

The shopkeeper attended his store whilst his contact in the police closed the door behind him.

Once outside, Boyd found himself in the rear lane. Soon, he thought. Something will happen soon but what are my options and how should I play the hand I've been dealt? Should we pounce on the Mercedes when it returns and lock the driver up for being in possession of a stolen car? If it's Edwards driving the Mercedes then he's also wanted on a warrant for non-appearance at Carlisle Crown Court. That leaves Crawford and Donaldson. Do we arrest them for loitering with intent and interview them as to their criminal intentions? No reply to every question comes to mind and it would leave us on a sticky wicket that might not lead to a conviction. The evidence is weak. Do I sanction the arrest of all three for conspiracy to rob on the basis that they are acting suspiciously in the vicinity of three banks? Well, it's the centre of a smallish market town so anyone who comes here is bound to end up near the Monument, all three banks, and a handful of building societies. So just being close isn't going to cut any mustard. The evidence is stronger if we can define the bank they are aiming for and catch them doing something that was going to lead to a robbery. Just standing around looking is not enough. It's not what I want. Are they armed? Not necessarily, pondered Boyd. It never stops raining in Carlisle. Maybe those raincoats are what they usually wear. I don't know. One thing I do know is that we need to protect Olly from being discovered by the opposition. Olly isn't going to give evidence so we must have this job sewn up tightly without him.

Boyd walked halfway down the lane and then turned suddenly into a narrow lane that led back to the main street and the site of the action.

Are the guns hidden in the churchyard? The detective wondered. Should I have deployed sniffer dogs there first thing this morning? What if, thought Boyd. The job is full of what-ifs. I told everyone to use first names on the radio rather than callsigns because we're all working in a tight area surrounded by shoppers. I don't want my team to be compromised because someone too close hears one of them talking in code or callsigns. I want a relaxed team. Is that right or wrong? What if they are suddenly exposed to the public by a trusted shopkeeper who suddenly changes their mind? I suppose I'm damned if I do and damned if I don't. The backroom boys will have a field day if this all goes wrong. They'll hang me out to dry because I accepted the risk that goes with raw intelligence and didn't wait for formal analysis and assessment.

Stopping close to the end of the lane, Boyd took the best advantage of the restricted view he was afforded to consider the situation on the footpath on the opposing side of the street.

Maybe I should have put two or three armed undercovers into each of the seven potential targets from eight this morning, thought Boyd taking a deep breath. Or even dressed them up as cashiers behind the counter. But this is Penrith and it's famous for gossip amongst the locals because it's a big village growing into a sizeable town. If it begins raining in one estate, then the neighbouring estate knows before the rain hits the pavement. That's what kind of place it is. Gossip travels faster than a downpour so changing faces in multiple buildings is like hoisting the Jolly Roger on the town hall roof and firing a cannon from the main street. How will this pan out, he wondered? Will they try and make a withdrawal or is it just a dummy run? Of course, they're so damned good that they might be testing us. They want us to show ourselves, rush out, and arrest them knowing they've done nothing wrong.

Detective Sergeant Terry Anwhari crossed Boyd's path and slunk into a shop seconds before Boyd took three steps forward and presented himself at the entrance to the lane. He had a commanding view of the entire street and surmised Terry would be checking out products for sale in the neighbouring shop whilst simultaneously keeping observations on the situation outside. Born in England, to Pakistani parents, Terry was not only bilingual he was experienced in the ways of surveillance too.

But Boyd's mind wrestled with the enigma before him. If it's a dummy run, why use a stolen car?

Taking a slight step back into the shadows, Boyd radioed, 'This is Boyd. I have control. All units, listen up. We are about to find out whether this is a dummy run or the Full Monty. Prepare to take a closer position to the plot and await further instructions.'

'We moved forward when the suspects were at the George Hotel,' replied Janice on the net. 'We're in the hold position.'

'I have that,' acknowledged Boyd. 'Dependent on their movements, we might have to blow our cover. I want them in the bank, not at the bank.'

A car engine fired. A safety catch was moved to the off position. A baseball cap with the word 'police' across the top was removed from a back pocket and made ready, and a streak of adrenalin rushed through the bloodstream of each of the watchers.

It was a waiting game that tested everyone.

Janice glanced at Colin, the youngest detective in her team. He was white about the gills, 'You okay, Colion?'

'Yes! Yes!' replied the young detective nervously.

'First time!' remarked Janice.

Colin nodded as his fingers curled around the trigger guard and he snapped, 'I'm fully trained.'

'I know. Relax!' offered Janice. 'Nothing prepares you for this. Take deep breaths. Get some air. Remember the training. Move your fingers. Take the safety catch off and breathe. If you're frightened, then join the club. Just remember that when you point your weapon at the robbers they'll be more frightened than you.'

'Thanks,' replied Colion. 'Yes, sorry! Deep breaths and squeeze the trigger. Don't pull it. Yes, I remember now. First time out for me on a real firearms operation.'

'Good! Easy now. Train hard, fight easy.'

Colin nodded and flicked the safety catch off with his thumb before saying, 'I'm good to go.'

'You bet you are,' smiled Janice. 'Listen up. You'll be fine.'

The net suddenly burst into life.

'Guvnor!' radioed Ricky almost panic-stricken. 'Loss of drone cover due to low cloud. I can reduce the height of the drone but it might compromise the operation if it becomes visible.'

'Hold present drone altitude,' ordered Boyd.

Martin reported from the bay window of the George Hotel, 'The Mercedes is back. It's pulling up near the NatWest at the bottom of St Andrew's Lane. I'm moving outside onto the street.'

'Negative!' ordered Boyd. 'Stay in the hotel, Martin. They've seen you once already. Give them plenty of room. All units, hold positions and don't take a step on the main street. So far we've got three gangsters eyeing up a bank. We've got nothing. Be patient. This is either a dummy run or the real McCoy. Stand by.'

Acknowledgements rippled across the network and the plain-clothed detectives began to tighten the net.

'Terry, return to your vehicle and make ready to block the Mercedes,' ordered Boyd. 'Anthea, move casually to support Terry. Natural and gradual manoeuvres, please. We'll do a cover and block in the first instance if we must. I have an eyeball on all three subjects. I confirm the driver of the Mercedes is Edwards. Ricky, confirm CCTV is running?'

'Ongoing from local origin,' replied Ricky. 'Quality is poor but smile for the camera.'

'I have that,' replied Boyd,

Leaning casually against the wall of the lane, Boyd watched the Mercedes stop outside the bank.

'Listen up! I have control,' radioed Boyd. 'The Mercedes has parked opposite the Monument. Its engine is still running and the brake lights are still showing from the rear of the vehicle. Edwards remains in the driver's seat. Crawford is walking past the car. He did not acknowledge Edwards. So far...'

Yard by yard, the surveillance team drew closer to the plot.

Boyd continued, 'So far... The brake lights are off. He's taken his foot off the pedal and switched the engine off. Donaldson has walked past the car and is near Barclays Bank. Hold all positions. They've three banks to choose from and it could be any one of them. Stand by. Hold positions!'

'With me, Colion,' whispered Janice. The feisty Scot ushered the young detective to her side with, 'We're going into Barclays Bank. Find the security guard near the entrance and get them to move all the customers away from the door. Just like the briefing. Nice and cool. Ignore the suspects on the street. Hold my hand. We're man and wife going to the bank. Come on.'

The duo stepped into the street and made for Barclays Bank. Hand in hand, they climbed the steps and entered the building.

Boyd's heart rate increased when he watched the two detectives walk straight past the suspects and enter the bank. Simultaneously, another couple walked out of the bank and down the steps before turning into King Street. Then a whistling postman bounded up the steps carrying a handful of letters. He pushed the door open and entered.

Boyd radioed, 'On target! I have control. I have the eyeball. The driver's door is open. The driver is Edwards and he's out of the car. Crawford and Donaldson are returning to the vehicle.'

The seconds ticked by and the hands of the clock on the Monument reached that excruciating position when the clock began to sound eleven.

Stepping further back into his hidey-hole, Boyd radioed, 'I have the eyeball. I have control. Edwards is at the rear of the vehicle. He's opened the boot. Crawford and Donaldson are joining him. They are all together. Wait! They're looking around. They're looking for us. Hold!'

Janice and company sneaked a covert yard. Martin vacated his table and sauntered to the hotel entrance where he stood in the porch. Terry wandered to the front of a shop and stepped into the street using a parked van for cover.

Boyd peered towards the vehicle.

Edwards reached into the boot of the Mercedes, uncovered two sawn-off shotguns, and watched as his two accomplices took possession of them. In a split second, each weapon disappeared into the folds of two long grey raincoats that hid the guns perfectly. They were deep poacher's pockets capable of hiding such weapons.

But in that same split second, Boyd noticed the expressions on their faces, saw the agile movement of the hands, witnessed the hiding of the guns inside the coats and radioed, 'Trigger! Trigger! Trigger! Crawford and Donaldson are now in possession of sawn-off shotguns. They have one weapon each hidden inside their coats. No small arms were seen. Sawn-off shotguns only. Hold positions! Stand by all units.'

The net went silent when Boyd's trigger message resonated across the surveillance channel. The team now knew for certain that they were involved in an operation relevant to armed suspects. The raw intelligence was being analysed on the street in real-time.

Edwards got back into the Mercedes and fired the engine.

Boyd radioed, 'Engine on! One in the car, two on the footpath. It's Barclays Bank. They're making for Barclays Bank. Stand by!'

Another safety catch was pushed to the off position on a police firearm in a nearby lane.

The raiders looked both ways and began to approach the steps to the bank. A step later they each removed a mask from their raincoat. The masks went from pocket to face in a matter of seconds.

'It's no dummy run,' voiced Boyd. 'Hold! Hold! Hold!'

Inside Barclays Bank, Colin withdrew a Gloch pistol from his shoulder holster whilst Janice unravelled a side by side shotgun from her clothing. Colin nodded at the security guard who pressed a button hidden beneath the reception desk and then beckoned all the staff and customers into a back room.

An annoyed elderly gentleman turned to confront the guard who quickly responded with, 'It's the police. Someone is raiding the bank. Now get in that room out of the way.'

Simultaneously, a silent alarm activated on a computer screen in the police control room two miles away. The words *Armed robbery in progress, Barclays Bank, Penrith* appeared on the screen.

Crawford and Donaldson climbed the steps to the bank wearing ski masks. A movement of hands inside raincoats signified access to the sawn-off shotguns.

Boyd radioed, 'All units! Strike! Strike! Strike!' and ran from his hiding place dodging traffic in the progress.

Controlled pandemonium and enforced mayhem hit the streets of the market town when Martin Duffy suddenly dashed out of the George Hotel and made for the bank. Terry fired the Saab and drove the car straight out of his parking place near the Monument. He bounced over the kerb, snatched the handbrake, and came to a standstill immediately in front of the robber's Mercedes.

Simultaneously, Anthea roared through the Narrows at tremendous speed, braked hard, and slid the BMW sideways thereby blocking the Mercedes escape route.

Crawford reached the top step. Donaldson kicked at the door. Both men entered the bank with their shotguns before them and the sound of an angry door hinge colliding with the wall.

'Everybody down!' screamed the robbers.

Janice stepped from the shadows and thrust both barrels of her shotgun into Crawford's temple with the words, 'No! You get down. Armed police. You're nicked.'

Colin followed suit and thrust his Gloch into Donaldson's ribs and said, 'Drop it! Drop the weapon!'

Total surprise accelerated across the faces of the county's most wanted. It was immediately followed by Boyd and Martin Duffy bursting through the door.

Crawford still felt the cold steel of Janice's shotgun hard against his temple but he turned slightly and immediately collided with Boyd who took him to the floor whilst Martin rugby tackled Donaldson from behind. In the ensuing tussle, the barrel-chested Crawford headbutted Boyd and slung Martin away before Janice stepped forward and slammed the butt of her shotgun into Crawford's face.

Turning to Donaldson, her fingers slid to the trigger of her weapon when she challenged him with, 'Your choice. On your knees with your hands clasped and behind your neck.'

Donaldson slid to his knees and complied.

'Do the honours, Janice,' suggested Boyd who stood back as Janice and Colin went through the arrest procedure.

Within moments, the rest of Janice's arrest team stormed into the bank to assist.

A siren sounded far away, and then another as patrol cars were diverted to the scene following the alarm activation.

On the street outside, armed detectives either bounded into Barclays Bank to assist their colleagues or surrounded the Mercedes. The driver of the getaway car, Edwards, remained nonplussed as multiple police weapons clattered against the windows and officers screamed for him to show his hands.

Terry Anwhari tried to open the driver's door but it was locked. Edwards hit the accelerator and he reversed into the gunmetal grey BMW blocking his escape. The rear of the Mercedes collided with the BMW and threw Anthea back in her seat. Terry withdrew a telescopic baton from his clothing, hammered it into the driver's door window, reached in, and grabbed Edwards by the neck.

But Edwards had other ideas and kept his foot on the accelerator gradually pushing the BMW further back.

A gap opened up. There was enough room for the Mercedes to break out of the block. Terry's arms pulled and the driver's foot reached for the accelerator pedal as his hand changed gear.

Nearby, on the pavement, people began screaming and running to safety when they realised what was happening.

There was a frantic heave resulting in the detective dragging Edwards out of the car via the driver's window. Edwards hit the tarmac and was immediately pounced on by other officers.

The cold snap of handcuffs could be heard when the first patrol car arrived at the scene and a dozen detectives made themselves known to the new arrivals by shouting, 'Special Crime Unit! Special Crime Unit! We're on your side!'

On the floor of Barclays Bank, more handcuffs found their way around wicked wrists. Two bodies were lifted from the ground and carried outside to join the other prisoners.

Three police vehicles arrived and the prisoners were bundled into the rear.

Anthea opened the door of the BMW and promptly fell out of the vehicle onto the road holding her neck.

'You alright?' shouted Boyd.

'I'll guess whiplash,' replied Anthea rubbing her neck. 'More of a twinge than an injury.'

Janice allowed her shotgun to drop by her side with the barrel pointed to the ground. 'My car! You were told, Anthea. It's wrecked. I told you to look after it.'

'Sorry,' offered Anthea. 'But I didn't touch your sweets.'

A scowl grew across Janice's face before a slight ripple of a smile broke through

'You okay, Colin?' inquired Boyd.

'I am now,' replied the young detective. 'Train hard, work easy, or something like that. I thought it was a crazy plan but it worked, Guvnor. It worked.'

'Good,' replied Boyd slapping Colin's back. 'Well done! By the way, no one came up with an alternative plan.'

A patrol car pulled up and Superintendent Fowler leapt out of the passenger seat and yelled, 'Boyd! What the hell is going on? I was told you were mounting an intelligence-gathering surveillance operation in the town centre. I wasn't told there would be a bloody armed robbery at a bank.'

'No one was hurt except me,' remarked Anthea stepping forward. 'Slight whiplash.'

'And I presume that's your car that has been written off?' voiced Fowler pointing at the crash site.

'Mine!' said Janice amidst a growing crowd of onlookers. The word was out and the cameras and mobile phone cameras were being put to good use. 'My car! Still, I'll just have to get another one, won't I? A Porsche this time. A black one with a magnetic force field around it. Now, sir, if you don't mind, we have prisoners on route to the nick and I need to be there.'

'Damn lucky no one was hurt,' snarled Superintendent Fowler. 'Everyone with guns! You'd think it was bloody Chicago! This is the sticks, for God's sake. Not America! It could have been planned better surely?'

'Probably,' admitted Boyd. 'But we don't run the show. They run the show because they are the only ones who know what they're doing. We just react to the situation.'

'In future, Commander Boyd, you will kindly inform me of any operational presence that you may have on my patch. Do you understand? I'm not being left in the dark again.'

'Absolutely,' remarked Boyd. 'I'll make a note of that. Excuse me, Superintendent Fowler. I want an ambulance for Anthea. That neck of hers needs looking at by the medics and I need to be at the station.'

Boyd engaged his mobile with three nines.

Janice brushed past Fowler and joined Boyd in Martin Duffy's car. The team set off just as a local journalist arrived and thrust a microphone at the local superintendent who reacted angrily with, 'There'll be a press conference in half an hour. Now get that thing out of my face.'.

'Let's get it done,' nodded Boyd to the team. 'Custody office, secure the evidence, trap the CCTV and drone coverage, witness statements and interviews. Crack on.'

'Attempted robbery, conspiracy to rob, theft of a stolen car, handling a stolen car, possession of prohibited weapons, unlawful possession of firearms, driving whilst disqualified, loitering with intent, going equipped for theft, failing to carry chocolate for sharing. Which one, Guvnor?' asked Janice.

'Reminds me of perm one from any seven,' chuckled Boyd. 'You and Terry can put the file together and pass it to Anthea. She's a tough old nut. I'm sure she'll be okay. Anthea can discuss the job with the prosecutors. One thing is for sure, Janice.'

'What's that?'

'They'll get years instead of months because we played risk and won.'

Boyd's mobile sounded. The name Antonia Harston-Browne appeared on the display panel.

'Antonia!' answered Boyd.

'You're wanted in London,' replied Antonia.

'It wasn't me. I'm innocent,' snapped Boyd.

'Not anymore,' chuckled Antonia. 'You are especially requested.'

'Why, when and where?' queried Boyd.

'To attend a security conference chaired by the Home Secretary at ten o'clock tomorrow morning in our briefing room. Maude Black wants a rundown on the threat from Boko Haram to the UK. I'm sure you're up to date with such matters of international importance or are you too busy chasing squirrels around the lakes?'

'Well, we did catch three squirrels today. They were robbing a bank so it hasn't been a waste of time. I'm not sure I can make it for ten in the morning. I'll have to sort a train out in time.'

'I can send the helicopter for you,' replied Antonia. 'Otherwise, can you make the night sleeper into Euston?'

'The night sleeper? Yes, of course. I'll be there,' replied Boyd. 'Ten sharp! See you in the morning.'

'Problems?' inquired Martin as Boyd closed his mobile.

'I hope not,' voiced Boyd. 'Although my wife will no doubt be annoyed that I'm travelling again. Still, I managed a month on home soil before the cage rattled. Take me to the nick, Martin. Then I can phone Meg once we've got everything sorted out.'

A short time later, Martin pulled into the police station car park and Boyd met with his team to ensure the evidential needs were being followed up.

In the cellblock, Edwards, Donaldson and Crawford were informed of their rights, searched, and then placed in separate cells.

As the night wore on, Crawford lay on his bunk and closed his eyes trying to relax. The arrest had shaken him to the core. All he had to show for the day was a cell and a bruise to the face where the butt of Janice's shotgun had impacted. He considered his freedom to be sacrosanct. There was nothing more important to him particularly as he considered this latest robbery to be their last. Over ten years, they'd carried out over thirty such robberies in Cumbria, Northumbria and the South of Scotland. They had enough money stashed away from all the other robberies to see them through for a lifetime. Bundles of cash were all nicely hidden away so that one day they could retire from a life of crime and jet off to the sun and a new beginning.

Unexpectedly, his hand felt the sharp edge of the wooden bunk upon which he lay. He sat upright and realised that there was more to the bed than he had imagined. Wondering if the last prisoner in the cell had not been searched properly, Crawford trickled his fingers along the slender piece of metal that had been embedded into the side of the bunk. He pocketed it in the folds of his waistband and eventually fell asleep dreaming of escape, freedom, and a secret hideaway where thousands of pounds lay undiscovered.

That night, a visit home was followed by a dash to the railway station where Boyd caught the night sleeper to London.

As Boyd settled into his accommodation in a snug railway carriage in Cumbria, Zak was asleep on a sofa in a house in Peckham. With only a thin blanket to keep him warm the man from Chad felt the cold that came from the lowering of the night temperature and the change in the climate.

The warmth of the African continent had left Zak in more ways than one. His memories of hot sunshine and a cool night breeze were overwhelmed by the nightmare that revisited his mind. Zak's troubled brain thought only of his home on the shores of a lake. The house was made from mud and stood one storey high with an open doorway and a dozen holes in various parts of the building that let in the light and air. His was the last house in the immediate area of the lake to be made of mud. A new regime was afoot and all the new homes were made of bricks and had pitched roofs. They were bigger than his house. He thought of the house that he had made from layers of fine mud, and a woman and three children who lived there with him. They were paddling in the shallow water of the lake with a ball. They were all so happy. Laughter prevailed but then the ball that they shared exploded and Zak's mind went into turmoil.

A cold swathe of perspiration swept across his body.

Zak was surrounded by evil and a man kneeling on top of him with a gun pointed at his head and an overabundance of words that he understood but did not want to hear. Then the man smiled and hugged him when Zag agreed to do his bidding. The evil wicked man who now hugged Zak like a close friend was called Malik. Now he was a friend of Zak. A pal! An important friend who taught him what to do and how to do it. But Zak's mind was troubled by all the pals he had made in recent days. Malik was a pal just like a taxi driver he had recently met, and the people who had let him sleep on a sofa in the house in which he now lived.

Even that policeman on the train was some kind of pal. The policeman had reached out a hand to him, but he was dead now. The offered hand had been too late.

They were all friends. All helping the man from Chad to do the job he was being paid to do. It was too much for Zak to bear.

Restless, mentally disturbed, Zak's mind turned over again, but Malik's gun bore into his temple and the barrel twisted once more, deeper this time, threatening, and entering the innermost sanctity of his skull. Then the evil individual removed the weapon and pointed it into the dark. A light shone and a woman and three children appeared. The woman was sobbing relentlessly. A house made from the mud was behind them. The children were screaming. The brute of a man pulled the trigger. There was no sound of a gunshot in Zak's mind, but the woman fell to the ground. The killer pulled the trigger again and the children screamed.

Zak suddenly sat upright. Breathing heavily, sweat poured from his skin and he felt his heart beating solidly within his chest.

Rolling from the sofa onto the floor, Zak felt a thin carpet and clawed at the threads of the weave to try and find reality. He was tired of the nightmare, frightened by the content, scared of the evil being he dreamt of and knew it would soon be time to move on to do his bidding.

What choice did he have? He knew the answer. There was no answer that satisfied anyone. Zak was bound by his word to follow Malik's orders. It was the way of the tribe who lived in the houses made of mud by the side of the lake. He would follow their way. He had no choice. It's what they did. It's what he had pledged to do.

The clock struck midnight when he pulled the blanket around him and sought to bring warmth to his terrified and tired body.

The hands of Big Ben neared midnight in the city of London where a dark-skinned female dressed in a body-hugging dress showed off her voluptuous curves to a man she had decided was worth the attention.

Her curvaceous body dazzled his eyes as she danced sensuously in front of the window and the moonlight invaded the office to cast her shadow on the carpeted floor.

'Come away from the window,' pleaded the man. 'Others will see you and I'd rather they didn't.'

Giggling, she placed a finger between her teeth and posed in idle playfulness saying, 'You mean, you want me just for you and no one else.'

'Come here,' he pleaded when he reached out to capture her.

With a hop and a playful step, she evaded his outstretched hand, wiggled her hips and swayed her body from left to right. She taunted him, drove him to distraction, and finally said, 'I'm tired of advertising, Dennis. It's time you came and caught me, Mr Butler.'

In a moment she was gone from the open-planned office and into a smaller office where she closed the door behind her. Perching on the edge of the desk, the dark-skinned beauty allowed the hem of her dress to rest high on her thighs. Conscious of the low-cut silk dress that she wore, she waited.

The door opened and Dennis Butler walked toward her.

She sensed the fire in his belly, saw the desire in his eyes, and scattered the contents of the desk onto the floor.

'Now,' she cried. 'Now.'

Big Ben chimed as Dennis used his heel to tap the door closed behind him. He took hold of the woman and crushed her to his body as they both dropped onto the desktop.

The night was yet young.

~

Chapter Five

~

The Secure Conference Room
The Special Crime Unit
London

Boyd was out of the taxi and climbing the steps to the office as the hands of Big Ben neared ten. He was late. Half an hour late to be precise. Clearing security, he entered the innards of the Special Crime Unit and took a lift down to the secure area of the building. Trotting along the corridor, he entered the secure conference room.

Antonia frowned at his late attendance, Sir Phillip smiled, and Maude broke into speech with, 'Ah! Commander Boyd! How kind of you to join us. I do apologize for arranging such an early appointment for you but then again, you have a track record of being late for such meetings, don't you?'

Boyd beamed a huge smile and replied, 'Home Secretary, I had no idea you were chairing the meeting otherwise I'd have been here at the crack of dawn. How are you, madam?'

'I'm well, thank you,' replied Maude Black, the Home Secretary. Settling her glasses on her nose, Maude twisted an air of sarcasm when she suggested, 'I understand you are late because you had to go to the bank.'

'No withdrawals were made, madam,' revealed Boyd. 'And no one was hurt in the process. Everything went well.'

'I'm pleased to hear it. Please convey my personal thanks to all concerned. In my position, it might surprise you to learn that I seldom hear of every armed police operation that takes place so, when good news crosses my desk, I'm keen to respond appropriately.'

'And from whom did you hear about this one?' asked Boyd.

'Me!' interrupted Antonia Harston-Browne. 'You're always late. Someone had to cover for you. It was the best I could do.'

Antonia was renowned amongst her male counterparts for her shapely legs and long red hair which flowed down her back covering her shoulder blades. With an hourglass figure, Antonia wore a dark blue, two-piece, executive-style suit set off with a silver brooch worn on the lapel. A highly educated and articulate individual with connections across a broad spectrum of society, Antonia was a senior Intelligence Officer and leading member of the Special Crime Unit. She was also in love with Sir Phillip Nesbitt K.B.E., the Director-General of the Security Service.

'You're so kind, Antonia,' replied Boyd who then mouthed, 'Grass!'

Approaching the Home Secretary, Boyd removed a bottle of Bushmills Irish whiskey from his pocket and handed it to her with the words, 'For you, madam.'

Surprised, Maude Black reached out for the gift but then withdrew saying, 'Oh no! I mean, I don't think I should, Mr Boyd. People might construe that this is a bribe of some kind. Do you think it's politically correct?'

'On your birthday?' queried Boyd. He removed his overcoat and hung it on a peg saying, 'It's a present from the unit to yourself, Home Secretary. Happy birthday! Your favourite, I believe.'

'You are well informed, Mr Boyd,' smiled the Home Secretary. 'Put like that it would be disrespectful not to accept. Thank you all so very much.'

Boyd handed the bottle over and it was finally accepted. He helped himself to coffee from a dispenser and went to sit beside Antonia.

The redhead looked at him contemptuously and whispered, 'Lackey! Flattery will get you everywhere.'

As Maude Black read the whiskey label, a well-dressed man voiced, 'Can we get on with it. It's like listening to a high school reunion. Please!'

'Of course,' replied the Home Secretary. 'Commander Boyd, I don't believe you know the recently appointed Secretary of State for Defence Mr Dennis Butler.'

'Pleased to meet you,' stated Boyd shaking hands with Butler whilst simultaneously nodding his presence to Sir Henry Fielding: an elderly gentleman who wore a three-piece suit and sported a walking stick to aid his mobility. He was the Secretary of State for Foreign Affairs. 'Sir Henry!' continued Boyd. 'I trust you are well?'

'No wonder we're behind time,' scowled Butler.

Boyd acknowledged the gathering and nodded a smile to some military uniforms sat next to the Foreign Secretary.

Maude Black slammed the whiskey bottle onto the table and announced, 'In which case, we shall proceed with haste. Sir Phillip, as per my recent memorandum, Her Majesty's Government need to know about Boko Haram and its current relevance to Nigeria and the United Kingdom. We are hosting elements of the Nigerian Government in the Lake District soon and need to be up to date with such matters.'

'The Lake District?' queried Boyd.

'Which is why we waited for you, Commander,' quipped the Home Secretary with a sly grin. 'Sir Phillip! Begin with a concise but relevant history, please.'

'Hot off the press,' whispered Antonia to Boyd. 'I'd no time to tell you.'

The Director-General of the Security Service, Sir Phillip Nesbitt K.B.E. was older than Antonia and in his early fifties. Of medium height with light brown hair and brown eyes, he was extraordinarily nondescript in appearance yet those who knew Phillip well would testify to his tenacity when chasing down a specific matter of importance to him. A 'Jack of all Trades' and 'Master of None', he enjoyed an uncanny ability to remember the slightest detail. Phillip would remind his closest friends that he had started on the factory floor and worked his way to the top of the tree. He'd enjoyed a long career in the service and specialised in both Irish and International Terrorism before rapid promotions followed in the realms of protective security and organisational administration. It was here that he gained a Knighthood and took the reins as head of the intelligence community. Surprisingly, Phillip was not the most popular man in the Service. He'd deliberately chosen his friends carefully determined to do the best he could in his chosen profession.

Clearing his throat, Sir Phillip replied, 'Boko Haram is a Nigeria-based terror group that wants to rid Nigeria of Western and secular institutions. It intends to resurrect the Kanem-Bornu caliphate that once ruled Nigeria, Chad, and Cameroon. The group began in 2002 when a Salafist cleric opened a mosque in Maiduguri and immediately enlisted several disgruntled adolescents living in the area. As you know, Salafism is an avenue of Islam that argues true Muslims should live as the Prophet Mohammad did fourteen hundred years ago. Apart from advocating Sharia Law for the masses, they tend not to get involved in mainstream politics.'

'But they are still extremely dangerous to society,' contended the Director of Special Forces, Major General Kenneth Armitage. 'As my man on the ground, Major Alexander Anderson, will tell you.'

'Alex,' corrected the SAS Major. 'Call me Alex. I am honoured to be with you all today. I am, of course, fully familiar with Commander Boyd and the Special Crime Unit, but my presence here merely reflects my deployment as a liaison officer to the Nigerian military. The incumbent, Captain Murray, recently returned to the UK to enjoy his well-earned retirement. I've served in the area before but it's my turn to take the reins now. I'm on a midnight flight from Brize Norton to Abuja, the capital. My first port of call will be Maiduguri. I do believe my official title is Military Attaché.'

The middle-aged Major General Armitage threaded his brittle moustache through nimble fingers and said, 'No disrespect intended to Captain Murray but you will kindly note that a high-ranking officer now has a responsibility to me for military operations in the region. He is our military attaché and we need him there. That is because when the stakes expand it is time to respond accordingly with increased resources and increased dependency. I require more, so should you. It's my remit to report to COBRA and yourselves in terms of both national and international responsibilities, which is why I have no hesitation in introducing Major Anderson to you. He comes highly recommended for the job at hand. The Major works at street level. When he is too old to fight, he will work at this level.'

'I'll second that,' interjected Boyd. 'His training regime in Hereford is legendary in our office.'

The Major General nodded in appreciation and continued, 'These responsibilities include the provision of training and support to the host nation as well as what I choose to call managerial overview, strategical management and tactical operations. MOST! Management! Operations! Strategy and Tactics!'

'Good!' intervened the Home Secretary. 'Indeed, excellent! As chair, I would like you to explain to me, and the gathering, how I might differentiate a Salafi Muslim from a Sunni or Shia Muslim. Is that possible?'

The two military officers gestured to each other before Major Anderson accepted the challenge and replied, 'Salafi-jihadists are what we need to worry about because they imitate the particular habits of the first Muslims of Muhammad's time. They dress like the Prophet by cuffing their trousers to ankle-length. These people also brush their teeth in the same way Muhammad did.'

'What?' from an astounded Maude.

'They use a twig called a miswak to clean their teeth,' replied Alex. 'It sounds rather archaic but it is medically approved and the best way to clean your teeth.'

Dennis Butler shook his head, clasped his face in two clenched hands, and said, 'Stories! Back to square one. Or is it me?'

'Possibly,' ventured Alex. 'I don't talk politics. I talk fact and you can make your mind up therefrom. The reality is that Boko Haram and ISWAP harbour activists that could change the world as you know it and take us back fourteen hundred years. What you see around you today will not be there under a Salafi administration.'

There was a pause in proceedings as those assembled around the oval table considered the words of Alex Anderson: a handsome, square-chinned, slender man in his mid-thirties who had joined the military as a degree entrant at Sandhurst and worked his way into the command structure.

'Why Maiduguri?' queried Butler.

'The city is the capital and largest city of Borno State in north-eastern Nigeria,' explained Alex. 'It was founded in 1907 by the British as a military outpost. Geographically, it's a handy location for me to be stationed. I'll speak with the team currently there.'

'I see,' replied the Defence Secretary. 'It was a military settlement originally. What is there now, may I ask?'

'Sir Phillip,' gestured the Major.

'Now it has a population of close to two million people,' revealed Sir Phillip. 'Most of them are Muslim but there is a fair smattering of Christians and multiple tribal groups of various ethnic persuasion. It is a notorious area polluted by many different political, religious and tribal concerns. The three main tribes are the Hausa-Fulani, the Igbo, and the Yoruba, but there are other tribes that are smaller in comparison. Some support Sharia Law, and some do not. The Hausa-Fulani are the largest and politically strongest in the area but once you understand and recognize the differences in the religious beliefs in play, you must then consider the disparities in their political aspirations. And there are many. You have multiple religions side by side with multiple political and cultural beliefs. It's a hotbed of violence, back-biting and problems. The area we are talking about is an example to other countries that multi-culturalism might look good on paper but in practice, it doesn't work. It hasn't worked there for hundreds of years.'

'Oh dear,' intervened the Home Secretary. 'I can hear the thunder of opposition parties already. Sorry, Sir Phillip, do continue.'

'Maiduguri sits beside the Ngadda River which flows into the swamps in the areas around Lake Chad,' continued Sir Phillip.

'I must confess,' admitted Maude. 'I had to get the map out to find out exactly where Chad is situated. Most of the country is slap bang in the middle of the Sahara Desert but I see that Lake Chad is close to the border with North-East Nigeria. It's hardly on the mainline into Europe, is it? Or anywhere else for that matter. Has anyone ever been there other than Major Anderson?'

Sir Henry tapped his walking stick on the floor and suggested, 'I wouldn't mention such a matter with the Nigerian ministers when they attend the conference, Maude. They are travelling a long way to speak with us. I advise against starting an argument with them about travel arrangements.'

'Yes! They are attending at our invitation and our expense,' chided the Home Secretary. 'A lot of this is new to me and will be useful in the coming weeks, Sir Henry. Now then, Sir Phillip, coverage! Do we have coverage in Chad?'

'We have people there from our sister service,' replied Sir Phillip. 'Primarily in the capital.'

'Thank goodness!' voiced Maude.

'May I ask why Chad and Boko Haram are so important at present?' asked Boyd.

'Dennis?' queried the Home Secretary. 'Your ground.'

'We are informed by America that the leadership of Boko Haram recently changed and we should expect a different pattern of attack from them,' explained the Defence Secretary. 'The yanks seem to think Boko Haram could go global like ISIS although I don't see any evidence of that. It's probably just warmongering humbug from the USA. However, as we are all attending a tripartite conference later this month, I wanted to be up to date with the latest situation.'

'Excuse me,' interrupted Boyd. 'What do you mean by tripartite conference?'

Maude black leaned forward in her seat and said, 'It's a meeting involving senior ministers from the UK, the USA and Nigeria. We shall be discussing terrorism in Nigeria and its neighbours and what further steps can be taken to address the problem. If you can bear with me for a moment Mr Boyd. I'll bring you up to date shortly.'

Boyd nodded and remained silent.

Butler, the Defence Secretary, continued, 'I've worked with the defence industry over the years but I'm new to the global politics that are an important part of the government. I'm aware we have military forces stationed in Nigeria but I'm not up to date as to why we need to deploy Major Anderson there. Can you bring me up to speed, Sir Phillip? I ask because as far as I am aware there is no history of attacks from Boko Haram in the UK. Surely America has it all wrong?'

The Director-General of the Security Service coughed politely and said, 'May I enlighten the audience?'

'Proceed, Sir Phillip!' declared Maude Black loudly.

'There have been several civil wars in Nigeria since the mid-sixties,' professed Sir Phillip. 'None of them have heralded an outright winner and a surplus of weapons has been in existence for over half a century. The region is awash with weapons. As a result, the aggressors, let's call them the long term armed rebels, have used those weapons and their bullying tactics to exploit the cultural, ethnic, and religious ties that Chad, Niger, and Cameroon share with northern Nigeria.'

Dennis Butler nodded with interest as Sir Phillip took a sip of water and continued, 'From the outset Boko Haram's strategy has been to build their foundations from the people born in Chad, Nigeria, and Cameroon. Make no mistake, it is a jihadist group that has exploited that region. It is an evil we need to eradicate. Cross-border smuggling of weapons and supplies is common and helped by the fact that Boko Haram has recruited fighters from neighbouring countries to fill its ranks. To do so, it has a history of paying young recruits to join them. That is one of their better-known tactics.'

'An extremely dangerous group by the sound of it,' ventured Butler.

'Yes,' agreed Sir Phillip. 'In 2009, the leader was killed by Nigerian security forces. A new trailblazer took over and has a reputation for the use of mass violence. In addition to targeting Christians and Catholics, who together represent less than a quarter of Chad's population, Boko Haram routinely targets Muslims who do not support their aims. This might explain why ISWAP is now a problem in the region.'

'ISWAP?' queried the Home Secretary.

'Islamic State in West Africa Province,' explained Sir Henry. 'Don't you read the weekly briefing notes, Home Secretary?'

Maude ignored the remark and gestured to the Defence Secretary who queried, 'Is ISWAP related to ISIS, Sir Phillip?'

'Yes,' confirmed the Director-General of the Security Services. 'It's a splinter group of Boko Haram and since 2015, these two extremist groups, which operate throughout the Lake Chad region, have killed hundreds of people. Over twenty thousand Chadians have fled the country, and almost a quarter of a million have been displaced. Sir Henry perhaps you'd like to inform the audience of the political ramifications.'

'Yes, I will,' replied Sir Henry. 'These devilish groups have caused immense challenges to stability in the region. They launch attacks on the neighbouring countries of Nigeria, Cameroon, and Niger. The Chadian armed forces were given the right to mobilize against the extremist outfit by Nigeria in 2015 following suicide bombings in the capital N'Djamena. There have also been multiple attacks on villages resulting in dozens of kidnaps and ransoms that are at epidemic proportions. When joined together, Boko Haram and ISWAP are a major headache for the Nigerian government. These two terrorist gangs have increased their attacks against Chad and Cameroon. Sir Phillip, what's the latest on territorial control there?'

'ISWAP controls the Lake Chad Basin area and Boko Haram controls land in central and southern Borno State as well as the Sambisa Forest. Corruption is plentiful amongst the police, politicians, and public services. The problem is that the Lake Chad area is a magnet for migrants looking for work in agriculture and farming. Boko Haram control the infrastructure and are providing jobs because government officials can't get into the area. They're too frightened and Boko Haram control the entrance points. Yes, ladies and gentlemen, a terrorist group has become so powerful that Nigeria cannot govern its people. As a result, recruits to Boko Haram are rife because the local population in the specific area to which I refer is more likely to look to Boko Haram for jobs, money, food and clothing than the government. That's the magnet. Now then, because the government is denied access to the area, the countryside is awash with self-governing militias trying to protect communities against these jihadist groups whilst those very same jihadist groups battle the militias to retain control. Meanwhile, the Nigerian security forces look for ways to infiltrate the area.'

'Surely the Nigerian army can track them down?' ventured the Home Secretary. 'What do you think, Major Anderson?'

'Sadly no, they cannot' explained Alex. 'Boko Haram hides in the swamps and on islands in the lake and is impossible to locate. Its headquarters seem to move like a snake in the grass. Unseen!'

'Can anything be done?' queried Butler.

Alex Anderson declared, 'In 2018, the first UK-Nigeria security and defence partnership came about. We have been helping Nigeria train over thirty thousand troops. The terror groups are responsible for the deaths of over twenty thousand people and the displacement of about two million. We've provided equipment and training for the military to help them protect themselves from the threat of improvised explosive devices used by terrorists. I know this has saved many lives from recent conversations with Captain Murray. He has fully briefed me and brought me up to date since my last tour of duty there three years ago.'

Interrupting, Sir Henry added, 'Our government is also in the process of delivering a programme to educate one hundred thousand children who live in the conflict zone. Some of the teachers have fled, schools have been destroyed, and the country is in turmoil. Interestingly, we've persuaded the Nigerian government to adopt a crisis response mechanism like our COBRA system. This helps them to respond to terror attacks whilst trying their utmost to protect its citizens and British nationals and businesses in the country. All these things ought to reduce the number of recruits joining Boko Haram by tackling the lies and false information spread by the group to attract new members. We're pushing out counter-narratives and drawing on the UK's experience of countering terrorist propaganda at home and as part of the global campaign against ISIS.'

'That's astounding,' remarked Boyd. 'I had no idea.'

'I wouldn't expect you to, Commander Boyd,' voiced the Foreign Secretary. 'Your team has enough on your plate in this country as it is. That said, you will be interested to know, I'm sure, that our arrangement with Nigeria also encompasses plans to strengthen policing, reduce piracy in the Gulf of Guinea, and tackle organised crime by directly challenging kidnapping and trafficking. There is a combined desire to stamp out corruption and a new civil asset recovery task force will help Nigeria recover stolen assets held in Britain.'

'If I have followed this briefing correctly,' ventured Boyd. 'I can see why Boko Haram and ISWAP have adopted a new reign of terror. Mass violence, you mentioned. It seems that is their response to the UK-Nigeria partnership.'

'That's exactly as how I see it,' intervened the Home Secretary.

'Why is there a conference in the Lake District?' queried Boyd. 'I would have thought the Nigerian Embassy or a conference centre in the city would have been more likely.'

Sir Henry declared, 'I thought it a wise and useful move to take our visitors, particularly the Nigerians, to one of the most beautiful areas of our country. I want them to feel relaxed and safe to the extent that we can easily discuss how much the current arrangements have worked and what we need to do to improve them. Success will be the result of hard work, not paper policies that are put in place and left to fester. Furthermore, the chance of a demonstration against our Nigerian guests is much reduced if we take them out of rent-a-mob London. The American Secretary of State, Nigel Vanderbilt, will be in attendance on behalf of the United States whereas Nigeria, Chad and West Africa will be represented by the President of Nigeria, Adebiyi Berundi. I'll be present to represent British interests.'

'I understand your point about any demonstration,' remarked Boyd. 'In London, you might expect a few thousand and some of them will be what we call weekend-demo people. They don't do the garden on a weekend, wash the car, or play golf. No! They go to whichever protest march is arranged. You're right, Sir Henry. If there was a protest of some kind in Cumbria, it's unlikely to involve more than a couple of hundred marchers at the most.'

'In respect of the conference, Mr Boyd,' intervened the Home Secretary. 'A portfolio of who's who will be with you tomorrow morning. It contains details of the guests, who they are, photographs, the usual. I want a discreet security operation from your team, Commander. The Special Crime Unit is my preferred choice.'

'Thank you,' replied Boyd. 'Can I ask you all if there is any recent intelligence that might indicate a terrorist attack will be mounted against the conference and the people attending it?'

'Not as far as I am aware,' replied the Home Secretary checking around the table. 'It should be a breeze but if anything comes up I'd be happy in the knowledge that the unit is already in position.

'Why the Special Crime Unit may I ask?' questioned Dennis Butler. 'Surely the local police can handle the conference if there is no likelihood of an attack and, as Commander Boyd states, any such protest march or demonstration is unlikely to cause staffing problems for the local police.'

Maude Black nodded in agreement with Butler but then said, 'The Special Crime Unit is a hand-picked team of detectives drawn from Counter Terrorist Command together with some top detectives from all over the British Isles and some hand-picked individuals from MI5 and MI6 as well as other national agencies appropriate to their duties. They are all experts in some field or other. The unit's remit is to police and defend the freedom of the nation and its people. Mr Boyd's speciality is running a stand-alone response team capable of running any major investigation anywhere in the country, and if necessary – elsewhere. If we are talking terrorism to the Nigerians and the Americans I want my best people there. The yanks will undoubtedly deploy an army of Secret Service personnel to the conference. Commander Boyd will run the operation and has experience in dealing with such personnel deployed on our soil whilst protecting their nationals. I want a low key visible response supported by a high-intensity background security surveillance operation. Boyd is my choice.'

'Marvellous what a bottle of Bushmills can do,' muttered Butler.

'I beg your pardon,' challenged the Home Secretary.

'Nothing,' replied the Defence Secretary. 'Nothing at all.'

A knock on the door heralded the delivery of a trolley laden with more tea and coffee. The meeting broke up for a short time whilst refreshment was taken.

Boyd and Antonia took the opportunity to approach Maude Black where Boyd asked, 'Are you sure there's nothing we need to know about the Lake District conference, Home Secretary? It is short notice if the truth is known.'

Maude Black studied Boyd and Antonia and replied, 'I'm sure it will be fine, Mr Boyd. It's just that one of the matters on the agenda is corruption and therein lies the weakness.'

There was a silence that betrayed the truth of the matter and Boyd responded to it when he looked into the Home Secretary's eyes and suggested, 'It's awfully stuffy in here. Would you care for a breath of fresh air in the rose garden?'

'That would be nice,' replied Maude. 'I've heard of it but never been invited to partake in its loveliness. The rose garden is quite special, isn't it? I think it is okay to take a short break whilst refreshments are taken.'

'Antonia,' remarked Boyd. 'Your service, I believe.'

The redheaded lady from MI5 smiled and said, 'Home Secretary, the rose is associated with state intelligence work. Sir Francis Walsingham, Queen Elizabeth I's spymaster in the 16th century, used it on his seal. What is said in the rose garden remains in the rose garden.'

'I understand,' replied Maude Black. 'I like a good rose.'

Moments later, Boyd opened a door in the corridor and escorted Antonia and Maude into the rose garden. They strolled in the small but quite divine area which lay at the centre of the building.

'We speak freely in the rose garden, Home Secretary,' revealed Boyd. 'No one takes notes, records the minutes or raises a formal objection. There is no recorder and no camera. You have my word on that, madam.'

Maude Black nodded and said, 'You missed out trust, Mr Boyd. It is a rarely used element of life these days. I have decided to trust you once more.'

'You have a point to make, I believe,' suggested Boyd. 'I'm guessing you distrust someone.'

'The Prime Minister forms the cabinet, Mr Boyd. I am part of the decision-making process but do not have the final say on who the other members are. Sometimes I find myself at odds with the beliefs and aspirations of others. That's all.'

'I take it you are not getting on with the new Defence Secretary,' suggested Boyd.

Maude Black shrugged her shoulders, looked at Antonia and said, 'What makes you think that, Mr Boyd?'

'Just an observation, that's all. I do not doubt Dennis Butler's sincerity but he was rather abrupt with you. Is he a problem that you need to deal with quietly but expeditiously?'

Turning to Antonia, the Home Secretary asked, 'Is he always so blunt?'

'Boyd is a detective, madam,' replied the redhead. 'He's not an intelligence officer like myself and he's not a politician. Boyd means no offence to your colleague but he has not been developed to a standard of political correctness that some would wish for.'

'Developed?' grumbled Boyd quietly.

Antonia glanced unsympathetically at Boyd and continued, 'You must forgive him but you must also rally to him if there is something on your mind because if you want the job done properly you need Boyd, not someone who will pander to everyone's political emotions.'

Maude Black bent down to examine a rose before revealing, 'The rose garden you say.'

'Indeed,' replied Antonia. 'Roses have no ears. Just strong stems.'

'The Defence Secretary is new to his job,' replied the Home Secretary engaging Antonia approvingly. 'He has no idea of who he is dealing with and is quite lax in everything he does. I consider him to be incompetent. Furthermore, he won't take my advice. Mr Butler tells me he doesn't need a crutch to walk on his own two feet.'

Boyd pursed his lips and nodded.

'He's not a bad person,' continued Maude. 'He's just inept and easily swayed when it suits him. The Nigerians have a security advisor that I am aware of from previous meetings. She has made overtures recently to Mr Butler. Perhaps sexual or suggestive, you understand. I'm not sure which but nothing would surprise me. She's using her position as security advisor to the Nigerian Embassy in such a way that she wants to know everything about other embassies and the security protocols in place. I've told Butler to ignore her but he is doing quite the reverse and I shudder to think what he may have told her already.'

Antonia and Boyd glanced at each other before Antonia asked, 'Is she a legitimate diplomat or hired by the embassy to do a job?'

'She's a hired hand, Antonia,' replied the Home Secretary. 'Our Mr Butler doesn't seem to recognise the difference between the two. I think he's becoming infatuated with her.'

'Is it that you don't trust the Defence Secretary or don't trust the security advisor?' probed Boyd. 'I'm picking up that your Mr Butler might be slightly naïve.'

'And you would be right in my opinion,' nodded the Home Secretary. 'His naivety doesn't help the situation. I would not be at all surprised to find that she may have direct access to the wrong people.'

'Boko Haram supporters?' suggested Boyd.

'Yes, possibly. Look, her details will be in the portfolio that you'll receive tomorrow morning. I think you should be aware of my thoughts and opinions. I want things to go well with the Nigerians and can think of nothing worse than our team shooting themselves in the foot.'

'Thank you,' smiled Boyd. 'Her name is…?'

'Ester Abara! Her photograph and details are in the portfolio.'

'Of course, many thanks.'

'Do not trust every politician who arrives in the Lake District, Mr Boyd. If the travellers from Nigeria have the wrong kind of friends and are engaged in loose talk then who else knows? It's a corrupt country. I'm just covering all the bases as I see them.'

'Understood,' replied Boyd. 'Perfectly put. I think you might have just given us a nightmare scenario if it all goes wrong.'

'A nightmare?' queried Maude. 'I hope not, Mr Boyd. I truly hope not.'

The trio returned to the room where the conference continued throughout the morning before ending at lunchtime.

Boyd and Antonia made their way from the conference room into Boyd's office where the Commander presented his colleague from the Security Service with a leatherbound armchair and a long sigh.

'What's the matter?' enquired Antonia, her long red hair falling neatly across her shoulder as she took the seat. 'It's a sudden high-level protection job that you should be pleased to handle. The Home Secretary wanted the unit. No-one else. There's not much time but we can handle it.'

'Anthea is in Cumbria nursing whiplash. Janice Burns and Terry Anwhari are putting a file of evidence together and I expect they'll prove that the Carlisle criminals they arrested in Penrith are responsible for at least another dozen armed robberies in the area. They are the team I need around me at this moment in time. My best selections, Antonia.'

'You forgot Bannerman,' revealed Antonia.

'No, I didn't,' replied Boyd. 'He's a six feet five inch giant with more experience in the Royalty and Diplomatic Protection Squad than the rest of the unit put together. I'll brief him on the show. DI Bannerman will be in charge of the protection issues. The last thing he needs is a situation between Ester Abara and Dennis Butler to sort out. Security advisors and Defence Secretaries do not seem to go well. Still, Bannerman can arrange a low-level covert operation against them both. It will be interesting to see if this Ester woman has any traces that are of interest to us.'

'Anything else?' probed Antonia.

'I want Bannerman to report directly to you and me because we need to be in charge of the intelligence assessment. And I want you to be responsible for that assessment. Not the local police, the military, the Americans, or any of the ministers and politicians who will be attending. Give such people an inch and they are likely to take a mile. I want the security angles watertight. No leaks.'

'My pleasure,' nodded Antonia. 'I'll make a start on the Ticker computer system shortly.

'I'll ring Bannerman,' voiced Boyd reaching for his mobile. 'We seem to have the Home Secretary's approval if we've been specially selected as you say. Let's use that authority. Bannerman can use any resources necessary including the Red Alpha teams.'

'Just one thing.'

'Go on, Antonia.'

'The unit has four branches. Your preferred team is tied up. Brief them and keep them up to speed. Once they're on top of the paperwork arrange for the locals to take over the administration and onward investigation into those historic armed robberies you spoke about. I presume they are working in tandem with locals from Cumbria already?'

'Of course,' replied Boyd.

'Good, then once they're ready to relinquish the file, and we're ready to muster the troops for the background investigations into the lakeside conference, we can call Anthea and the team back into the limelight. How does that sound?'

'Fine! We'll do that. I'll circulate the job in hand, keep them up to date, and hope we never need them. According to the Home Secretary, it should all go well anyways.'

'You can always have faith in our senior politicians, Boyd,' chuckled Antonia. 'What would we do without them?'

Boyd paused for a moment before replying, 'Be happy with a permanent state of unauthorised anarchy?'

'Just don't put them in charge of the unit,' frowned Antonia as she turned to a standalone computer system. 'Your starter for ten. The plan, please.'

Sitting down, Boyd said, 'We are told there is no threat against the conference but then we are warned that some of the people attending may be corrupt and untrustworthy. Let's suppose the enemy is planning to attack the conference?'

'Okay! That sounds reasonable given what Maude Black has just told us.'

'Go back three months looking at APIS: the advanced passenger information system. Anyone arriving in the UK legitimately should be recorded in those lists. I want all the travel routes investigated from West Africa into the UK. Include cargo flights and pre-booked train and bus tickets from Europe. I want a list of passengers available for cross-reference as we develop this enquiry. Simultaneously, double-check individuals moving through Europe who originate from West Africa. Concentrate on Nigeria, Cameroon and Chad. I'm sure the Americans will automatically be screening similar flights from their neck of the woods.'

'Three months? That will take three months,' argued Antonia. 'Can I suggest we start at one month and work backwards towards three months?'

'Agreed!' nodded Boyd. 'I want us to suppose that we're looking for a professional hitman possibly supported by three or four others. Male or female, I don't know.'

'A traveller?'

'Yes! Look for people travelling all together or people travelling separately who all leave the same place and then arrive at the same location in the UK within forty-eight hours of each other. It's just a gut feeling I have because of the nature of the West African problem.'

'Your health issues have always worried me,' chuckled Antonia. 'Do you have a degree in flying by the seat of your pants?'

'Not yet, but I'm working on it,' laughed Boyd. 'Sometimes my gut feelings are spot on and other times they are miles out. It's the nature of being a detective I suppose. Look, Antonia, when the portfolio from the Home Secretary arrives I'd also like the team to check out all the attendees, not just Ester Abara. Double-check bona fides. Don't share anything with the Americans without my say so.'

'Sir Phillip may disagree.'

'Then I'll listen to his argument,' explained Boyd. 'But I'm not trusting anyone until we've cleared the list of guests and that includes the Americans. If we've got dodgy politicians talking to Boko Haram then so could the Americans. Step by step, please. Furthermore, I want all the CCTV from the Nigerian Embassy area in Northumberland Avenue examined. Compare images with known ISIS sympathisers and any suspect travellers on the lists you are about to scrutinise. Do we have any regulars out on the streets watching the embassy to report back to their paymasters as to what they see in the vicinity? I want to know if there's anyone out there watching us watching them. Same with the protection teams for the Prime Minister, the Home Secretary and the Foreign Secretary. Do any of our people have a new suspicion, a new face, a strange or weird connection that has suddenly appeared recently? Rattle the cage, Antonia. I want to see what drops out.'

'That's all well and good,' suggested Antonia. 'But if your imaginary hit team exists then we probably won't find them listed on a ship coming out of Lagos or Calabar.'

'I know but we need to eliminate the obvious first,' argued Boyd. 'There has to be a West African connection somewhere along the line. We need to dig for it.'

'I'll check our current operations,' replied Antonia scribbling notes. 'We have several small surveillance teams running against a host of interesting individuals. They monitor targets who are of lesser interest to us than others.'

'The Red Alpha surveillance teams?' queried Boyd.

'That's the ones. They have the necessary authority to mount audio-visual surveillance on specific targets as designated by a Home Secretary's warrant. We seldom get anything hot from it. That said, Home Office Ministers tend to agree to the warrants when a strong argument for gutter-level intelligence is required.'

'Good!' replied Boyd. 'Sometimes the best intelligence comes from the gutter.'

'You mentioned legitimate passengers. What about illegal Channel crossers?' suggested Antonia.

'How do you mean?' enquired Boyd.

'Most of the Channel crossers originate from either Dunkirk or Calais,' explained Antonia. 'They buy their way across on a dinghy and usually land on the Kent coast between Margate and Dungeness. That's the main stretch of land they target. Once in a while, a different departure point or a bad storm might push them further south towards Rye or Hastings.'

Boyd nodded as he listened closely.

'It's all the rage and it would be no surprise to me if that was the method of entry for a team from West Africa.'

'I bow to your historic wisdom in respect of such matters,' replied Boyd. 'I suppose it depends on how astute they are. Plane, train or boat?'

'If you want to bypass tickets, credit cards and CCTV then a dinghy is the best way to enter the country,' suggested Antonia. 'It all depends on the mental capacity and educational attainment of the attacking group.'

'Ouch!' replied Boyd. 'Well, they don't seem to be famous for their planning aptitude, so far.'

'Right now,' continued Antonia. 'Boko Haram has no history of attacks here, so I'd say they were second division players trying to enter the Premier League. The Channel, Boyd! It's worth a shot.'

'Second division or not, they only need to win once,' nodded Boyd. 'Okay! I'm going to link up with Joe Harkness and see what his detectives on the south coast have to say about such people.'

'Detective Inspector Joe Harkness is a former member of the Kent Serious and Organised Crime Unit, a surveillance officer and a financial investigator,' remarked Antonia. 'All before he joined us here at the Special Crime Unit. Are you bringing him into the game?'

'Yes! I'll phone him shortly,' nodded Boyd. 'I think we'll split his team. One half can help you with the nitty-gritty and the other half can deploy to Calais, liaise with the French, and find out who the main players are over there in the people trafficking racket.'

'The West African connection,' remarked Antonia. 'You're right about one thing, Billy. The Channel crossers initially began with people escaping war zones in Syria, Libya and elsewhere. Places like Bosnia and Serbia. A lot of them didn't want to be captured and identified so they spent their time running and hiding once they'd arrived on the beach. There were a lot of Iranians involved, to begin with. Did you know?'

'I didn't,' replied Boyd. 'Is it still the same?'

'No!' voiced Antonia. 'Now the Channel is full of people who want to get caught. The French don't seem to do anything to stop the Channel crossers. The whole issue has become a political football that the two governments use in their various arguments over trade, the EU and whatever else is the flavour of the month. I don't like it. I think you should tell Joe Harkness to watch his step.'

'You mean do a Maude Black and warn him that his fellow police officers over there in France may not be trustworthy?'

'I'll leave you to sort that out with Joe,' replied Antonia. 'But yes, that's right. The Channel is full of economic migrants from Africa and Asia who want to be rescued. No one runs and hides anymore. They want to be captured and they want the benefits of a western lifestyle here in the UK.'

'Provided they can keep their own culture, religions, language and obsessions, without giving a thought to integrating into our way of life.'

'Now you're being a racist.'

'No, I'm telling a version of the truth, but it's not that important at the moment. Query Ticker, Antonia. Who's most likely to be involved in people trafficking in France? Anyone on the system?'

'I can tell you that without looking,' replied the redhead. 'Louis Martin is the main man in Calais and Dunkirk.'

'Bingo!' snapped Boyd. 'That's our first port of call.'

'Nope!' chuckled Antonia. 'Louis Martin doesn't exist. The French can't find him.'

'You mean the French police say they can't find him. Presumably, the Channel crossers have his telephone number.'

'Apparently, you just mention the name Louis Martin in the camps and in the streets where the migrants are and he appears, or rather, his team appears. If he does exist, he's one cool customer, I can tell you.'

Stroking his chin thoughtfully, Boyd nodded and said, 'If he does exist... Interesting. I think we'll put an undercover on the job. I want someone to hitch a ride from Paris on a wagon, arrive at Calais, and mooch about the camps for a Channel crossing. No connection to the French police. Entirely undercover for a short term. Let's find the Louis Martin connection. Who do you suggest?'

'What about Eddie Chandler?' suggested Antonia. 'One of your new detectives. He's done a stint undercover before and if remember correctly, Eddie is a lorry driver as well as being able to pilot a small aircraft. He's very versatile.'

'Ah! Bond,' chuckled Boyd. 'Eddie Bond.'

'No!' challenged Antonia. 'Eddie Chandler! That's why you recruited him to the unit. If he can penetrate a drugs gang for months on end, I'm sure he'll manage a couple of weeks in France. He'll just need a good brief.'

'And a bank account in a European country other than France. Can you oblige?'

'I'll see what I can do. Leave it with me for now.'

'And no identification papers,' remarked Boyd. 'False identity, access to cash, and an unbreakable life story if things go wrong.'

'Completely undercover, almost a black operation?'

'Absolutely! Untouchable and untraceable. His undercover experience to date will have equipped him with his legend. Check it out and tidy it up if you must but Eddie is my choice. I want him on the streets of Paris as soon as possible. Not Calais. Get him on the next available flight once he's been fully briefed. Work him into the Calais area posing as a refugee or a migrant. The man's a master at what he does. Give him free rein and a 24/7 emergency phone number to call if it all goes wrong. He can memorise it. I want Eddie at the water's edge looking out at the Channel with a sack full of information in his hand and all there is to know about the Louis Martin trafficking operation.'

'Oh! He's going to love you for this one,' replied Antonia. 'Either way, it will save him dropping his passport in the Channel on the way over. That's what they're told. Don't carry anything that identifies you if you're illegal.'

'Excellent!' replied Boyd. 'A lorry driver as well as a pilot! Well, I hope he remembers which side of the road to drive on in France. Now, what does this multimillion-pound state of the art computerised intelligence system tell us about Boko Haram personalities in the UK?'

Turning to the keyboard, Antonia interrogated the Ticker system and replied, 'It begins with the basics and tells me that Boko Haram, when translated, means Western education is forbidden. That's why Boko Haram is well-known for kidnapping schoolchildren. They teach them about Islam and tell the kids that their land was an Islamic state long before it was turned into the land of the kafir: the infidel. The current westernised education system over there is contrary to true Muslim beliefs.'

Boyd nodded with interest as Antonia continued, 'Kidnapping is the most lucrative industry in Nigeria and Chad.' Her fingers trickled across the keyboard as she continued, 'Here's a list of schools recently targeted by Boko Haram. Do you know what it does to the population? It causes desperate parents to sell their homes to pay the ransom and free kidnapped children.'

'Not a holiday destination then,' grimaced Boyd. 'It sounds like the devil's very own nest.'

'Good description,' suggested Antonia as she and Boyd interrogated the intelligence system to understand the complexities of a terrorist organisation based in West Africa that was now being assessed for its potential threat to the UK.

'What a nightmare of a place to live,' suggested Boyd.

On the sofa of a living room in a house in Peckham, Zak tossed and turned in his sleep as his mind played turmoil and cast his memory back to the lake, the children, the woman, and a man called Malik. The room was silent but inside Zak's head a man was screaming at him, a gun was pressed into his temple, and he was on his knees nodding, listening, learning what to do, and figuring out what was expected of him in the days ahead.

How did I get involved in all this, thought a worried Zak? Where did it all go wrong? They told me what to do and how to do it. Now I must kill for them. I will. I will kill because I have been trained to do so. When will they give me a gun? Or will it be a bomb? And who will deliver the weapons to me?

There was a knock on the front door and Zak slid from the sofa and scurried behind the furniture to hide. He'd been told to sit tight and wait there. Who was knocking at the door?

Zak peeped through the window from behind a curtain and saw one man climbing into a dark blue van. The vehicle drove off and the street was quiet.

Shaking, cold, numb and feeling abandoned, Zak lay on the floor at the foot of the sofa and closed his eyes. His mind spun into overdrive once more and quickly took him back to the nightmare that was now so much part of his life.

Elsewhere in a makeshift observations post, a middle-aged man engaged his throat mic and radioed, 'This is Red Alpha Four. No change at the target address. Stay awake, I say again, No change.'

Moments later a dark blue van swept across the surveillance officer's line of vision and continued down the street.

A woman turned the corner and walked purposefully along the footpath until she reached her destination. Knocking on the door, she glanced around, looked over her shoulder, and smiled when a fellow Nigerian opened the door and welcomed her with, 'Ester! At last. Come on in. About time too.'

'Abe!' acknowledged Ester. 'It took a little longer than I expected but I got there in the end. This won't take long.'

Ushering Ester into the house, Abe then peeped out and looked both ways. His eyes traced the full length of the empty street before he closed the door and went to join his visitor.

In the nearby observation post, Red Alpha Four engaged his computer system and printed off photographs of Ester and Abe. Diligently, he adjusted the volume control on his console and radioed, 'All units stand by. We have an unknown female in the plot and she has been admitted to the house by the target known as Abe. The subject is referred to by Abe as Ester. Audio-visual is operating. Follow the subject Ester when she leaves. All respond!'

As the radio waves were filled with acknowledgements, Red Alpha Four listened to the audio product now whistling through his ears.

'The conference will take place in a Lake District hotel in Cumbria,' revealed Ester. 'I do not yet know its precise location but it has a conference facility and borders directly onto the lakeside.

There are hundreds of such hotels in Cumbria but only a few have land that runs right down to the actual lake. I've narrowed it down and made a list. Here, check this out.'

Ester handed Abe a piece of paper and an ordnance survey map and nodded to three men sat a table.

The taller of the three, Kareem stroked his beard and took the map from Abe's hands before introducing himself. He gestured to his colleagues saying, 'This is Yan and Moussa. We've heard about you, Ester.'

'And I know all about you and your friends, Kareem,' replied Ester.

'Which is your favourite?' probed Abe as the map was unfolded. 'Where do you think the conference will take place and when?'

'My guess is Ullswater in the next week or so!' replied Ester.

'Well, what do you know,' laughed Abe. 'That's one hell of a ride from one lake to another. Our man from Chad just loves the lake, or so I'm told.'

'I heard on the grapevine that we lost three in the Channel recently. Where is the top man?' asked Ester.

'Close by,' replied Abe.

'Fully trained and totally committed, I take it?'

Kareem nodded and said, 'He took a cop down the first day he was here. A cop I tell you! But right now, he's resting under our control. He's a valuable weapon and we're looking after him. Okay?'

'Great!' replied Ester. 'Not my problem then. Yours! Do you know how to get to Cumbria? It's near Scotland.'

'Yes, I know where it is,' replied Kareem. 'I've lived in England a long time. We all have, or did you forget?'

'Always in Peckham?' probed Ester.

'It's where most Nigerians settle when they arrive in this country. Now sit down and tell us everything you know, Ester. We'll do the rest.'

The audio device recorded the conversation in the house as Ester joined the group sitting at the table pouring over the ordnance survey map of Cumbria's Lake District.

Adjusting his headpiece, Red Alpha Four breathed out heavily as he listened to the conversation, wrote down some pertinent notes, and decided he needed to ensure Bannerman was aware of the situation. Locating his mobile, he put in a call whilst tapping on the computer keyboard and reporting the live conversation to the Ticker intelligence system he was privy to.

In the Savanna in Lake Chad, tall, scattered trees provided an extensive canopy that grew close to the swamps surrounding the lake. The lake provided almost the entire country with freshwater, enjoyed hardly any salinity, and did not drain into the sea. Lying south of the Sahara Desert, Lake Chad basked in a tropical climate.

Beneath the canopy, in a dry clearing festooned with mud-built huts, Malik dominated the kidnapped schoolchildren when he strode amongst them and barked, 'Ibrahim! Dress them all in the grey hooded suits and give them food and water. Once that is done have them kneel before me. Tell them that I am their saviour and that I am going to teach them the ways of jihad.'

'Yes, master,' replied Ibrahim as he ran around removing clothing from the children and handing out baggy grey one-piece tracksuits from a score of cardboard boxes.

'Wear this,' ordered Ibrahim. 'And listen to Malik. He is your master now. Do what he says.'

Working his way through the throng, emptying clothing from the boxes, Ibrahim gradually presented the horde with identical clothing.

'You want the girls in a different colour, master?'

'No!' barked Malik. 'Only if we need to sell them. Not yet! I will tell the children about the Sixth Pillar of Islam when I read the Quran to them. I will tell them of the struggle they are now part of. I will teach the ways of the Prophet Muhammad and his early companions. It is the basis of our faith, our future, and the path we must take. This is the way, our way, not the way of the infidels. Prepare them for the words I speak. They will all be equal in my eyes. Dress them in grey tracksuits. Quickly!'

As Malik, the warlord, strolled around the clearing, his men busied themselves dragging the children into a crescent-shaped huddle. By the time his minions had finished, a wall of three hundred children faced Malik. Beneath the grey hoods, their faces were full of fear. Eyes flickered from left to right not knowing where safety lay. Remembering the murder of their teachers and the destruction of the school, they grew fearful and weary when they watched the armed guards surround them.

Dominating proceedings, Malik, the monstrous warlord of Boko Haram, stood ready to taunt the children in their hour of need.

'Allah be praised,' bellowed Malik. 'Listen to me! Learn my words! I will teach the world, one by one, the great words of the Prophet which were unheeded by the infidels of the west. Let my teachings begin.'

In the mud-built huts that formed a haphazard border to the rear of the children, a score of women with their babes in arms ventured from their abode to hear the words of the great master. He was their leader, a killer of men, women and children, who was now embarked on teaching others the way of his world, Malik was renown for training a select few to do his evil work far from the swamps that surrounded them.

There was a slight rustle in the leaves of the trees that straddled the savanna and bore witness to the psychological brutality that one simple terrorist could bring to bear on one of the most vulnerable sections of society.

A bush elephant parted the tall grass, skirted the village, and disturbed a herd of antelopes on its journey to the next watering hole. This was Chad, West Africa, and the world of Boko Haram situated slightly over three thousand miles from Carlisle, England.

~

Chapter Six
~

Carlisle Magistrate's Court
Special Hearing
The Next Day

The court building dominated the street in which it was located and was approached by a fine array of concrete steps complimented by a ramp for the less able members of the public attending proceedings. Four courts were sitting on the day in question. Court four was for juveniles, court three for traffic offenders, court two for minor criminal offences and court one for the more serious cases where bail applications were heard. The building was a myriad of rooms and corridors that housed solicitors, witnesses, journalists, police officers, and the public. Adjacent to the courthouse sat the city police station and an underground corridor that facilitated the movement of prisoners from the police cells to the dock of courtroom one.

In court one, the case against Crawford, Donaldson and Edwards was reaching its conclusion. The three men sat reluctantly in the dock where they faced the bearded and bespectacled solicitor who represented the Crown Prosecuting Service. Each of the prisoners was individually handcuffed to a security guard as they listened to the allegations made against them. The handcuff is a restraining device designed to secure an individual's wrist closely to the other wrist. They consist of two cuffs that are linked together by either a chain, a hinge, or a rigid bar. Both wrists are fitted with a cuff. Each cuff has a rotating arm that engages with a ratchet that prevents it from being opened once closed around the wrist.

Crawford spread his fingers out trying to force a surge of blood into his fingertips. He felt the cuff restrain the movement, closed his eyes, and shrugged.

'To sum up,' declared the solicitor. 'The three men before you are charged with an attempt to rob a bank in Penrith. Armed with loaded sawn-off shotguns they were intent on carrying out a malicious criminal act with little or no thought for the safety of others. I must inform you that enquiries continue into the ownership of the firearms used by the accused as well as ownership of the vehicle in their possession when arrested. The prosecution suspects that both the shotguns and the vehicle used in the attempted robbery were stolen from others. Indeed, your worships, I am aware that searches of houses and a garage are taking place and they are an important part of the prosecution case. And of course, a great deal of forensic investigation applies to this investigation. I ask you to remand the prisoners in custody whilst further enquiries are made.'

The Chairman of the Magistrates nodded and gestured to the defence solicitor to reply.

A younger, fresh-faced man rose from the front benches and began his argument.

As the court proceedings continued a thin piece of metal held precariously between the finger and thumb of Crawford's right hand journeyed back and forth along the shallow slender channel that held the ratchet in his handcuff in place. Covered by his other hand, Crawford worked tirelessly with the hairclip he had found embedded in the bunk of his cell on the day of his arrest. He worked the metal clip, wondered as to what kind of longhaired teenager had worn such a convenient device, and then felt the retaining pin surrender and release the handcuff's ratchet.

Deliberately, and loudly, Crawford coughed and bent forward in a display of unexpected pain as he covered his wrists with his stomach and shook the handcuff loose before clasping it closed in his fist. At last, he was free from the handcuff and knew only of the red blemish on the skin of his wrist. It had all begun in his cell and it had taken him over an hour to accomplish the feat.

Both solicitors glanced at Crawford before returning to the business of the court and engaging the bench.

A security guard bent low to look Crawford in the eye but, in so doing, did not see the result of the manipulation of the hairpin.

'Are you alright?' whispered the guard.

'Yes! I'm okay. Wind I think,' replied Crawford.

Donaldson and Edwards glanced at each other, glimpsed at Crawford's wrists, and then shuffled forward slightly to hide the matter from the other two guards.

In the courtroom, the arguments continued before the chairman announced, 'I don't think we need to retire, my learned friends.' He sought the gestures of his fellow magistrates and whispered, 'All agreed?'

There was a nod of agreement from the lady to his right and the man to his left before the chairman addressed the accused specifically and announced, 'Please stand.'

In the dock, a handcuff slipped from the hand and clattered against the side of the booth where Crawford sat.

'We decide to remand you in custody for seven days.'

Crawford sideswiped his guard with a humdinger of a right, leapt across the dock that denied his freedom, and tumbled awkwardly to the floor. Unbalanced, he fell backwards hitting his head against the foot of the dock.

Surprised, stunned, the magistrates shrunk in their seats. The prosecutor's jaw dropped and the defence solicitor screamed, 'No!'

Regaining his feet, Crawford jumped onto the front bench of the court and bounded down the wooden structure scattering papers everywhere whilst hastily pursued by an out of condition guard who bellowed, 'Stop!'

Crawford jumped from the bench, landed squarely on the floor, and shoulder-charged a policeman out of his way as he sprinted for the exit and a pathway to independence. The loose cuff rattled dangerously through the air when it enjoyed its freedom and narrowly missed a clerk's face.

Turmoil erupted in the court when the clerk reached beneath his desk and activated an alarm bell that shrilled harshly throughout the building. A red light pulsated in the corridors of the courthouse and a guard at the entrance rushed to lock the front door.

Meanwhile, a journalist sitting in the aisle at the rear of the court set down his notebook and stuck out a foot trying to bring down the absconder. Skipping over the protrusion, Crawford barged through the door into the corridor and made for the exit pushing everyone out of his way. People stood back and watched. It was as if Moses were parting the waves of the Red Sea when Crawford reached the top of the staircase, leapt three steps at a time to the next landing, and eventually arrived in the entrance hallway. The bolt on the front door of the court building shuddered into position with a final rasp when the burly guard rammed it into the lock and then flattened his back against the thick wooden structure.

Turning, Crawford tore down the corridor chased by three guards shouting at him to stop.

A row of red lights flashed from the ceiling in liaison with each other. The alarm continued to shriek and echo from chamber to chamber. People screamed and ran from the man wielding a loose metal cuff that hung dangerously from his wrist whilst a criminal element, there to support their mates, merely stood in silent admiration.

The escapee suddenly stopped, kicked a door open, ran into an office, and threw himself through the window. There was a thunderous explosion of glass when Crawford exited the building and landed on the footpath outside.

Bent low, Crawford glanced at the building, saw the guards gather in the void, and realised the immediate chase was over because no one was following him. Ignoring the shouts from the guards, Crawford stepped into the roadway, stopped the first car headed his way, and dragged the driver from the vehicle.

Moments later, Crawford gunned the car down the street and onto the nearby dual carriageway laughing as the loose cuff clattered against the steering wheel and the sight and sound of flashing lights and noisy alarm bells shrunk away.

Back in an office within the court building, a security guard dialled a number on the phone and reported, 'This is Court Security. One of the robbers has escaped from custody. He's made off in a blue Ford Focus. The car has just made the dual carriageway. It's travelling westbound at speed.'

The guard listened, nodded, and replaced the telephone.

On the dual carriageway, a blue Ford Focus driven by Crawford thundered past a police patrol car entering the road system from a different access point.

'Jeez!' remarked the policeman. Snatching a lower gear, PC Mark Howard squeezed the accelerator and gave chase. Out on the overtake, Mark radioed, 'In pursuit of a blue Ford Focus westbound entering Wigton Road. Speed over six zero miles per hour. Am engaging! Assistance required!'

When the telephones started ringing from the courthouse again, the operators in the police control room realised PC Howard was chasing the car that Crawford had hijacked.

As Crawford gunned the stolen car west towards the Caldew Fells, the police poured over their maps and considered the options they had to try and recapture Carlisle's most wanted.

The sound of squealing tyres spitting loose gravel from the side of the road filled the air when Crawford negotiated a roundabout and headed towards Workington. A glance in the mirror confirmed the presence of three chasing police cars, a row of blue lights, and the constant wailing of deafening sirens.

A mile ahead, a tractor emerged from a field, bounced awkwardly onto the tarmac, and turned to face the oncoming cavalcade of vehicles. Its load of hay wobbled slightly when the long-wheelbase trailer gradually heaved its entirety onto the roadway. The driver's jaw dropped when he saw the line of police vehicles chasing a Ford Focus.

Checking his mirrors, Crawford adopted the offside of the road and made for the tractor with his foot hard down on the accelerator and his hands gripping the steering wheel. His remaining handcuff hung loosely and gently clanked against the dashboard. Only the handcuff appreciated that a head-on collision was imminent.

At over eighty miles an hour, and on the wrong side of the road, Crawford travelled towards the tractor with a line of police cars chasing him.

The tractor driver screamed when he swung the steering wheel to avoid a collision. The trailer baulked, unsettled the load of hay, and wobbled dangerously as Crawford blared his horn and drove past the tractor missing it by inches.

Hay slipped from the trailer, landed on the tarmac, and exploded in a hazardous mountain of straw, grass and fodder.

Crawford was through the gap but PC Mark Howard was in danger as the tractor and trailer slewed to the side and toppled over blocking the highway.

PC Howard snatched the handbrake whilst simultaneously slamming the brake pedal. Swinging the steering wheel to his left, he felt the police car hurtle around and face the direction he had just come from. There was a loud crunch of metal when the rear bumper of the patrol car collided with the front of the tractor and then slid into the mound of hay.

The pursuing police cars shuddered to a standstill as Crawford disappeared from view and sped west at ninety miles an hour.

'Crash! Crash! Crash!' radioed PC Howard. 'I've collided with a tractor. The road is blocked. We've lost contact with the stolen car!'

The police radio network fell into silence allowing one supervisor to approach a map on the wall and query aloud, 'Where has the escapee gone? Where is he now?'

A short time later, Crawford turned into a garden centre near the Orton Grange Residential Park and slowly negotiated the car park until he saw a couple leave their vehicle and head into the building.

Parking the Ford Focus nearby, Crawford approached the couple's vehicle, tried the driver's door, and realised he couldn't break the lock. He looked around, saw a quad bike parked near the staff entrance, and mounted the vehicle.

Firing the quad bike, Crawford headed back to the main road. Traffic westbound was non-existent. The road was closed.

Smiling, Crawford began whistling nonchalantly as he drove west before taking the road to Caldbeck and an array of narrow leafy lanes that guided him towards the Lake District and a taste of freedom. But for Carlisle's most wanted crook, there was more than freedom at stake. There was over a quarter of a million pounds hidden in Lake Ullswater and he was the only free man who knew where it was. The problem for the other two was that they were still incarcerated in the cells. He was free.

'My prize!' he laughed aloud. 'It's my money now. Those two can rot in hell. Here I come.'

~

Chapter Seven
~

The same day
The University Library
N'Djamena, Chad, West Africa

Wearing a white linen suit set off by a light blue cotton shirt and matching blue tie, the middle-aged Roger Buckley was regarded as one of the so-called educationalists who had been drafted into the region by Her Majesty's Government. His brief was to help the Nigerian administration and its neighbours to bring a fresh approach to educating the youngsters in the region. There had been a marked movement away from the teaching of Sharia law and various religious and cultural ideologies in favour of a more western approach to modern-day living. Seen by many as an affable observer, Roger was a key representative who travelled throughout the area meeting teachers and administrators working in the field. His Oxford accent was well known and held him in good stead in the community which he had penetrated on behalf of the British government. Unbeknown to the masses, Roger was the only MI6 officer in Chad and he was stationed at the British Office in N'Djamena where his unofficial title was Barracuda.

Reading the D'jamena Hebdo local newspaper, Roger cast his eyes over the headlines which included references to an international budding geniuses' competition as well as an article calling upon Christians to take responsibility in society. On the inside pages, he read an article about three hundred children who had been kidnapped by Boko Haram from a Christian school in the Lake Chad area. Two of the teachers had been murdered by the kidnappers and the headmaster had been deliberately untouched so that he might deliver the ransom note to the government. The newspaper revealed that the children were offered for ransom and it disturbed Roger slightly since the matter was not on the front pages. Of course, part of the reasoning for his presence in Chad was to realign the media so that terrorism was given less attention whilst education and other matters relevant to the type of society wanted were given pride of place. The joint Nigerian-British plan was to push terrorism out of the top spot and carefully slide the importance of a good education into place.

Roger shook his head and reminded himself that he was in Chad, not Nigeria. However, the matter of the school kidnapping had been carefully hidden amongst matters of lesser interest.

The library was quiet, thinly populated, and convenient for Roger who heard footsteps approaching. The lowering of his newspaper introduced him to Professor Bakar whom he was cultivating as a source for British Intelligence.

Roger stood up and shook hands with his guest before taking a seat. Only the table laden with recent publications separated them.

A Professor of languages, Bakar was of a similar age to Buckley, spoke good English as well as French and German, and was a thinly built gentleman who lacked an aura of physical fitness.

Bakar seldom began a conversation and Roger found himself leading the way as usual. After a smattering of small talk and pleasantries, Roger asked, 'Anything of interest this week, Professor?'

'In which way do you mean?' came the reply.

'Oh, you know. The people, the students, gossip!' explained Roger. 'What's new in the world? Or to be more precise, what's new in Chad?'

'Nothing earth-shattering, Mr Buckley. But I will say your idea that more people should take an interest in the ways of the western world is catching on.'

'Why do you say that?' probed Roger.

'Just an observation, that's all. About half a dozen local men signed up for English lessons recently. That is not unusual but the individuals are interesting.'

'Really, in what way?'

'I noted that a few of our hardliners are catching on and have recently abandoned their old traditions in favour of the English language. A cultural development I think you might call it.'

'Do you mean a move from Islam to a Christian culture, Professor?'

'For some, yes, that is the case,' nodded Bakar. 'Months of gradually introducing new subjects that are fresh and interesting are finally attracting the locals. Not all of course, but certainly some.'

'Good!' smiled Roger who leaned forward, frowned, and replied, 'Now tell me what is bothering you, Professor Bakar. Some months ago you told me an identical story. You related to me that quite a few men from the Lake Chad area had taken up English lessons because they wanted to know more about England and the language. I asked you why but you had no answer then.'

Professor Bakar averted his eyes from Roger and fidgeted with a magazine on the table.

'I've known you long enough to know that something is afoot. What's on your mind.'

'Nothing at all,' replied the Professor nervously. Looking around, assuring himself that he could not be overheard, Professor Bakar continued, 'For every student of the English language we gather we seem to lose the same amount to Boko Haram.'

'Who did you have in mind?' probed Roger.

'I know a man who was learning English at the university. I was surprised when I learnt he had made friends with people who preached the Sunnah, which is the main body of traditional social and legal customs and practices of the Islamic community. Do you know what I mean by the Sunnah, Mr Buckley?'

'Along with the Quran and Hadith: the recorded sayings of the Prophet Muhammad, the Sunnah is a major source of Sharia law,' nodded Roger. 'I don't suppose there is anything wrong in learning about English culture and Christianity at the same time as learning about Islamic law. Our desire is not to prevent the population from learning about Islam. Our wish is to teach such people that there is more to life than just one God and one set of teachings. Maybe it's good that your man is extending his knowledge. What do you think?'

Professor Bakar did not reply but merely looked into Roger's eyes for a moment before replying, 'His name is Zakaria and he is a married man with three children. I don't ask my students questions, Mr Buckley. I just listen to them talking in their social groups. His full name is Zak Zakaria. He has disappeared from his home by the lake. I heard that he has joined Boko Haram.'

'Who told you that?' asked Roger.

'No-one! Just gossip I overheard.'

'How did he physically join the Boko Haram group?'

'He was seen boarding a minibus that was headed for the Sahara Desert. Not by me, you understand. It was something I heard in a passing conversation.'

'And you believe it to be true?'

'Absolutely! The people I heard talking about it were local villagers.'

Roger Buckley removed the magazine that the Professor was fidgeting with and said, 'Tell me more about this Zakaria man.'

'He was born in the village of Sangari near Lake Chad. His father was one of the village elders. It seems Zakaria has been selected by the leaders of Boko Haram to join them. Zakaria is living right in their heartland so it's not a surprise to me. I thought it might interest you, that's all. It's another name for your membership list, is it not? It's not earth-shattering like I said, but it is another member of Boko Haram to look out for.'

'There's more to life than putting people into pigeonholes,' replied Roger. 'What else do you know about him?'

'I knew his father. They are from the Kanuri tribe. Chad is occupied by over two hundred tribes which explains why there are so many diverse social structures in this neck of the woods. They have an economy that is mainly based on agriculture. Zakaria speaks Kanuri, Nigerian and English. His parents taught him some English when he was younger. Although the Kanuri are Muslims who trace back to the nomadic tribes of the Sahara, the Zakari family have never been great followers of Jihad and Boko Haram. Zak puzzles me because his parents did not bring him up that way.'

'That can be said for many people in the country.'

'Yes, but I'm wondering why it has taken him all this time to become a militant and join Boko Haram. He has denied its presence and turned a blind eye to that organisation all his life. Why has he changed I ask myself? And the answer is that I don't know why, Mr Buckley. I have watched youngsters pass through this university for many years. Most of them seldom change their culture, their beliefs, or their religion. They just grow up and become adults but they seem to retain their core values. People like Zakaria are just the kind of people you want to nurture and develop into the ways of the west. For some reason, Boko Haram recruited him into their way of thinking and he has joined them without reservation.'

'Where is he now?'

'I've no idea. Not at the university, that I can tell you.'

'Still in the country though?'

'I don't think so but I'm not sure. If he has joined Boko Haram for all the wrong reasons then he could be anywhere doing their bidding. I'd guess he's been taken into the Sahara, trained in their ways, and then released to attack a target of their choosing.'

'You read people, don't you, Professor? That's a pretty bold statement to have made about one of your former students.'

'I've thought long and hard about this before deciding to tell you about him. I hope he's driving a supply wagon around the desert for them, but the bottom line is that I think he and his fellow tribesmen may have been recruited to carry out a particular assignment in Nigeria, Cameroon, or elsewhere.'

'Can you trust local politicians?' probed the MI6 man.

'Some, not all,' declared the Professor. 'There are so many tribes and rivalries in play. Different cultures, beliefs and aspirations are rampant in Chad. Why do you ask? Are you going to try and trace Zakaria via the usual government channels?'

Roger did not reply.

'It's just that if you are,' suggested Professor Bakar. 'Then I'd think your biggest hurdle might be either here in Chad or Nigeria. If Zakaria has gone over to the other side then it would not surprise me if there was a dubious politician involved.'

'In what way?'

'Free passage out of Chad and no records relevant to Zak Zakaria in government circles. By that I mean no questions asked when he is moved through all the various checkpoints that different tribes and groups lay down throughout the country. Someone in government who is in cahoots with Boko Haram will have a key to the safe passage route from here to the rest of the world. Perhaps I'm wrong. What would I know?'

'More than you are telling me?' insinuated Roger.

'I'm still working you out, Mr Buckley. We both know you are not just working as a Director of Education. My problem is that I need to be able to trust you if our relationship is to bear fruit.'

Gesturing in agreement, Roger remarked, 'You mentioned fellow tribesmen. Are you suggesting there are others involved in jumping ship and joining Boko Haram?'

'I heard that a few from the same village had joined him but I don't know any of them by name. They aren't university students. They are from the Kanuri tribe like the Zakaria family.'

'How many?' probed Roger.

'Three from the same tribe but it's my understanding that Zakaria is the main man. That's who they wanted.'

'Thank you, Professor. I wondered if you might have a photograph of Zakaria, one from his earlier days in the university?'

'I thought you might ask,' replied the Professor as he reached inside his jacket and removed a manilla envelope. Sliding the package across the table, the Professor said, 'You didn't get this from me.'

Nodding, Roger offered a grateful smile and pocketed the photograph with, 'Sometimes we cannot afford to take chances. Thank you, Professor.'

'That works both ways,' came the reply.

'Can you tell me about the Kanuri tribe?' enquired Roger. 'I'd like to know what makes them tick.'

'The Kanuri people are an African group living largely in the lands of the former Kanem and Bornu Empires in Niger, Nigeria, Sudan, Libya and Cameroon,' revealed the Professor. 'They consist of several subgroups and their most common bond is the Kanuri language. The tribe can be traced back to the medieval Kanem-Bornu Empire which dominated this part of the world before the German, French and British joined the race to rule Africa. Traditionally, the Kanuri are peace-loving people, pastoralists, who emerged from the Saharan desert and now engage in farming and fishing in the Chad Basin, as well as salt processing and rice production. They are not a warlike tribe.'

'But if I were recruiting for Boko Haram I would happily remind such people that Africa was stolen by the British, the Germans, and the French. Is that why you also speak German and French, Professor?'

'Not at all! The same countries brought Africa out of the backwoods, colonised it, and made it great,' argued the Professor. 'And rich!'

Roger smiled and replied, 'I had my Boko Haram hat on. It would be one way to convince people to join the brigade. What else can you tell me about these people, Professor?'

The meeting wore on finishing half an hour later when Roger Buckley bid farewell to the Professor and made for his office in N'Djamena. Entering a secure part of the building, he engaged an encrypted message facility and sat at the desk. For a moment, Roger recounted what he had been told by his source whom he had coded *Bookworm*. Following security protocols, Roger entered a password into the system and typed a message into the device.

The message read:
Source Report: Bookworm.
Handler: Barracuda.
Subject: A developing target of interest

The following individual has left his home in Sangari, Chad having been recruited by Boko Haram to engage in terrorism.

ZAK ZAKARIA, born circa 1996, six feet tall, broad build. Caution is advised since Bookworm suggests the subject may have been recruited to carry out terrorist attacks in South West Africa, Europe, or elsewhere. It is suspected that he has been transported to the Sahara for advanced terrorist training. He may be accompanied by three males from Lake Chad Basin and the Sangari region, of similar age, no further description. All four subjects are of the Kanuri tribe.

Provenance low. There is no further intelligence data that lends support to the proposition made herein.

Submitted to Central HQ, London and the Military Attaché Office, Abuja, Nigeria for information regarding

membership database and travel watch procedures and restrictions.
Attachments:
1. Historic photograph of Zak Zakaria
2. Report re Kanuri tribe titled 'tribal instincts and origins.'
Ends: Barracuda.

Roger read the report again and wondered how important it might be. Would a fellow intelligence officer be interested? Zakaria's details would be entered into a list of suspects who were thought to be members of that group and his name would be added to the watch list. Was it akin to adding another item on a weekly shopping list next to the vegetables, fruit, meat, groceries, and household goods? It was hardly earthshattering in the scheme of things. But is it useful intelligence, thought Roger? Or merely a justification of my mundane inconsequential presence in Chad?

He pressed the button and the report migrated into cyberspace.

~

Chapter Eight

~

Later, the same week
France

Eddie Chandler was no stranger to undercover police work. A recent addition to the Special Crime Unit, Eddie had transferred into the team from Merseyside Constabulary having proved himself working undercover on the docks. In his early thirties, Eddie had spent his time watching the comings and goings of people working in the area. He'd made friends with the good, the bad and the ugly and gradually penetrated the drug gangs that were importing their evil trade into Merseyside. It had taken him over two years before he'd been accepted and was able to walk the gangplank to help unload a ship from Colombia and then drive it away in one of their wagons. It was the first of many shipping vessels that he was to become aware of in the months that followed. His work had resulted in the recovery of millions of pounds worth of drugs and several high-grade convictions of those involved. A single man, Eddie was used to living under a false identity and had been recruited by Boyd when the details of several cases he had been involved with had crossed the Commander's desk.

But Boyd was nowhere to be seen when his preferred undercover officer arrived in Paris from a flight out of Bristol.

Cautious in his planning, Eddie landed legitimately in Paris and immediately posted his true passport back to his home in the UK. Without a tattoo or blemish on his skin, he carried not one piece of paper that would betray who he was or what he was up to. Travelling light, with only a change of clothing, he dressed in an airport washroom and then hitched a ride into the French capital.

Once on the streets of Paris, Eddie Chandler introduced himself as Marius and posed as an unemployed Romanian heading to London to look for work.

Initially, Eddie made for the area of the Louvre Art Gallery where he decided to penetrate his target. Working in tramp-like conditions between Place de la Concorde and the Arc de Triomphe on the Champs-Élysées, Eddie quietly begged his way up and down his target route dodging the gendarmes, the army, and any authority figure that might seek to challenge him. He kept himself to himself, to begin with, acted in a reserved manner, seldom acknowledged others, and gradually built a unique facade around him. Gradually, he loosened up and soon became a regular in a group of migrants who were inhabiting the streets of his target area.

It wasn't long before the dishevelled Eddie was sleeping on the pavements of the city next to his newfound friends. Without saying much, the man they knew as Marius unwrapped the national flag of Romania from his bundle. It was a tricolour with vertical stripes in blue, yellow and red and had seen better days since it was grubby and well worn. He used it as a blanket at night and wore it to display himself as a Romanian Although he was wise enough to steer away from other Romanians, and there were only a few, he felt happy in the comfort of others who were making for England. As the hours passed, the detective worked out who he was most likely to get along with, and who knew more than they were saying.

Eventually, Eddie begged enough money to buy his closest friend, Adrian, a cup of coffee from a street takeaway near Place de la Concorde.

'Sugar?'

'Two!'

'Milk?'

'Just black,' replied Adrian.

Handing one of the cartons to Adrian, Eddie said, 'Let's walk. They want our money but they don't want us sat next to their van.'

'Walk? I've been on my feet all day. Where are we going?'

'Calais!' chuckled Eddie. 'I'm tired of Paris. Isn't everyone? Why do they all talk about going to England yet they sit around being moved on by the gendarmes every hour or so.'

'They've no money for the journey.'

'Oh! I never thought of that. But they had enough to get from wherever they once were to Paris?'

'Looks like it, Marius. I reckon they just hitched a ride to get here or walked all the way. Why are you getting so agitated? Relax man! Take it easy.'

'I can't take it easy,' scowled Eddie. 'I hitched a ride from way back where and got dropped off here but I need to get to Calais. I want a boat to get across the Channel.'

'Are you headed for England for a reason, Marius?'

'Yeah! I need the work and they say there's money to be made.'

'How are you going to get a boat ride?' probed Adrian.

'Not sure, but when I get to Calais I'll find out. Are you coming with me or what?'

Adrian nodded, looked over his shoulder, and replied, 'I can get people over the Channel if they've got the money.'

'How?' questioned Eddie as he took a drink of his coffee and stepped back into the shadows when a police car entered the roundabout.

'I have friends,' replied Adrian. 'Connections.'

'Me too, but right now they're a few thousand miles away and no damn good to me. I'm not going back, Adrian. Not to Bucharest or anywhere else in Romania. They don't want me back.'

'You mean you're a wanted man?'

Eddie offered no reply but dropped one hand onto Adrian's arm as the police car paused in traffic directly opposite them.

'This is not a good place to be either,' whispered Eddie. 'Come on. Down here! Quickly!'

Gesturing Adrian to follow, Eddie strode down a narrow alley that led into a shopping mall.

'We just need to keep out of sight for a while,' explained Eddie. 'I don't want to be part of the furniture here. Once the police get used to us they'll recognise our faces and we'll be running here, there and everywhere to get out of their way. Look, Adrian, who do I see in Calais? Don't bullshit me with the migrant camps. I want to know the truth. Where do I go? I need to know. I'm going there with you or without you. What do you say?'

Adrian stopped suddenly and demanded, 'What are you wanted for? You mentioned Bucharest. What did you do there that makes you want to get to England now?'

'None of your business!'

'It is if you want my help,' barked Adrian.

'In that case, I don't need your help. I picked you out as a friend. I was wrong. I'll get to Calais and make my way from there. I don't need you anymore, Adrian. Take a hike.'

'You reckon? I'll say you're a fool because you'll need a lot of cash to get a boat across the Channel. Look at you. You haven't washed for how many days? When did you last shave because that's no beard on your face? It's just a pile of stubble being fed by drips of coffee every time you miss your mouth.'

'Shut up!' scowled Eddie. 'I thought you might be able to help. I was wrong. You're just an aimless drifter like the rest of them. Go jump in the Seine.'

Eddie stormed off with Adrian quick to follow. He grabbed hold of Eddie's arm and said, 'I can help you but you'll need five thousand Euros at least.'

Pausing, Eddie replied, 'Five thousand?'

'It's all about money, Marius. If you haven't got the cash don't bother. They don't want you in Calais.'

Nodding, Eddie glanced around before asking, 'Who's they?'

'You don't need to know. Just connections!'

'But I need to know if I'm to get across the Channel.'

'You've no money, Marius. Stop dreaming the dream. Look at you. You're a tramp. No one is going to take you across the Channel. You're a worthless piece of shit.'

'I've got money.'

'Give it a rest, Marius. It's never going to happen. You're just a bummer like the rest of them.'

'No, I've got money but I can't spend it in Romania.'

'Yeah! And pigs will fly around the Eiffel Tower at midnight.'

'I've got the cash,' revealed Eddie. 'I can get it.'

'Are you going to rob a bank?'

Eddie looked the other way before glowering at his friend.

There was a pause in the conversation before Adrian quietly chuckled and suggested, 'So that's it. You robbed a bank. You robbed a goddamned bank in Bucharest. Well, get you, Marius.'

Eddie shook his head with guilt.

'How much did you get?'

'Not here, follow me.'

Eddie grabbed Adrian by the arm and dragged him down into an alcove where he laid his pack down and removed his shoe. Digging his fingers into a compartment built inside the heel, he hooked out a Romanian identity card and a bank debit card. They were both the same size and made from laminated plastic. Eddie held the cards up and said, 'Take me to someone who can get me into England and I'll get you the cash.'

Reaching for the cards, Adrian asked, 'Let me have a look?'

Relinquishing both items, Eddie remarked, 'The money is in a bank in Bratislava.'

'Where's that?'

'Slovakia! I did what I had to do, crossed the border into Ukraine, and then reached Bratislava. Come on, Adrian. That's all you need to know.'

'Ukraine! Russian connections or just luck?'

'I can't say,' replied Eddie. 'Maybe both! Do you want the money or not? All I need is a bank in Calais and I'll do the rest. I'll soon knock the cash together.'

'Is this your real name?' enquired Adrian studying the identity card.

'Yes! I'm Marius Luka!' replied Eddie. 'Don't ask another question, Adrian. There are close to one hundred thousand Euros in that account. Stop playing games with me or I'm walking away. Yes, or no?'

Thoughtfully, Adrian fidgeted with the debit card, studied Eddie, and returned the card with, 'Yes! You need Louis Martin. He's in Calais and he'll need ten thousand Euros for the crossing.'

'I thought you said five.'

'I work on commission,' replied Adrian. 'Come on. We need a wagon driver I know. If we set off now, we'll be in Calais by morning.'

'I could drive the wagon.'

'There's no need.'

'In that case, England here we come?' suggested Eddie.

'England!' remarked Adrian. 'The south coast to be precise.'

~

Chapter Nine
~

The South Coast of England
The Weary Sailor Public House,
Dungeness, Kent

Boyd and Joe Harkness travelled south along the main coast road, took a left down a narrow lane leading to the beach, and found a car park next to the Weary Sailor pub close to Dungeness Point. Both detectives were aware of the nearby military training camp at Lydd and the Dungeness nuclear power station. It seemed an unlikely location to attend the meeting of a group of voluntary channel-watchers. However, the fact remained that, in a twenty-four-hour period, the beaches in the immediate vicinity had recently experienced the arrival of over four hundred and twenty-five illegal migrants from the other side of the English Channel. It was a hot spot of migrant activity.

Opening the driver's door, Boyd felt sand beneath his feet before stepping onto the gravel pathway that led to the pub's entrance. A glance at the incoming tide suggested the sea was less than fifty yards from the building but had reached the high point in its journey.

Joe pushed the pub's front door open and entered the lounge. He heard dominoes clacking against a table in one part of the room and table skittles collapsing elsewhere followed by a roar of approval. The pub was packed with both drinkers and those having a meal.

In the far corner, a man in his sixties wearing a dark suit set off by a brilliant white dog collar was remonstrating with a group of men sitting at a table that was covered with maps, beer bottles, and pint glasses.

'What are you having?' asked Boyd.

'A pint of lager,' replied Joe. 'Get them in, Guvnor. I'll catch up with you shortly.'

Boyd approached the bar and ordered the drinks whilst Joe strolled to the table, tapped the vicar on his shoulder, and said, 'Tom! You're under arrest for disturbing the peace again.'

The Reverend Thomas Grey looked up, burst out laughing, and replied, 'Joe Harkness! Well, I'll be damned by all the Archangels in the heavens above. Long time no see, how are you?'

Shaking hands, Joe said, 'I'm well, and you?'

'Good!' replied Tom gesturing to those sitting at the table. 'I take it you've come to lock up everyone here. About time too. These reprobates are plotting a revolution.'

'Still?' chuckled Joe. 'What happened to the last one? How are you all? Mike? Pete? Bernard?'

In the moments that followed, Boyd returned with the drinks and noticed how everyone present knew Joe who was shaking hands with people around the table.

'I'd like you to meet my boss,' explained Joe eventually. 'The Guvnor here wants to know all there is to know about Channel crossers. Where do they arrive? What time of day? What kind of vessel are they in? Where have they come from? How do they arrange transport across the Channel? What do they do when they get here and where do they go? The works, gents, everything you know if you don't mind.'

'How long has he got?' came one reply.

'Mr Boyd has all afternoon,' revealed Joe.

'In that case, mine will be a Guinness with a couple of pickled eggs,' from Mike.

'It's all old hat by now, Joe,' voiced another. 'We're all tired of writing to the local MPs telling them of the problem and suggesting they need to get to grips with it. If your boss is just a pair of deaf ears sent by the Home Office to placate us then, no disrespect intended, but tell him to get lost.'

'It's not like that,' replied Joe.

'Then again, I do like a steak pie with a pint of bitter. The Faversham Red, please.'

'A pint of Kent Gold for me,' declared Pete. 'It will oil the larynx as well as the brain.'

Boyd smoothed his way into the company buying a round of drinks and emptying the pie and pickled egg displays on the bar. Eventually, he sat amongst the group and said, 'Joe tells me you are the leaders of the various groups that watch the Channel for illegals up and down the Kent coast. I understand you go searching for them when the boats are spotted.'

'He's right,' replied the Reverend Grey. 'I wouldn't call them leaders, by the way. They're community volunteers. You see, Mr Boyd, I keep advising my flock that they must learn to accommodate their fellow man as opposed to hounding them on the beaches.'

'That's all well and good but once they get off the beach they used to nick our cars, bikes, clothes of the line, anything not screwed down, vicar. It's not as bad as it was but we can't be nice to them when they're not nice to us,' argued Bernard, a giant of a man with a big belly and size twelve wellington boots.

'Not all of them are like that.'

'Oh yes, they are. That's one reason they dump their passports in the sea and we've had a crime epidemic for the last ten years. It's not good enough. It's a national tragedy. It's a bloody disgrace. It's an invasion and no one cares.'

'They are all weary sailors,' ventured the Reverend Grey with an engaging smile.

'Yes, but they don't run and hide anymore. They used to when it first started. Now they hold their hands up and surrender to the police, the coastguard, Border Patrol, and anyone who they bump into. That's all they want these days. A home in England.'

Within minutes a full-blooded argument had broken out between the vicar and the Channel watchers. It was only subdued by the provision of more beer, and a rush to locate more pickled eggs in the refrigerated stockroom. As the session continued, the two detectives listened to more stories from the gathering of watchers.

'Okay! I see the picture,' revealed Boyd eventually. 'Things have changed from running and hiding when they hit the beach to surrendering to anyone in uniform. Thank you and cheers.' Boyd raised his drink and was happy to see half a dozen other glasses raised to join his, including one held by the vicar. Continuing, he probed, 'Can any of you recall capturing a group of three or four men who were perhaps just a little out of the ordinary?'

'What do you mean by out of the ordinary?' asked Pete, a slender man who wore a bobble hat and a roll neck jumper.

'To cut to the chase,' interrupted Joe. 'The Guvnor means something recent when people who didn't want to be captured ran away and hid from you guys and the authorities. You've just explained that most of them today land and give themselves up. We're looking for those who run and hide.'

'Do me a favour, Joe,' suggested Mike. 'That's well and good but you're out of touch. Those days are long gone. They dance on the beach with each other once they've landed.'

'Rye!' whispered Bernard. 'There was that one at the Golf Club at Rye not so long ago.'

'What did you say?' asked Joe.

'Rye!' replied Bernard. 'My team searched Camber Sands near Rye recently. I remember it because I was with them.'

'Isn't that out of the usual catchment area?' questioned Boyd.

'There was a storm that day,' explained Bernard. 'A dinghy was sighted approaching the coast. It bucked up and down in the waves and then overturned when it got in the way of the big ships.'

'Then what happened?' asked Boyd.

'Hard to tell,' revealed Bernard. 'It disappeared below the surface. Whether it rose again half a mile further down the Channel or not, I don't know. The team couldn't see.'

'Survivors?'

'I don't know that either but would expect they went to Davy Jones's locker. That's not unusual. Some of them never make it.'

'Rest in peace,' voiced the vicar as he made the sign of the cross in the space before him. 'All of them.'

'One made it,' revealed Bernard. 'We missed him, I'm sure of that. I've wondered since if he hid in the dunes that day. He can't have been alone in the dinghy so somewhere out there at the bottom of the ocean is another boat full of dead bodies being eaten by the fish. Sorry, vicar, but that's the way life is. God doesn't save them all no matter how many times you pray at church on a Sunday.'

The Reverend Grey nodded his understanding, tugged at his dog collar, but did not reply.

'Ask the cop from Dymchurch,' suggested Bernard. 'He's lucky to be alive.'

'Dymchurch?' queried Boyd.

'It used to be the smuggling capital hereabouts,' explained Bernard. 'Way back in olden times smuggling was rife all along the south-east coast of England. Dymchurch was the place to land if you were a smuggler. Such long beaches. Anyway, I think the one we lost from the overturned dinghy that day was the same guy who stole a motorbike from the golf club and was caught by the cop who lives in Dymchurch. Sorry, I don't know his name but he chased someone from the golf club who was on a stolen bike.'

'Police Constable John Sanderson,' explained Joe. 'He's stationed at Rye but lives in Dymchurch. It's been in all the local newspapers and on the television.'

'The story goes,' continued Bernard. 'That the thief jumped a train while he was being chased by the Dymchurch cop. I think the thief might have been the man we lost on the beach because the timescale fits. Anyway, I heard the thief jumped onto a goods train. The cop tried to follow suit and was promptly kicked off the train by the bike thief. The cop nearly broke his back.'

'I heard he'd been killed to start with,' remarked Mike.

'He survived,' declared Joe. 'But you're right. He was initially thought to be dead at the scene. Luckily, he was unconscious and pulled through.'

'Did you guys get anyone for it?' enquired Bernard.

'Not yet but we're working on it, as you can see.'

Boyd took a sip of his orange juice and remained silent listening to the story and the gossip that followed. An hour later, it felt as if he had been educated in all there was to know about the life of a newly arrived Channel crosser.

'We'll meet again, I'm sure,' remarked Boyd as the session ended. 'Thank you all for your valuable contribution.'

Handshakes and friendly banter followed before the two detectives finally returned to the car park where Boyd rested his hands on the roof of the vehicle and leaned across to engage Joe.

'It's beginning to fit,' declared Boyd. 'I think it's a great big jigsaw puzzle and your friends in the pub just threw a few pieces at me. That has brightened my day, Joe.'

'I know this stretch well,' replied Joe. 'They're not a bad bunch. They mean well even though they regularly fall out with the Right Reverend Tom. Can you fill me in on the big picture as you see it now, Guvnor?'

Opening the car door, Boyd slid into the driver's seat as Joe took the passenger side. Boyd fired the engine and said, 'It's not proven, Joe, but recently I read a report on the Ticker computer system from an Intelligence officer in Chad, West Africa. It tells of four men recruited by Boko Haram who are suspected of travelling out of West Africa to commit terrorist attacks.'

'In the UK?'

'Not known,' replied Boyd as he drove the car back towards the main road. 'Could be anywhere in Europe. I understand there's a new man in charge of Boko Haram and he's changing the agenda. There's a photograph of one of the individuals attached to the Intelligence report. His name is Zak Zakaria if I remember correctly.'

'Interesting! Kent CID has the image of a man wanted in connection with the assault on PC John Sanderson,' explained Joe. 'The same man is wanted for burglary and theft at Rye Golf Club, and theft of a scooter.'

'Assault? I thought it was attempted murder?'

'Could be,' replied Joe. 'But it's not my case.'

'I wonder,' mused Boyd as he drove. 'Anyway, one of the Red Alpha teams reported they were monitoring a house in Peckham. They're covering low-level Boko Haram traces. A woman we're interested in showed up and coverage of a conversation she had with the occupants indicated that the main man had arrived from Chad. Boko Haram lost three operatives in the Channel in one day! Apparently, the main man took down a cop shortly after he arrived. Now correct me if I'm wrong, Joe, but could the assailant have been Zak Zakaria? There are some similarities between this report and what your mates have just told us. Was he the survivor that Bernard says he missed on the beach the day that dinghy overturned and the traveller arrived? Is Zak Zakaria the man who burgled the golf club at Rye and bumped John Sanderson from the train? Or am I making it all up because it all fits this crazy jigsaw puzzle?'

'All jigsaw puzzles are crazy until you get the last few pieces together, Guvnor.'

'I'll phone Antonia, Joe. The incident on the train with the policeman will be on the Ticker intelligence system. We just haven't made the connection until now.'

'That's because you can put it on the computer but there's no guarantee someone will see it. You need a dedicated Ticker operative on that system, Guvnor, if you don't mind me saying.'

'You're right, Joe but instead of increasing our budget, they're holding it where it is. No forward progression. Maybe I need to argue the case on the top landing. Still, we'll find the incident on the computer system and go from there.'

'I can do better than that, Guvnor. Turn right at the junction ahead.'

'Why? Where are we going?'

'Dymchurch! It's ten miles away. If anyone can help then John Sanderson can. You've got a photograph of the man from Chad. John Sanderson has body-worn video footage of the man he tussled with on the train. Are they both Zak Zakaria?'

Boyd checked the traffic and gunned the car towards Dymchurch with, 'Let's find out.'

More than three hundred and fifty miles to the north, in the Lake District, Crawford was still at large. He'd reached the Caldbeck area and dumped the stolen quad bike in a quarry about five miles from the village. He smashed the loose handcuff from his wrist using a rock taken from the rugged landscape that defined the area and then made his way on foot over the moorland and into the settlement.

Approaching a line of terraced houses, Crawford crept low, climbed over a wall, and stole a pair of jeans and a couple of tee shirts from a clothesline. Within minutes, he'd changed and stolen a woollen jumper from another line close by. Half an hour later, his minor crime spree came to an end when he entered a telephone kiosk and forced open the cash box. He emptied the contents into his pockets and set off deeper into Caldbeck regularly glancing over his shoulder in the quiet secluded village that was often referred to as Cumbria's hidden emerald.

Crawford reached the bus stop in time to catch a ride to Ullswater via Keswick and Bassenthwaite. He paid the fare before snuggling into a seat in the rear of the coach and gazing out of the window. The vehicle trundled out of Caldbeck and headed west before cutting back towards Penrith.

Exhaling, wiping the unseen emotions of dread and fear from his brow, the heavily built Crawford drifted into sleep as they negotiated a score of twists and turns on the roads.

The prize, he dreamed. It's hidden in the boathouse and it's all mine because, as sure as hell, Donaldson and Edwards weren't going to share their ill-gotten gains. They were in the pokey and had not taken their chances to escape.

No, his mind told him. No, not for them. The prize is mine now. Hidden in a double layer waterproof dry bag, the contents were the proceeds of twelve months of armed robberies at building societies and banks in the area. It was he who had decided that stolen cash should be well secreted and not taken home where the police might come and search the house for the proceeds of crime. It was Crawford's idea to penetrate that boathouse on the shores of the lake and hide the stolen money, below the waterline, in the recess next to the rear stanchion in the jetty. Years of being a joiner and a bricklayer had paid off in his criminal years.

It was a great place to hide the cash, they had decided. Because it could not be seen from the jetty or the boathouse.

Crazy? No, over the previous months, the police had searched their houses, their gardens, their cars, and their garages, and found nothing incriminating. All he had to do was to reach the destination, enter the boathouse, and retrieve the bag from the waters beneath the building.

The monies and the false identity papers hidden with the cash would guarantee his safe delivery to shores far from the United Kingdom. It was all to play for and Crawford was ahead in the game.

There was a jolt in the journey when the coach driver slammed his brakes on as a deer strolled across the tarmac.

Shaking his head free, Crawford gazed out of the window and took his bearings. He was almost there.

~

Chapter Ten
~

Peckham
London.

Detective Inspector Bannerman shuffled into a seat next to the Red Alpha team leader and said, 'Morning, Henry. What's cooking?'

Gesturing to a full coffee pot, Henry replied, 'Help yourself! The woman is back and she's not talking about breakfast.'

'Again? I got your Red Alpha Four report by the way. Thank you! You've just sent us a low ball that has thrown us into turmoil. Is she a spy, a diplomat or a well-placed activist of some persuasion? I wasn't expecting Ester Abara to be worthy of further enquiry.'

'Well, it's her. Make no mistake,' replied Henry. 'Repeatedly followed and housed at the Nigerian Embassy in Northumberland Avenue.'

'Who's on the plot?'

'Red Alpha One, Two and Three, that's all. We housed her at the Ministry of Defence in Whitehall recently.'

'Interesting? gestured Bannerman. 'She has no official connection there according to our records.'

'She's a good-looking woman,' offered Henry. 'At least that's what the Defence Secretary thinks.'

'And he's right but don't tell me Dennis Butler has visited the target house here in Peckham.'

'Not yet,' chuckled Henry. 'You briefed me to monitor Ester so we've accommodated your wishes. Butler was the focus of a discussion between Ester Abara and the subject we know as Abe who appears to be the main man in the house. Here, put the headphones on, Bannerman. Why don't you listen to an earlier recording I made? It's a conversation between Abe and the Abara woman. It's all about love and the infamous Dennis Butler.'

Bannerman nodded and put the headphones on saying, 'Thanks! Interesting?'

'Oh, it's interesting alright,' remarked Henry pouring coffee for two. 'Love at first sight even!'

'Well, well, well!' Bannerman shook his head. 'Sounds like everything we didn't want to hear. Here we go.'

A switch on the control unit was pressed and the detective who had once served in the Special Escort Group of the Met's Royalty and Protection Squad listened to the recording.

Bannerman shuffled his feet and accepted a coffee as he adjusted the sound. The feet wore size ten shoes and he stood six feet five inches inside them. Broad across the shoulders, he was quite muscular despite a slight paunch around his midriff. A chiselled square chin gave him the appearance of a man older than he was whilst a crop of microscopic ginger hair sprouted from a rounded skull and crept dangerously towards his ears. From a distance, he looked almost bald. Up close, no one told him so. His friends called him 'the big man' but enemies called him 'the screaming skull'. He was an ex Cumbrian officer and one of Boyd's historic connections.

'Why Peckham?' queried Bannerman as he listened to the recording. 'I mean why is Peckham so important to this crew?'

'I'd say it was because it's in their backyard,' explained Henry as he checked a bank of closed-circuit television monitors. 'It was heavily redeveloped in the 1960s. It was a good place to live in those days. Mainly high-rise flats replacing older dilapidated houses. But as you can see, not now. High unemployment and a lack of economic opportunities have made it one of the most deprived residential areas in Western Europe. Vandalism, graffiti, arson attacks, burglaries, robberies and muggings are commonplace.'

'Wow!' remarked Bannerman holding the earphones closer. 'Sorry! Carry on, Henry.'

'I told you it was an interesting conversation,' remarked Henry.

'Peckham!' replied Bannerman.

Henry slurped his coffee and said, 'The government ploughed millions into the area but it didn't stop the locals rioting a decade ago. Anyway, the point is, Bannerman, the British Nigerian population forms a sizeable chunk of the community here. The area is often dubbed Little Lagos.'

'Lagos! Nigeria's largest city?'

'That's the one.'

Bannerman removed the headphones and said, 'Well, I never. Ester Abara mentions Lagos whilst talking to Abe. She's told him that Lagos is where she got the job as a security advisor to the Nigerian Embassy in London. Someone called Malik arranged it all.'

'We'd do well to find out who Malik is,' remarked Henry.

'But the secret is out too. She's been having an affair with Dennis Butler for some weeks now. What do you make of that?'

'It's not a secret to what I will now call the Peckham Boko Haram team,' replied Henry. 'When I listened to the live feed, I worked out that it's been their long term objective to penetrate both the Nigerian government and the British government by using a woman to bend everyone. That Ester has used her manipulative charms to bring the Defence Secretary under her wing. Butler doesn't realise it, but Ester has suckered him well and truly with her hourglass figure, good lucks and sexy hip-swaying in the office. She's gone out of her way to hook Butler and reel him in.'

'Absolutely,' nodded Bannerman as his right hand pressed tight against the headset.

'I don't know what you think, Bannerman but I reckon Boko Haram set their stall out to get him and they succeeded because she discovered how to twist Butler around her little finger.'

'She certainly has. Her weapons appear to be a voluptuous body, a sexy voice, and a clever interplay with Butler. He's keeled over for her, hasn't he?'

'Yep! He's gone for her like a fox chasing a rabbit and he's deliberately tried to impress her by tipping the cart over and telling her some secrets about the government's response to Nigeria, Boko Haram, and so on. She's a masterpiece. A honey trap who has plied him with sexual come-ons for weeks before he finally surrendered.'

'Married with two kids and a mansion in Surrey, I believe,' added Bannerman. 'Why are MPs one of the most vulnerable sections of society?'

'Because they've no idea who the real enemy is. When you've finished listening to the audio recording, I'll pack it off to my boss. My director needs to know we've got evidence that the so-called security advisor from the Nigerian Embassy is a spy working for Boko Haram and not the Nigerian government. We need a strike team to move in, arrest her, search the house and her home, and take the team down. It's a feather in the cap for the Red Alpha squad.'

'Not yet,' advised Bannerman. 'Your director knows why we are interested in Ester Abara. We've been tipped off that she might not be what she claims to be. Moving in too soon will upset the apple cart. No, let it run for a while. I'm sure there's more to discover.'

Henry grimaced and replied, 'Are you sure? Why don't you check with Boyd? I thought our job was to trap spies and catch the enemy at work.'

'It is but Ester Abara is just one and right now Abe and Ester are the best leads we've got to a hitman who has been directed to attack a conference in the Lake District.'

'Ullswater to be precise, as per the audio recording,' reminded Henry.

'Correct,' nodded Bannerman. 'I'd like to know more about Kareem, Yan and Moussa too.'

'We have them on record. They are low-level activists. What worries me, Bannerman is that one day these people are of little interest and the next they are the prime target. We can't watch them all despite all you might read in the newspapers. There's not enough of us to keep an eye on these low levels and not enough of us to make enquiries and bring everyone up to speed in the shortest time possible.'

Bannerman nodded and said, 'My brief is to protect the conference site and all those attending it. Our problem is that we don't know if we're looking for a gang, a professional hit team, or one individual. Look, Henry, you've done a great job, but I'll have a word with your boss. Let the operation run. We need to find out all we can. You've unearthed the Peckham team and I'm glad you did.'

'I suggest you switch seats and go live,' remarked Henry. 'Abe and Ester are talking about the attack and how it will be done.'

Bannerman changed seats, plugged into the live system and listened to the conversation in the Peckham house.

'Our man from Chad is the walking time bomb,' revealed Abe as he threw his feet onto the edge of a table and leaned back in an armchair. 'Kareem, Yan and Moussa are his support.'

'Where are they now?'

'Gone!'

'Including the cop killer?'

'They're on their way,' replied Abe checking his watch. He pulled a magazine towards him and began leafing through the pages as he remarked, 'He was collected this morning from a safe house around the corner. You can tell Malik we're clean. Relax, Ester. Now you know we're up and running, there's no need to visit the house anymore. Once they've arrived things will go back to normal. No visitors until Malik sends the messenger again.'

Bannerman turned to Henry and said, 'How many houses are you watching in Peckham?'

'Just this one, why?'

'Because there's going to be a suicide attack in the Lake District and the people we're looking for left a different house in Peckham earlier today. They're calling the main man the cop killer.'

'Who did he kill and where?'

'I don't know,' replied Bannerman. 'It's news to me. Boyd has the bigger picture. Abe also mentions someone called Malik and an un-named messenger. I'll update Boyd. Meanwhile, keep an eye on Abe for me, please, Henry. He's going to be the only one left in Peckham by the sound of it. If he moves, follow him. I'll ask for a full surveillance team to assist. If the audio suggests the messenger from Malik has arrived, I want him photographed, followed, housed, and identified.'

'Will do,' nodded Henry.

'Malik is a strange name,' remarked Bannerman. 'I presume it's from Africa.'

'I looked it up,' replied Henry. 'It's Chinese and is derived from a Sea Goddess.'

'So Malik could be a woman,' proposed Bannerman.

'Who knows? In Japanese, Malik means *in first place*.'

'Well, the Japanese version fits. He or she is first in line, that's for sure. We've no idea who we are looking for.'

'I wonder who Malik is?'

'We'll work on it,' replied Bannerman. 'I'll be in touch. I've got a helicopter ride to Ullswater to look forward to.'

'Hang on tight.'

'Will do, but before I go, do you have a list of vehicles attributable to the occupants of the house? Do Abe and his mates have a motor car, for example?'

'No, but one of them has a motorbike that is kept in the yard at the back.'

'A motorbike! What kind?'

'A black Kawasaki 500. It has black panniers fixed to it but it's never moved whilst we've been watching the house.'

Bannerman nodded and said, 'Never moved? Interesting! Parked out of sight for a reason perhaps. Is it on the Police National Computer as of interest to us?'

'Funnily, enough, Bannerman, I did that first thing this morning. It's on the system as *Sightings only to be reported to DI Bannerman, SCU*. It will be in the daily Red Alpha surveillance report which you'll receive tonight as usual'

'Thanks, Henry.'

'By the way, forget the helicopter ride, Bannerman,' suggested Henry. 'Why not take a taxi? There's one just pulled up outside the target house. Stand by. Yep! It's Ester Abara.' Henry engaged the surveillance radio system and ordered, 'All units! The female is out of the house wearing a long red dress. She's entering a taxi. Red Alpha Two and Three follow and house. Over!'

The radio crackled, 'Red Alpha Two I have that. I have an eyeball on her. She's taken the rear offside seat in the black taxi now leaving the target house. To you Red Alpha Three.'

'Red Alpha Three I have the eyeball. I designate the taxi Victor Six. Just passing my position and heading into the city. I'm on it.'

Henry glanced at Bannerman who chuckled and gestured with a thumbs-up as he engaged his mobile and arranged the attachment of a full surveillance team to the operation.

Ester Abara took a mirror from her shoulder bag and checked her lipstick as the taxi came to a rest in a line of vehicles held at the traffic lights.

In Calais, a white taxi screamed around a corner on the wrong side of the road causing Eddie Chandler to glance up from his table at a pavement café and watch proceedings. He heard the siren, saw the blue lights, and then watched two police cars hurtle around the corner in pursuit of the taxi.

'A police chase, Marius,' declared a clean-shaven man wearing dark jeans, a dark long-sleeved sweater, and a typical French beret. 'I'll guess the taxi is stolen. What fun. I saw you flinch when they all appeared. Did you think they were coming for you?'

Another police car swept around the corner and joined the chase as the entourage disappeared and the atmosphere returned to normal.

'I'm not in Romania anymore,' explained Eddie. 'And you! You didn't budge an inch.'

'Why should I?'

'Because you are the most wanted man in France. The famous Louis Martin! The traveller's favourite man.'

'Call me Marty.'

'You're the guy everyone wants on their side. How many people have you trafficked across the Channel today?' smiled Eddie.

'Marius!' scolded Adrian. 'Careful what you say. Marty is just my contact. That's all.'

Eddie studied Adrian and then set his eyes on Marty before saying, 'I don't care who he is. I want to be in England as soon as possible. Safe passage is what I want. Nothing less will do, and I'm told Louis Martin is the man to get me across the Channel and anywhere I want to be in England. No questions asked. Now stop playing games and tell me how much you want.'

'Who are you and where are you from?'

'I've told you once and I'm sure Adrian will have told you all about me before he arranged this meeting.'

'Okay! How did you hear about me?'

'From others on the trail.'

'Who?'

'I don't know their names,' replied Eddie. 'They were going to Peckham.'

'Romanians?'

'No, Nigerians.'

'I don't think I can trust you.'

Eddie stood up as if to leave and then said, 'Marty! You're not Louis Martin. No way. But let me tell you that if you can move Africans out of Chad and Nigeria then you can damn well move Romanians out of Romania. Yes! I want to be in England. Edgware to be precise. Burnt Oak is where most of my Romanian friends want to go. The problem is, Marty, they don't know how to get across that stretch of water without being grilled by everyone between Bucharest and Calais. Are you with me so far?'

Marty did not flinch but continued to study Eddie before saying, 'What do you want, Marius?'

'Free and safe passage for a line of friends coming over from Bucharest. They've got the money. To be truthful, I've got their money. I never robbed a bank. That was a lie to get me here close to you. I want a business relationship with Louis Martin that will make us a million Euros or more. I'm the middleman. You're a middleman. Get me to Louis Martin. That's who I want to talk to. Not one of his lieutenants. Do you get the picture, Marty?'

'Have you got a long line of Romanians wanting to settle in England or a line of wanted crooks from Eastern Europe looking for a secure passage? A passage that is unknown to the authorities and needs to be well funded.'

'Both!' replied Eddie.

'Male or female?'

'Exclusively male! Mainly Romanian but some are East European, I'll put it that way.'

'How much you got?'

'How much do you need?'

153

'One hundred refugees at five grand a time from Eastern Europe and a hundred grand for every wanted man and false papers on arrival in England, and not before. Fifty per cent down within twenty-four hours of every movement and the rest upon arrival. No ifs, no buts. Simple as that.'

'No deal!'

'Why not?'

'I want the Louis Martin route. Not yours. No ifs, no buts. Simple as that.'

'It's one hundred grand cash for that route, Marius.'

'Done! Half now and half at the meet?' suggested Eddie.

Adrian asked, 'Why didn't you tell me all this before?'

'I thought you might have been a police informer, to begin with, so I told you lies. Sorry, but I had to test you out and make sure it wasn't just idle chatter.'

'Do you trust me now, Marius?'

Eddie paused for a moment before replying, 'I'll take a chance on you and your mate.'

'What makes you so confident?' probed Marty.

'Because Adrian has never been out of my sight since we arrived in Calais. I can tell from talking to you and watching you that you're not Louis but you're damn close to him.'

The beret nodded and Marty glanced at Adrian before declaring, 'Stay here. I'll be back shortly.'

Adrian watched Marty disappear before engaging Eddie with, 'He's gone to make a phone call. I take it you want to do business with Louis and no one else?'

'That's right. I want the main man, not his helper.'

'You don't want much,' admonished Adrian.

'Just enough,' replied Eddie.

Moments later, Marty returned, pocketed his mobile phone, and said, 'We're on. I'll get back to you when we're ready. As soon as you get my call, follow the instructions immediately. Take the cab from Rue Descartes and leave the rest to the driver. He'll know who you are and will be expecting you. Understood?'

'Perfectly!'

'Bonne journée, Marius.'

Marty was gone from the street leaving Eddie Chandler and Adrian with cold coffee and a vacant seat at the café.

~

Chapter Eleven
~

The Ullswater Hotel
The Lake District, Cumbria
The following day.

The blades of grass parted when Eddie Crawford crawled through the field that descended gradually to the hotel, the jetty where his treasure was hidden, and the sparkling splendour of Lake Ullswater. In the distance, the lightly brushed snow-capped Cumbrian Fells provided a heaven-sent backdrop to the picture-postcard scene that filled his vision.

Scanning the car park, Crawford saw several men and women clustered near a dark coloured van. The rear doors of the van were wide open. A male occupant sat on the tailgate talking to the gathering. Then he pointed to a house next to the hotel and jumped casually from the vehicle allowing those present to begin unloading the contents.

From his position, Crawford wondered why the people he was watching did not enter the hotel. Rather, they carried cardboard boxes into the house and disappeared. Except for the lady who was last to enter. Crawford recognised the woman as the one who had smashed the butt of her shotgun into his face when he was arrested for the bank robbery in Penrith. She was the Scottish detective who had hijacked them in the bank.

They are all detectives thought Crawford. It's that team who locked us all up that day. But why are they here, he puzzled.

A speedboat turned from the centre of the lake and headed towards the boathouse where Crawford's money was hidden in the depths beneath. The vessel was blue and white and sported the word POLICE on the bow as it docked at the boathouse.

Finally, the penny dropped and Crawford rolled over onto his back to gaze into the grey wintery sky above. They've done a deal, he thought. Donaldson and Edwards have done a deal with the cops.

Shaking his head, annoyed, angry, Crawford rolled over again and lay on his belly studying the house where the detectives were.

Thinking things through, his eyes focused on the police boat now tied at the jetty close to the boathouse where he knew his treasure trove lay. There were over two hundred and fifty thousand pounds in a watertight dry bag buried near the rear stanchion of the boathouse. Had Edwards and Donaldson done a deal with the detectives? Is that why they were there? Were they waiting for him to turn up and retrieve the stolen money? They've sold me and our nest egg for either a reduced sentence or a get out of jail card free. And I thought I could trust them when, all this time, they've traded the secret of the whereabouts of a quarter of a million pounds in exchange for a better life. A shorter sentence, I bet, decided Crawford. But how much have they told the police? Everything or almost everything? I need to think this through. How do I get into that boathouse and retrieve the stolen money without getting caught by the cops? And what did they take from the van to that house? It can't have been food when there's a hotel twenty yards away.

As he studied the scene, the first fall of snow gently fell from above and settled its thin white sheet across the landscape.

Of course, figured Crawford. Surveillance equipment. Cameras and the like. Those detectives haven't been told the full story by Donaldson and Edwards. Maybe my pals are trying to get a better deal without disclosing where the money is. Here am I free yet caught in the jaws of a dilemma of my own making. What have my two pals told the police? The cops have a van load of technical equipment that they're putting together in that house, and it's all designed to catch me walking up to the boathouse and getting the stash of money back. Or is it? Have they already found the cash, thought Crawford? No, that cannot be. They've just arrived. A van full of cops, surveillance gear and a police boat, and they've all arrived at the same time. What's going on? Is it all about catching me or is it something else? I need to watch these people and work it out for myself. They're not going to stop me.

Determined not to be caught, Crawford gradually slithered away from the scene on his belly.

Puzzled, slightly confused, Crawford eventually jumped to his feet and made his way towards the road that bordered the lake and the adjacent woods. In his wake, Crawford's bodyweight lay down a visible imprint that followed him. A thin ribbon of guilt meandered behind him and portrayed his presence.

Inside the house, next to the hotel, Boyd helped Detective Sergeant Ricky French unpack the boxes he had taken from the van. The contents were half a dozen close circuit television screens and as many computers. They would soon dominate the sprawling lounge of the building that Boyd had secured as a temporary operational centre.

Helping to set up the system, the red-headed Anthea Adams was Boyd's second in command and knew the procedure well. By nightfall, the hotel complex and its surroundings would be covered by CCTV whilst a set of standalone computers linked to the global Ticker intelligence system would be tried, tested and in use by the incoming staff.

'I've briefed a plainclothes dog handler to begin a visual sweep of the perimeter, Guvnor. It will be a while before the system is up and running.'

'Good!' nodded Boyd. 'We need some protection for the computer system. It's worth a fortune.'

Anthea smiled and replied, 'I was thinking more of the conference and the personal security of those attending.'

'Ah! Good point,' chuckled Boyd. 'People are much more important than computer systems. By the way, can you link through to the Home Office and the Foreign Office Secretariat Division?'

'Absolutely,' replied Anthea. 'Ricky will sort it shortly. He's the gizmo man. We'll have you talking to the Moon before long, Guvnor.'

'Brilliant! Personally, I still can't change a plug.'

'I must say it's good to get out and about again,' ventured Anthea. 'Putting the file together against Donaldson and Edwards was no easy task. That little trio has been busy, I can tell you.'

'I read your report,' offered Boyd. 'Remanded in custody to Durham with a date to be fixed for trial. A guilty plea is anticipated but Crawford is still wanted. Any idea where he is?'

'Workington! Whitehaven!' replied Anthea. 'I only say that because when he escaped, he headed west. The reality is that we have nothing in the intelligence system that denotes he has contacts in West Cumbria. He just outran us.'

'I'll speak to my informant,' nodded Boyd. 'Maybe there's something from the past that we need to know about.'

On a wall in the operations room, one of the detectives pinned a selection of photographs taken by the Red Alpha team in Peckham. The images also included one of Zak Zakaria. It was the photograph of the man who PC John Sanderson had encountered on a train near Rye. Above the photographs, a succession of clocks had been fitted to the wall. Each clock told the time it was in a different location, namely London, Paris, Washington, Chad, Nigeria and Cameroon.

The photographs and the clocks were all positioned directly in front of the briefing area that Boyd used to brief the team.

The unit continued to assemble the operations room as Ricky took charge and began linking the electronic systems together.

On a lakeside path, John Reed zipped tight his anorak and stepped across a puddle as the sleet changed to snow and his dog, Lucy, turned inland to avoid the pier.

The temperature had plummeted, and the plainclothes officer reflected on how unwise he had been to volunteer for the first perimeter patrol in this miserable weather. The mountains overlooking Ullswater were now snow-capped, and the lake was grey, choppy, and unfriendly in its appearance. Reed cut inland as an eight-seater Agusta 109 helicopter appeared in the sky and navigated towards the hotel.

Adjusting his earpiece, Reed heard the radio transmission, 'This is Control. Callsign Charlie Tango Charlie is approaching the helipad. He is clear for landing. Ground crew stand by to receive.'

Reed watched the helicopter land, then he turned and made his way uphill. Lucy was slack on the leash enjoying herself as she ploughed furrows with her nose in the shallow snow.

Inside the operations centre, Anthea radioed, 'Go ahead, Antonia. I hear you loud and clear. Multiple channels are linked here. I take it that's Bannerman in Charlie Tango Charlie?'

'Multiple channels confirmed, also the international channels requested as well as Ticker. We're good to go,' replied Antonia in the London office of the Special Crime Unit. 'And yes, that's Bannerman in the response helicopter. He has an update on the situation for Commander Boyd. How are things in the Lake District? What do I need to know about Ullswater? I have it mapped on my screen.'

Boyd leaned across Anthea, engaged the radio, and replied in a posh and learned voice, 'Madam, it's the second largest lake in the Lake District. It's about nine miles long and three-quarters of a mile wide in some places.'

'Get you, Mister Teacher! How deep is it?'

'About one hundred and ninety-seven feet. It's what they call a ribbon lake,' explained Boyd. 'You'd best bring your wet suit if you fancy a swim, Antonia. Plus, it's snowing.'

Boyd released the radio as he winked at Anthea who continued the commentary with, 'Ullswater was formed after the last ice age by a glacier scooping out the valley floor. The lake was formed by three glaciers which explains why the surrounding hills give it the shape of an extenuated Z. The origin of the name Ullswater might originally have been Ulf's Lake from the Old Norse language. Legend has it there was once a Nordic King called Ulf who ruled the area. There was also a Saxon Lord of Greystoke called Ulphus. His land bordered the lake so we're not sure who it's named after.'

'Wow!' voiced Antonia. 'Are you both on your holidays? I'm wondering if you've done anything other than study local history whilst you've been there?'

'Nope,' chuckled Anthea. 'It's written on a plaque in the hotel lobby.'

'Oh! I see,' replied Antonia. 'I'm impressed.'

'I'll catch you later,' interrupted Boyd. 'I see Bannerman arriving.'

'Don't forget Superintendent Fowler is now fully appraised of the operation,' declared Anthea. 'He's on route here for a meeting with you about manpower requirements. We'll need public order trained officers to deal with any demonstration that might impact us.'

'Thanks! Got that! Let's hope it doesn't make the press.'

'We'll prove the transmission links while you are away,' remarked Anthea. 'And then position the wildlife cameras in the trees and the bushes. It will be like making a documentary about nature if we're lucky.'

'Wildlife cameras! Nature! What next?' queried Boyd.

'I am the gizmo man, Guvnor,' voiced Ricky French. 'It makes a change from drones that get blanked by low clouds.'

Lucy began wagging her tail and scampered back to John Reed who bent down and tousled her neck before guiding her away again. The dogman followed with the leash now straining in his hand and Lucy pulling him up the slight incline to the top of the hill.

Footprints in the snow!

They were plain for all to see and distinctive enough for Lucy to reckon she had found something out of place.

Reed bent down and studied the footprints that were gradually being filled by the falling snow. Standing, he followed the track and saw that they stopped at a dry-stone wall. Beyond the wall lay the main road and then another stretch of meadow that gradually rose into the woods.

Has Lucy got a scent, thought John? Surely not in this weather. She's just playing.

A glance behind indicated a clear line of sight from the crest of the hill to the hotel and the house where the operations centre was situated. There was a disruption in the snow where the footprints ended, and a shallow trough was visible.

Read used a pair of binoculars hanging loosely from a cord around his neck. He scanned the wooded area before he radioed an update to the controllers.

'Footprints in the snow lead into the wood one mile from the hotel,' radioed John. 'Looks like we've had a recent visitor who has been watching us. Turn the dog team out. I'd like to scour the woods. I think we have company.'

Anthea acknowledged the signal and reached for a map replying, 'Probably kids, possibly walkers who got lost. Did you copy the last from the security patrol, Guvnor?'

'All received,' radioed Boyd. 'Keep me informed. John Reed has ground control. Give him what he wants and launch the helicopter to assist.'

'Roger!' replied Anthea. 'Charlie Tango Charlie prepare for take-off. Engage search pattern at the request of John Reed. He has ground control.'

On the road that bordered the lake, Crawford flagged down a car, spoke to the driver, and got into the passenger seat. The vehicle set off south towards Kirkstone Pass.

Bannerman and Boyd strolled around the grounds of the hotel as the two men updated each other on recent events in Peckham, Rye and Dymchurch.

Moments later, the helicopter took to the skies again.

'Ester Abara!' voiced Boyd. 'Well, I never.'

'We could block her now or arrest her,' proposed Bannerman. 'She's acting in a manner prejudicial to the interests of the State. If the Defence Secretary has been leaking information to her, who else has he been cosy with? Is he bent or just a naïve idiot that needs to be put out of office? I think we need a team on him. What is he doing on a regular basis that he shouldn't be? As it is, I've told the Red Alpha team to carry on watching the plot. We should let it run for a while. Henry and MI5 have uncovered what I call the Peckham team, and we need to know more about them. All we have so far is a set of photographs from the Red Alpha surveillance team. They'll be on the ops room wall for your next briefing. The one from the Dymchurch cop is amongst them too. I see it like this, Guvnor. An alternative course of action is to lock them all up and thereby disrupt their activities. We might not get the right conviction if any, but we'll have stopped them for the time being.'

'I agree with you,' nodded Boyd. 'We've proved Ester is connected to the team that is planning to hit the conference. If we move in now, we might end up with only her and not the people we want. It's one thing to have intelligence on the subject but intelligence doesn't always equate to evidence, and I don't want to burn the Red Alpha teams just to get Ester Abara in the frame. No, she can wait. I want the hit team, not just Ester Abara and the Defence Secretary. She's running messages between this Malik you mentioned and Boko Haram activists in Peckham: the Peckham team. We need to use our contacts to find out more about Malik. I want his photo on the wall next to the others so that everyone knows who we are looking for. I'll settle for the whole of the Peckham team and anyone who gets in the way and nothing less. We'll put Malik through the Ticker system when it's in place.'

'Great minds think alike, Guvnor,' chuckled Bannerman. 'How do you see it now that we've got Ester and the Peckham connection?'

Boyd stroked his chin for a second or two before replying with, 'At the briefing later today, I'm going to update our team so that they know we've got a game on. I need to remind them that they're no longer well-drilled doormen. It's a conspiracy to murder that we're dealing with. You see, Bannerman, if we put it together, it comes out like this. A Channel crosser gets caught in a storm and lands on the Kent coast. He burgles a golf club in Rye and steals a motorbike. The local police get onto him. He legs it when he's involved in a road accident. An officer gives chase. Our man climbs on board a train and the cop falls from the train and is lucky to be alive. It's initially thought that the policeman died when he was pushed from the moving train. Initially, some thought he was murdered. That's not the case. That cop now identifies the bike thief as Zak Zakaria who, according to intelligence sources in Chad, left that country recently to be trained by Boko Haram in terrorism. Zakaria heads for Peckham. He's the man the activists there are looking after and he's the man who has been trained to kill. That's the hitman who is going to destroy the conference. He's almost certain to have a support team with him, probably Kareem, Yan, and Moussa from the Peckham house. It must be them because we know from the Red Alpha team watching the house that only Abe is there now. For all we know, Zak could turn out to be a shooter or a suicide bomber.'

'Or a wild man with a samurai sword,' offered Bannerman.

'I don't know,' countered Boyd. 'But keeping Ester Abara and Dennis Butler under surveillance might give us more to go on. Find Zakaria and we can save the day.'

'I arranged a bigger surveillance team to help out Henry in Peckham, but Abe hasn't moved and the other three are gone. I've diverted the resources onto Butler and Abara. You okay with that?'

'Oh yes,' replied Boyd.

'How about a false story in the media?' proposed Bannerman. 'We could say that Zak was missing from home and we are concerned about his welfare. Publish his photograph and wait for the phone to ring.'

'It has its merits,' nodded Boyd. 'But I think we'll wait for him to turn up here. I'm not even going to circulate his photograph to the uniform department. It's only for our unit and no one else. These leads emanate from the intelligence community and their sources must be protected. The less that know the better. We'll keep it under wraps. One bonus we have is that the conference hasn't been featured in the press. If we can keep it that way, this man Zak ought to stick out like a sore thumb. Let it ride for now. We've got both Peckham and the conference covered. Keep the cards close to our chest. I'll update the Home Secretary and the Commissioner's office but it's just a game of poker at the end of the day.'

'Understood! Have you considered that the footprints in the snow may have been an indication that an advanced party from Peckham is already here?'

'It is a possibility, but I think it's too soon to tell. The conference isn't until later this week by which time the photographs of our suspects will be burnt into everyone's minds. You're right though. Where is Zak Zakaria now?'

Slow moving traffic on the M6 motorway had encouraged Kareem to detour onto a service area and take a break. Together with Yan, Moussa and Zak, they sat at a table overlooking the carriageway and drank coffee.

'How long before we get there?' enquired Zak.

'A while yet,' replied Kareem. 'Don't concern yourself with the time. We've got a way to go before we reach Glasgow.'

'Glasgow!' queried Zak. 'Where's that?'

'Where we'll all be kitted out,' replied Kareem. 'You in particular. No sweat. We have friends there who are helping us. Take it easy and do as you have been told. All will be well. Just remember what you have been trained to do and everything will be fine. Be like us, Zak. No one here knows you. No one knows us. Relax. Be yourself. Understood, Zak?'

'Yes, yes of course,' nodded Zak with a forced smile.

'Glasgow,' declared Yan. 'Is everything in place?'

'The diversionary tactics are coming into play soon,' replied Kareem. 'Now drink your coffee and get something to eat. We've got a long day and a long night ahead of us before we're finally ready to move in.'

When dusk arrived over Ullswater, sunlight was leaving the sky and night was edging closer. The kestrels and buzzards had soared on the last of the thermals but now retired to their nests on Plaice Fell until the morning. Only the night birds emerged to see Crawford making his way down the edge of the lake.

Dressed in a dark tracksuit and trainers, Crawford crouched low when he neared the hotel complex. He waited for the light to disappear altogether as he studied the layout of the land and gradually allowed his eyesight to adjust to the dark.

No guards, he thought. And no dogs barking. That means the CCTV is operating and I'm not on camera. They won't see me in the water, that's for sure. I'm as black as the night.

Beneath his outer clothing, Crawford wore a wetsuit he had stolen from Ullswater yacht club. It was dark blue, skin-tight, and was fitted with a long zip running the length of his back. He reached behind and pulled on the tab before sliding into the water and submerged to shoulder height.

With only his head above the waterline, Crawford swam gently towards the pier where his money was hidden amongst the brickwork. Gradually, he made progress careful not to disturb the water too much and make waves.

The offside stanchion from the lake viewpoint, he remembered. That makes it the one nearest to me.

In the control room, the duty operator saw a light flash on the console and realised the passive infrared detection system had been activated. He engaged the keyboard and directed a CCTV camera towards the area.

The controller engaged the radio with, 'DS Anwhari! I have a PIDS activation about fifty yards from the pier. No traces on the CCTV system but can you check it out? Probably wildlife.'

'Crocodiles,' replied Terry Anwhari. 'I'm on it.'

The controller chuckled at the thought of crocodiles in Ullswater and continued to pan the CCTV along the shoreline.

Crawford reached the pier. The structure was a solid wooden walkway supported by a dozen brick stanchions that sprouted out of the water and held it tight in selected places. It was wide enough for a score or more of people to walk on and regularly entertained speedboats and yachts that berthed there during the day for a short time.

Finding the target stanchion, Crawford checked the surrounding area. The police speedboat was anchored nearby, and the area was silent and as still as the night. Only the gentle ripple of the waves from his body movements gave testimony to his presence.

Crawford took a deep breath and fully submerged near the brick pier support.

Moments later, some two feet below the waterline, Crawford's hands finally found the false compartment built into the brick structure. He eased his fingers into the crevice at either side of the metal shelf and pulled. The compartment did not budge. It was held fast from a long period of solidarity in its environment.

Crawford tugged again and eventually felt the brickwork crumble in his hands. The compartment was opening. He felt the dry bag and knew the money was still there.

He tugged again.

Detective Sergeant Terry Anwhari made the pier, flashed a torch from left to right, and satisfied himself that there was no intruder. He turned to go.

There was a mighty commotion when Crawford ran out of oxygen and emerged from the water with his lungs crying out for immediate rescue. Water cascaded from his body like a waterfall and his voice croaked as he wheezed loudly and took in a lungful of air.

Stunned, Terry Anwhari spun around to see a human figure surface from the lake as if it were a monster rising from the depths to devour him. He dropped his torch, took a step back, and promptly lost his footing and fell into the lake.

Crawford shook his head and a thousand drops of water exploded into the atmosphere. He saw the torch flashing as it dropped into the lake, heard the man gasp with shock, and watched him fall backwards from the pier into Ullswater.

Glancing at the man in the water, Crawford looked down towards the brickwork below the surface, realised he hadn't time to finish his task, and struck out in a front crawl to escape.

'Intruder! Man down in the lake! Intruder!' screamed Sergeant Anwhari.

The detective floundered in the water, couldn't find his torch, but felt his feet hit the bottom of the lake and stabilise his body. Glimpsing the intruder swimming away from the pier, Anwhari leapt forward and began swimming after the trespasser.

Within a few yards, Anwhari's clothes became waterlogged, and he felt himself being dragged down into the depths of the lake.

The sound of running footsteps could be heard as Crawford dived to the depths, swam underwater as far as he could, and then surfaced to take in more oxygen some twenty yards later. He peeked over his shoulder and saw half a dozen people running onto the wooden pier.

A lifebelt was thrown. Terry Anwhari caught it, secured the belt to his body, and felt himself being pulled towards the shore as his colleagues rescued him from the lake.

Making inland, Crawford reached dry land and ran as fast he could along the shoreline and into the darkness of the night. Only the sound of his squelching trainers accompanied him as water dripped from his thin tracksuit and laid down a watery path for others to follow.

A CCTV camera panned the area, captured a dark shadowy image running towards the roadway, and then lost contact when the intruder disappeared into the woods bordering the highway.

~

Chapter Twelve
~

Penrith Railway Station
The following morning.

Parking his Porsche Cayenne in the station car park at Ullswater Road, Penrith Boyd wandered into the building. Casually dressed, he strolled the full length of the platform making himself clearly visible.

Olly sat in the waiting room and watched Boyd. The two men ignored each other.

Boyd's mobile phone rang and he answered it with 'Morning, Ma'am,' and listened before murmuring a reply and closing the call.

Checking the area, Boyd approached a notice board, paused for a while as he examined the contents, and then left the railway station. He crossed the road and entered Castle Park and the site of Penrith's now-ruined medieval castle.

Walking through the park, Boyd took a seat on a bench and waited.

'All secure,' radioed Anthea. 'Target approaching. He's clean. No followers.'

Boyd heard the transmission in his earpiece and saw Olly approaching. He stood up and joined his informant as the two men meandered through the park.

'All well?' enquired Boyd.

'Yep! No problems,' replied Olly. 'I got the early train. You wanted to see me. What's up, boss?'

'Yes, thanks for coming,' nodded Boyd. 'Crawford is still at large. I wondered if you'd heard anything on the grapevine.'

'No! Not a thing. I heard he'd done a runner from the court. Couldn't believe it myself but I read in the paper that he'd thrown himself through a window otherwise he'd never have made it.'

'That's right. He was determined to get away. If you were me, Olly, where would you be looking for Crawford?'

'Spain, somewhere hot and out of the way. Inland, probably in the mountains. Some tiny village twenty miles from Barcelona. That would be my guess.'

'Barcelona! Spain! What makes you think that?'

'The money! Come on, man. Haven't you worked it out?'

'What do you mean?'

'I read the newspaper,' revealed Olly. 'You guys have charged Edwards and Donaldson with twenty-five armed robberies over the last ten years.'

Boyd nodded in agreement.

'And conspiracy to rob in case you can't prove them all,' chuckled Olly.

'It's the easiest to prove,' remarked Boyd. 'Tell me, Olly, what haven't I worked out?'

'How much money did you recover from all those raids?'

'Other than the last job at Penrith, not a penny.'

'Haven't you stopped to think what they did with it?'

'Spent it I guess.'

'Nah! Not those three. They've stashed it somewhere. Crawford loves Spain. That's where you'll find him.'

Olly stood to go but Boyd touched his arm and said, 'Sit down, Olly. Tell me what else you know. Where did you hear that?'

'The city pubs! The ones they used to hang out in.'

'Did they have any connections in West Cumbria? Crawford in particular?'

'Not that I know of. They never needed anyone to dispose of the gear, boss. They only nicked money. One thing I did hear though.'

'What was that?'

'Don't know if it was right or not but Willie Hodgson is Crawford's cousin.'

'Willie! Yeah, I know him,' replied Boyd. 'What about him?'

'He was drunk one night in the Crown, and I heard him talking to Donaldson. Something about the last job they would be doing.'

'You mean the Penrith job?'

'Yeah! Craic was they were going to retire.'

'And you believed him?'

'I wasn't talking to him. I was just listening to the conversation like you told me. I thought that's a load of crap. They're in it for the long run. Now I'm not so sure.'

'Why?'

'If Crawford is on the run and you're nowhere near catching him then he's making for Spain on his own with a stack of cash the three of them pinched from the robberies. Simple really, unless you're going to tell me you've got a lead on a bank where the money might have been deposited.'

Boyd studied Olly for a moment and said, 'Now that's got me thinking. What about Ullswater? Did they ever go down there? Did you hear anything about any of them visiting Ullswater in the past?'

'These three robbers you caught are from a gang of joiners, brickies, labourers, and scaffolders,' replied Olly. 'Anything that needs physical labour they'll have a go at. They're money men, boss. Hard graft equals hard cash. But Ullswater? You must be joking. They're city robbers, not country bumpkins. There are no banks to rob in Ullswater.'

'No, but it might be a great place to stash the cash,' suggested Boyd.

'Now, you got me thinking, boss.'

Boyd chuckled and said, 'Well, you always get my mind working, Olly. Ullswater?'

'Crawford might have done some work at the yacht club when it was done up.'

'Do you know for sure?'

'Nah! But that yacht club advertised for labourers when they refurbished the spot years ago. I suppose Crawford and his mates might have been involved.'

'How long ago was that?'

'Nine, ten years ago, something like that.'

'Just when the robberies started,' remarked Boyd.

'For what it's worth,' offered Olly. 'You might be talking a couple of hundred thousand quid. How much did they steal over the years?'

'Not sure, but I'd say you were pretty close with that figure.'

'I'd say they splashed some of the cash on drink, horses, and gambling. I reckon most of it will have been hidden somewhere. I know Crawford went to Barcelona a few times on holiday. He loves the place. Have you tried one of the Spanish banks there?'

Boyd nodded thoughtfully and replied, 'Thanks, Olly but I can't see how he would be able to take a huge wad of cash out of the country and bank it in Spain. Look, if anything comes to mind ring the number I gave you and leave a message for me. Okay?'

'Yeah! Will do. Same meeting place?'

'For now, yes. Just keep an eye out for yourself when you're on the train. If there's anyone you know then don't board it. Get the next one. Stay safe.'

'Will do.'

Boyd handed some money over and said, 'Keep building that nest egg, Olly. Half now and half in the bank for you.'

Olly crumpled the notes into his fist, pocketed them, and made for the railway station with, 'Cheers! I'll catch the northbound to Carlisle in five minutes.'

Boyd watched him leave before radioing to Anthea, 'Closure! All done here!'

Anthea replied, 'Walk on through the park and I'll join you.'

Five minutes later, Olly was on his way to the city and Anthea and Boyd were discussing the meeting.

'Did you get anything useful?' asked Anthea.

'Nothing concrete,' replied Boyd. 'But he has activated my mind something rotten.'

'In what way?' asked Anthea.

'Ullswater! At the briefing this morning I heard about the intruder at Ullswater Hotel during the night.'

'They were lucky whoever they were, Guvnor. It's my fault. I should have told the staff to be on their toes from the word go. The raider got away because we were asleep and not up to the job at hand. We are so focused on the actual conference that we've forgotten the basics. That's zero out of ten for security in my book.'

'It happens occasionally, Anthea. There's no harm done. Most times we win. Last night we lost. The unit will have to do better next time, that's all.'

'The fact is, Guvnor, Terry Anwhari suggests the intruder might have been Zakaria visiting us last night and if it was, we missed him. If it was Zakaria or any of his team, what were they doing in the lake under the pier? Looking for the shortest way possible to get into the hotel from the lake without being seen, or planting a bomb underneath the pier?'

'Good thinking but none of our delegates are arriving by boat when the conference starts. They are all coming in by car, except the Americans, of course.'

'They'll be coming in by nuclear submarine, I presume,' offered Anthea with a twisted smile.

'Helicopter.'

'You know what the yanks are like, Guvnor. By the way, I've asked Lancashire to send a diving team pronto. I want the pier area checked above and below the water line in case a bomb has been planted there. They are in Lake Vyrnwy in Wales, at the moment, but they'll be with us tomorrow afternoon at the latest!'

'It's unlikely that there's a bomb there and such a device probably wouldn't have a blast radius that would take the hotel down. But get it done, just in case. If nothing else, it may well be a diversionary tactic. They might set a bomb off at the pier expecting us to rush there when their real intention is to attack elsewhere. They could half our security response merely by causing diversions.'

'I'm on it and I'm beginning to think that whoever decided Ullswater was a good place for a conference of this magnitude made a mistake. They should have stuck to London.'

'It was a government decision supported by myself. I made a mistake,' replied Boyd. 'Earlier today I took a call from Maude Black: the Home Secretary.'

'What did she want?'

'To tell me that the government have authorised a shoot on sight policy in the event of an attack on the conference.'

'Shoot on sight is pretty close to shoot to kill,' proposed Anthea. 'Did you agree?'

'I noted the instruction, that's all,' replied Boyd. 'Now I'm beginning to understand why they picked this venue in Cumbria. It's nicely out of the way and not in the public eye.'

'Remote!'

'Yes, but I wonder if we are being used as pawns in a game. Why Cumbria? Yes, I know elements of our organisation deploy protection officers to multiple private visits to individuals from across the globe who are at threat in accordance with the personal protection system. You need to be at a proven threat level before you receive authorised protection. It costs over one million pounds a year for a protection detail. I often question the document I receive in the post and deny them a positive response. It's political at times and not based on intelligence or a true reflection of present-day affairs. Some of the instructions we receive seek to promote individuals into the protection system at our expense. I see corrupted power when others see a need to comply. Political parties sometimes wrongly adhere to protective issues for their politicians when in reality no threat exists. But photo opportunities with protection officers in the background are good for political parties. That's why governments often send me misleading information that does not match our intelligence database analysis. We are pawns in a game that I refuse to play.'

'You'll not hear that anywhere else, Guvnor. But as one who has walked with you on that journey, you're right.'

'Maude Black would say that our government seeks to work closely and harmoniously with the Nigerian government. The UK has extensive interests throughout the African continent and doesn't want a lengthy trial that will drag the two nations through the mud and cause frustration if we were to arrest someone attacking the conference. They want a quick solution.'

'She means shoot to kill?' proposed Anthea.

'Mmm,' nodded Boyd. 'Something like that.'

'I don't like the sound of that. Let's get back to the hotel, Guvnor,' voiced Anthea. 'I need to tighten things up.'

'Have we got any local contacts connected to Ullswater Yacht Club?' probed Boyd.

'Fowler!' replied Anthea. 'Superintendent Roy Fowler.'

''The Commander at Penrith who joined us after the attempted bank raid?' remarked Boyd.

'That's him. He's the President of Ullswater Yacht Club.'

'Is he really?'

'Why do you ask?'

'I want to know if Donaldson, Edwards and Crawford worked on the yacht club refurbishment about ten years ago. The club might have records, invoices, photographs, whatever. If they did, then Crawford knows Ullswater.'

'I thought Crawford was on the back burner until the conference was over?'

'He is but Olly activated my mind.'

'In what way?' probed Anthea inquisitively.

'If I told you that my mind is considering the possibility that last night's intruder was Crawford hoping to get into the hotel to retrieve a hidden stash of stolen money, you'd just laugh, wouldn't you?'

'Probably,' chuckled Anthea. 'Did Olly tell you that?'

'Not in so many words. Why do you ask?'

'Because the yacht club is on the other side of the lake from our location. How did you work out that he knows our hotel? It's either beyond me or you are flying by the seat of your pants again.'

'I agree, Anthea, but Olly just got my mind functioning at full capacity. If Crawford knows the area because he was working here for a few months, then who knows? He may well have made friends and contacts with people in this neck of the woods, not just the yacht club.'

'He doesn't show on any of the people in the area we've run a check on. The villages are full of negative traces as far as we are concerned. There's no one of adverse interest recorded on our databases. It's a clean area as far as our targeting system is concerned. Ullswater's biggest political problem seems to be foxhunting, not Chad, Africa, global politics, or political activism.'

'Good! Thanks for that. I'm keeping an open mind. I still think it might have been Crawford, and his stash is somewhere near the hotel.'

'Or under the pier,' suggested Anthea.

'I doubt it. More likely to be in the hotel somewhere. But who knows these days?'

'This job tells me you should never leave a stone unturned, Guvnor. I'll bottom it out with Superintendent Fowler.'

'Please do, thank you.

'In fact, I'll pop into town and see him now,' declared Anthea. 'I'll catch you at the operations centre later.'

'That's a done deal,' replied Boyd. 'Have a good day. I'll catch up with you tonight.'

Nightfall crept across Ullswater when Crawford paddled a stolen fibreglass canoe across the lake from the yacht club towards the hotel and the boathouse.

The moonlight glistened on the quiet waters as a buzzard skimmed low and climbed towards its nest on Plaice Fell. Now it was time once more for the night birds to bid farewell to the buzzards and kestrels who dominated the skies through the day.

Crawford neared the boathouse and stopped paddling. Trailing the oar behind the canoe's stern, he steered the vessel towards the middle of the pier where he ducked low and positioned himself directly beneath the wooden walkway. His free hand shot up and caught the structure bringing the vessel to a standstill.

On the hotel grounds, silence ruled. No lights were shining onto the tarmac other than the security lamps that beamed down from the roof onto the forecourt area. The house nearby now boasted a fully equipped operational centre that was occupied by the Special Crime Unit. Other than a couple of saloon cars parked outside, the building was lit but very quiet.

Crawford's eyes grew accustomed to the scene as he watched a uniform security patrol venture towards the hillside and the woods. They moved away from his location leaving him unseen and undetected. A glance elsewhere revealed the police boat anchored in the lake about fifty yards from the shoreline. The vessel was deserted and in darkness.

Feeling safe, Crawford ran his hands along the underneath of the pier, found the stanchions that held it upright in the water, and began to count the bricks from the top of the pier to the waterline. He smiled on realising that despite all the recent floods, the snow, and incessant rain over the years, the depth of the lake had hardly changed.

Fifteen bricks down, thought Crawford as he gradually worked his hands below the surface. But it's cold, so damned cold, he decided.

Sliding out of the canoe, he found the bottom of the stanchion and then sought a line of brickwork that stood out from the rest and represented the opening to a shelf that bore the dry bag containing the money.

Crawford found the brickwork and tugged at the shelf he had embedded there ten years ago and which he had used as a depository on an annual basis ever since.

The metal shelf fully exposed itself when he removed the outer brickwork. A sealed dry bag lying on the shelf then presented itself and brought a huge grin to Crawford's face. He tugged at the bag and prised it from its safe place.

Surfacing for a moment, Crawford inhaled and captured a lungful of clean oxygen. He submerged once more, seized the dry bag again, felt the bulging contents in his hands, and took the bag and himself to the surface.

With the canoe held tight beneath the pier and the dry bag now resting on the wooden platform, Crawford removed the bag from its waterproof covering and unzipped it. Hundreds of banknotes were folded into bundles and held tight by rubber bands. Every one of them was as dry as the day he had put them there.

Crawford used the paddle to manhandle the canoe into a manageable position. He heaved the bag from the pier into the canoe and leaned over pushing the dry bag into the space that was the bow of the canoe. Then he manoeuvred along the wooden platform and began to ease himself into the canoe.

A klaxon sounded from the police boat and rushed through the atmosphere in a deafening crescendo. Simultaneously, a figure on the bow of the police boat directed a powerful beam of light onto the pier area.

Flummoxed, Crawford realised he was caught in a floodlight that enveloped his very being. He glared at the police boat but had to cover his eyes as the beam bore into his senses. Then he heard the thunder of running feet.

The wooden pier bounced under the weight of Terry Anwhari.

'It's Crawford!' screamed Anwhari. 'It's Crawford. We've got him at last!'

The detective knelt and grabbed the wanted man by his neck before pulling him out of the canoe and onto the decking. Ricky French followed on behind Terry and joined in as a tussle took place. Crawford refused to go quietly and lashed out at the two men whilst the police boat neared, its beam now more intensive and its klaxon screaming in the dark of the night.

'Stand still, Crawford!' shouted Janice Burns from the bow of the police boat. 'You are surrounded.'

Ducking beneath Anwhari's grip, Crawford sank a clenched fist into the detective's stomach before kicking out at Ricky. The melee continued with the men swopping blows and Crawford struggling to keep his feet on the sodden slippery deck.

A push from Cumbria's most wanted criminal witnessed Terry Anwhari tumble into the lake leaving Ricky brawling with Crawford. A headbutt from Crawford connected with Ricky who couldn't get a tight hold of Crawford's wet suit and promptly fell to his knees.

Crawford moved forward in a bid to escape but Ricky grasped his legs and brought him to the ground kicking and struggling for all he was worth. The two men grappled with each other, rolled over, and then crashed unceremoniously into the watery depths below.

Janice swivelled the floodlight on the bow of the boat and targeted the three men in the water lighting up the entire pier area as if it were daylight. Seconds later, she fired a flare into the sky and watched as the heavens turned red and the flare exploded into a hundred pieces of fiery magnesium.

Turning to the cabin, Janice gestured to the skipper that they move closer, and then shouted, 'Crawford! You are under arrest. Give yourself up! There is no escape!'

The skipper of the police boat ran from the cabin, threw another lifebelt into the lake, and then returned to the controls where he gently pushed the throttle forward and took the boat closer to the action.

Undisturbed by the floodlights, the noisy klaxon, a red sky, and the imminent presence of dozens of individuals from the Operation Centre, Crawford placed one hand on the stern of the canoe and pushed it out into the lake. He swam behind the vessel determined to escape with his ill-gotten gains.

Terry Anwhari identified the getaway route, took a deep breath, and plunged at the canoe's bow delivering all his weight on the vessel. The bow dipped. The stern rose. Terry bounced on the bow again and then submerged into the unknown.

Crawford momentarily flew high into the sky having lost control of the canoe. He landed with a huge splash and watched the canoe wobble. It was close to overturning.

Janice guided the boat nearer and threw another lifebelt into Ullswater. There was a splash when the buoyancy aid landed next to the trio of fighting, squabbling men.

Ricky punched out at Crawford and missed. Crawford retaliated by kicking the assailant in the stomach before renewing his quest to escape.

Terry Anwhari's feet found the lakebed. Squatting down, he leapt upwards striking the fibreglass canoe in its underbelly with his fists. Unbroken, the canoe denied the ferocity of the strike but gradually overturned depositing the dry bag into the lake.

One by one, bundles of banknotes dribbled from the dry bag and meandered into the lake.

Crawford screamed in anger and swam towards the police boat. Using every fibre of his body, he launched himself out of the water and grasped the vessel's deck with both hands. With a deep breath, he heaved himself onto the deck only to be repelled by Janice who shoulder-charged him back into the lake.

Ricky and Terry clambered on top of Crawford when more detectives, leapt into the lake and helped to overpower the escapee. Janice drew alongside and helped haul Crawford aboard where he was taken into custody and manacled.

Boyd and Anthea arrived at the pier.

Looking at the red sky above, Boyd chuckled, 'Janice did say that she could provide plenty of distractions.'

'She thought the klaxon and the lights would be enough to panic Crawford into submission, but it didn't work,' remarked Anthea. 'Still, we got him in the end.'

A patrol car arrived at the pier and Crawford was secured into the rear of the vehicle before being taken to Penrith police station.

As the police boat closed with the overturned canoe, Anthea nudged Boyd and said, 'You were right, Guvnor. Olly got your mind going. You thought it might have been Crawford and if it was, he would return. Flying by the seat of your pants again, but we got our man.'

'It was our turn to get lucky,' replied Boyd. 'I thought he would make for the hotel but it was the pier where the money was hidden.'

'I'd never have thought of that in a million years,' replied Anthea. 'I wonder how much money was involved?'

'The next hour or two is going to be interesting,' declared Boyd. 'Janice and the crew are going fishing.'

The canoe continued to float upside down as it discharged more banknotes from the dry bag and Janice and her colleagues used a fishing net to catch Crawford's treasure trove now gradually covering the surface of the lake.

Ullswater was awash with banknotes.

~

Chapter Thirteen
~

N'Djanema
Chad, West Africa

The slenderly built Professor Bakar left his language class earlier than usual and walked briskly to the Safari Restaurant and Coffee Shop that was situated close to the King Faisal University.

Bakar had delivered both French and German lessons that morning using a chalkboard and textbooks in need of updating. Nevertheless, observers knew he spoke good English and was a widely read individual who enjoyed a thirst for knowledge. Folded under his arm, the Professor carried a copy of the local Hebdo magazine: a weekly offering of local news.

Entering the café at a steady pace, somewhat agitated in his demeanour, Professor Bakar soon espied Roger Buckley. He made his way to Roger where he slapped the magazine down on the table in front of him and said, 'Have you seen this?'

'And good morning to you, Professor Bakar,' smiled the MI6 officer. 'Settle down and slow down. You seem hot under the collar today. I've just ordered a pot of coffee for us. It won't be too long, I'm sure. Now then, what is it that has caught your attention? It's not like you to be so anxious.'

'Page seven!' replied the Professor who quickly presented a news article for Roger's sight. 'Inside pages as usual. I thought you should be brought up to speed on this.'

Wearing his usual white linen suit set off by a light blue cotton shirt and matching blue tie, the middle-aged Roger Buckley casually, but quickly, appraised himself of the article.

'A couple of weeks ago, three hundred children were kidnapped from a school near Lake Chad,' declared the Professor. 'The kidnappers wanted thirty million nairas. They got a lot more than that. Three million American dollars to be precise. What the hell is going on? I thought you were an advocate of the non-payment of ransoms to terrorists?'

'I am,' murmured Roger as his eyes continued to scan the page. 'Unfortunately, I'm not the Chad government. This is a regular occurrence, Professor. Please, settle yourself.'

'You don't understand, Mr Buckley,' argued the nervous Professor. 'If you read the article to the end you'll see that only two hundred and ninety-seven children were released.'

'Do they want more money?'

'No, the three children still held in captivity are Zak Zakaria's kids.'

'How do you know that?'

'The canteen is buzzing with it. The kids who have been released have all been taken to a care centre for examination and health checks. Zak's kids aren't amongst them.'

'Where's Zak's mother?'

The coffee arrived and delayed a timely response before Professor Bakar was able to say, 'She's nowhere to be seen. I can tell you that she wasn't at the school when Malik kidnapped the kids. I'd say she's gone over to them. She's Boko Haram through and through just like Zak. She must be. I'd go even further, Mr Buckley. I'd say she was part of the conspiracy. She arranged for the kids to be taken from the school. You know what I mean, she was the insider. The one who set it up and pointed the finger.'

Roger finished reading the article, placed it in his briefcase, and replied, 'Fascinating, but also very sad. Three hundred children were kidnapped, two schoolteachers murdered, and three kids still missing. There's a mystery to solve.'

'There's no mystery, Mr Buckley. Zak's Mum's is involved. Malik will have paid her for the tip-off about the teachers and security at the school. You keep forgetting that Chad thrives on corruption. It's that simple.'

'Is there anything particularly special about the Zakaria children? Are they connected or related to any government ministers, for example? Is there anything that makes those three children stand out amongst the three hundred?'

'No, not that I'm aware of.'

Raising his coffee cup, Roger nodded and replied, 'The mystery may be more complex than you think. We'll see, Professor. It needs investigation, that's for sure. Will you excuse me for a moment? I need to make a call.'

'Of course,' replied the Professor.

Roger stepped away from the table and walked outside where he used his mobile to update Major Alexander Anderson on the situation. The conversation continued for some time before Roger stated, 'Yes, Alex! The mud huts at Sangari near Lake Chad. I want you to take a patrol and find out if the Zakaria woman is still in those huts waiting for her family to return. Or has she gone too? Find out what you can, Alex.'

Returning to the company of his guest, Roger said, 'A friend of mine is heading that way, Professor. He'll let me know what the situation is at the Sangari mud huts as soon as possible. More coffee? Perhaps a cocktail to soothe your nerves?'

'Does anything ever upset you?' probed Professor Bakar. 'When I read that this morning, I thought you would need to know. You can't defeat terrorism by paying off the men with guns and bombs. That said, I thought you'd be pleased that I'd confirmed that the Zakaria family are members of Boko Haram. They are followers of Malik.'

'Yes, of course, Professor. I am deeply gratefully for both your concern and your information. Do you know Malik? Is he an ex-pupil?'

'No! He is not. He's originally from Nigeria, just over the border. He is a feared individual running a brutal regime of terror in the area. It is said that he is the brain behind the recent school kidnappings. He's the new leader and don't we know it.'

'In which way is he different from his predecessors?'

'His eyes and his desires stretch way beyond the likes of Chad. He supports ISWAP locally but sees ISIS as a global organisation and, for what it's worth, they say he plans to take Boko Haram much further than the shores of Africa.'

'They?' cautioned Roger. 'Did someone tell you that, or is that an analysis from yourself?'

'I heard. I worked it out. You are a visitor. I live here every day and I sense the change in the wind. I'll tell you now, Mr Buckley, the wind of change is likely to be an unrivalled thunderstorm if he's not brought to book soon.'

Roger drank his coffee, patted his lips with a napkin and replied, 'Thank you, Professor. Now shall we start at the beginning? Malik! Everything you know about him. Slowly and concisely please.'

The jug of coffee was replenished as Roger asked his questions and Professor Bakar responded.

As the meeting between the two men went on, an unmarked blue and white Dauphin helicopter, nicknamed Blue Thunder, took off across the skies and headed for Sangari. In the Savanna which was the area of Lake Chad, tall, scattered trees provided an extensive canopy that encircled the swamps surrounding the lake.

Major Anderson sat in the front passenger seat, studied the map, and instructed 'Touchdown' when the lake, the mud huts, and the swamps, came into view.

Within seconds of landing, the six troopers aboard the helicopter had disembarked and advanced on the target area.

A gloved finger pushed the safety catch of a semi-automatic weapon to the off position. The soldiers moved forward and eyed the scattered trees that provided a jungle-like terrain and offered no welcome to their presence

Three hours later, Roger Buckley sat in his secure office in the capital and took a call from Major Anderson. The two men discussed the military operation at length, the findings, and things that needed to be done in the days ahead before Roger ended the call and activated his stand-alone secure computer.

According to the Ticker reports on Boko Haram, thought Roger. Elements of the Nigerian government are visiting the UK for a tripartite conference on terrorism. The report doesn't reveal where in the UK but asks that if new threats or associated intelligence becomes apparent regarding terrorism in the Nigeria/ISIS/ISWAP area of interest, then they are to be reported directly to the Special Crime Unit which is responsible for security at the event. I've never heard of that unit but here am I, thousands of miles away, sitting with the knowledge that at least one local from Chad has gone missing having been trained by Boko Haram in terrorism. Well, Zakaria might have been an irrelevant suspect before, maybe of minor interest, but now it looks as if the whole of the Zakaria camp has gone over to Boko Haram, and no one knows where they are. And Malik? Malik is said to be an up-and-coming leader with aspirations well beyond Chad. I wonder. Is this me being led down the garden path by my wandering mind, or is it me utilising the skills that are part of me? The ability and willingness to second guess what is going on in the world that I watch every day? Is this spying or passing on tittle-tattle? I don't know but others might have the answer. Do it anyways, thought Roger. What have you got to lose?

Roger concentrated his mind and then transmitted the following encrypted message to the organisation he served.

The message read:
Source Report: Bookworm.
Handler: Barracuda.

Subject: 1) Change of Leadership BOKO HARAM, Lake Chad area.

Subject: 2) Further re ZAK ZAKARIA

I refer to my report of the 8th instance entitled, 'A developing target of interest' Bookworm advises me that three hundred children were abducted from a school in the Sangari area. The school was attacked by a Boko Haram mobile brigade, destroyed by fire, two schoolteachers murdered, and the children held for ransom. The Chad government are reported to have paid three hundred American dollars to the kidnappers who, earlier this week, released two hundred and ninety-seven children into the hands of the Chad authorities. This has been verified by independent government sources. The three children who have not been released are the children of ZAK ZAKARIA (hereinafter referred to as ZZ) whose wife is also missing from home in Sangari.

(Cross-reference previous report on ZZ and Kanuri tribe)

The military intervention resulted in a visit to ZZ's home in the mud flats near Sangari. Major Alexander Anderson confirms the village is empty. There is no trace of ZZ's mother.

Bookworm reports / suggests ZZ's wife is involved in the kidnapping and is a member of Boko Haram. For this reason, the Zakaria children have not been liberated by the kidnappers. Rather, Zakaria's wife and children have relocated to the current Boko Haram HQ in the swamps. (Precise location not known)

The kidnappers are led by a man known as MALIK who recently took command of the local Boko Haram Brigade. This is a fully armed, well equipped mobile force that is known to travel the region extensively. Malik's photograph, description, and history are recorded in an article in this week's HEBDO Magazine.

Provenance High.

Intelligence suggests that data herein supports Bookworm's assertion. Continued enquiries into the whereabouts of Malik are now a priority for this station.

Submitted to Central HQ, London and Military Attaché office, Abuja, Nigeria for information re membership database and travel watch procedures and restrictions.

Attachments:

1. Hebdo Magazine (Diplomatic Bag Protocols apply)
2. Report on currently known biography of MALIK.

Ends: Barracuda.

Within the hour, the message had been deciphered in London and was being read by Antonia Harston-Browne who sat at her Ticker console in the London office of the Special Crime Unit.

Antonia dialled Boyd's mobile.

'Boyd!' came the reply.

'You'd better sit down, Billy. I'm reading an intelligence report from Chad about the Zakaria family and the new Boko Haram leader in the area. His name is Malik.'

'Malik! How strong is the provenance and who put that on Ticker?'

'Provenance is high and the origin is classified Top Secret Omega Blue. You don't need the name of the sender, but the originator of the transmission has the same security clearance as yourself. The sender is from Chad and has an impeccable record. But I didn't tell you that.'

'Understood,' replied Boyd. 'Your thoughts, please. Could Malik be travelling to the UK?'

'Indeed he could,' confirmed Antonia. 'I'd be surprised if such a man did but you never know. I'll commence a rapid analysis of recent air passenger movements. A pound to a penny says that

Malik may well be the Malik mentioned in the reports by the Red Alpha teams at Peckham. So such a journey cannot be overruled.'

'I'll say,' remarked Boyd somewhat stunned at the news. 'Chad! West Africa? Are you sure?'

'Yes, there's only one such place on the planet,' chuckled Antonia. 'The report tells me Malik and his brigade are responsible for kidnapping three hundred kids from a school in Sangari where Zak Zakaria lives. The school was torched, two teachers murdered, and three hundred children kidnapped. To cut a long story short, Malik lifted three million American dollars in ransom money and released all but three of the kids.'

'Tell me he wants more money because they are the local government minister's kids?'

'That's not on the table. The three kids that have not been released are Zak Zakaria's children.'

'Interesting! Maybe they'd already escaped,' suggested Boyd.

'I doubt it, and there's nothing in the report to suggest any such likelihood.'

'But we don't know whether or not they escaped before the ransom was paid for the others,' argued Boyd.

'If the intelligence report is correct,' proposed Antonia, 'And the Malik in Chad is the one mentioned in Peckham then that surely confirms the conference is in imminent danger of attack from Boko Haram.'

'Could be! Probably is!' nodded Boyd thoughtfully.

'And that attack is led by Zak Zakaria as you thought, backed up by a support team financed from the mother ship in Chad.'

'But what about Zak's wife?' probed Boyd.

'As I said, the three Zakaria kids and his wife have disappeared too. That's confirmed by Major Alex Anderson whom we met at the Home Secretary's conference a while back. Looks like they've all gone over to Boko Haram. I think we might have a problem, Billy.'

'Yes, I can see that, Antonia. It's difficult but I don't want to jump to conclusions. Sometimes raw intelligence must be analysed properly.'

'That sounds bizarre when I know that you thrive on raw intelligence. You have a track record of refusing to wait for the analysis to be done. You normally just accept it the way it is and fly by the seat of your pants.'

'Yes, I suppose you're right, but that's usually because I am the producer of the intelligence. When it comes from a source not known to me I can be sceptical.'

'It's simple, Billy. Boko Haram are intent on attacking the conference in the Lake District. What more do you need to know?'

'Whether or not the report is correct.'

'You mean is it raw or has it been fully analysed? Reel it in, Billy. You had a good day locking up Crawford now don't get above yourself and make a habit of criticising impeccable sources. You put me in charge of the intelligence assessment and I've just given it to you. It's as plain as a pikestaff. You're under attack. It's going to happen. Sort it, Billy. Otherwise, the Home Secretary and the Defence Secretary will destroy you. You would be happy if it had originated from one of your informants. But oh no, it's come from someone you don't know and will never know so you don't like it and choose to question it. Get real!'

'Analysis,' queried Boyd as he closed the call.

Boyd walked out towards the lake, alone in his thoughts, gazed upon the Fells that surrounded Ullswater and allowed his bizarre, often complex mind, to analyse the report he had just received.

Sitting by the water's edge, Boyd said aloud, 'A lot of that report is from an article in a magazine. What's really happening? Why did they keep hold of Zak's kids and where is his wife?'

In an office in Whitehall, London, Sir Henry Fielding, the Secretary of State for Foreign Affairs, sat at his desk reading and signing documents as required. There was a knock on the door before Penny, his secretary, entered carrying a flimsy message.

'I thought you should see this one sooner than the others, Sir Henry. There is a digital file on its way to you in due course but I thought you might appreciate this hot off the press, so to speak. It's from our man in Chad and it may impinge on the tripartite security conference in the Lake District.'

'Thank you, Penny. Letters from Chad, would you believe. I never expected such a global remit when I took on the job of overseeing the Secret Intelligence Service and GCHQ,'

Penny smiled and closed the door behind her when she left.

Sir Henry read the message and rang the Director of Special Forces, Major General Kenneth Armitage.

'Sir Henry! How may I help you?'

'Kenneth, are you in receipt of the message from Chad concerning the new leader of Boko Haram, a man called Malik?'

'Yes, I am, Sir Henry. I received it only moments ago.'

'Good! I want you to send a detachment of special forces to the area and assist Major Anderson. He's looking for Malik and if we can find the new leader of Boko Haram quickly then that may well do much to restrain this man's quest for international glory.'

'I will redeploy B Squadron from a training exercise in Cyprus directly to Chad. One hundred troops! They can be there by tomorrow morning, Sir Henry.'

'Excellent! Just one more thing.'

'Go ahead.'

'Upon arrival, have the commanding officer report directly to Major Anderson. I know he has commenced questioning the children who were kidnapped. Hopefully, they may well have some memories of the place Malik took them to. Any such lead might project our people in the right direction at an early stage. B Squadron can assist in that questioning, afford additional security, and engage in any follow-up operations that may need to be actioned. Understood?'

'Perfectly, Sir Henry.'

'Good! Thank you! Cocktails at the club tonight?'

'Absolutely! Eight o'clock.'

'Indeed! See you then.'

Sir Henry closed the call and incinerated the flimsy in a shredder. An electronic copy would be filed securely and there was no need to keep unnecessary paperwork

In the hours that followed, at a hospital ward in N'Djanema, Chad, Major Anderson and a team of interviewers began questioning the kidnapped children as to what had happened to them whilst they had been imprisoned by Malik.

The interviewers gradually put together a picture of where they were taken, and what had happened to them in the hands of a brutal regime.

~

Chapter Fourteen

~

Rue Descartes
Calais, France
(The same day)

Eddie Chandler checked his wristwatch. It was time.

Enjoying the morning sun, the undercover detective set down his coffee cup and paid his bill at one of the many pavement cafes that littered the streets of Calais. He nodded his thanks to the waiter and made his way to the roundabout where the Avenue Louis Bleriot, Rue Descartes, and various other streets met in a roundabout configuration near the canal. He walked slowly, as instructed, and knew within himself that his every move was being watched.

Close to the roundabout, a dark blue coloured Renault taxi sat with its engine idling and a thin output of white steam escaping from the exhaust pipe.

Interesting, thought Eddie. If the taxi has been sitting outside on a street all night, then condensation has built up inside the exhaust system. Starting the engine warms the condensation and turns it into white steam. It will disappear soon, but the steam tells me that the taxi hasn't been driven far to get to this location. Less than three miles, I'd say.

The rear door swung open. Marty leaned across and beckoned him into the taxi.

'No beret today, Marty,' chuckled Eddie as he ducked down and into the Renault.

As soon as he sat down, he felt a pair of hands slide a black pillowcase over his head. He tried to remove the blindfold but felt the muzzle of a handgun drill into his ribs followed by the words, 'Sit still! Remain quiet and you won't get hurt.'

Eddie nodded and heard the same voice order, *'Conduire!'*

There was a gentle lurch forward when the taxi took off and travelled north towards the port.

Eddie began to count in his mind. He hadn't expected to be kidnapped, blindfolded, and driven off in such a manner but it had happened. Counting the seconds might indicate how far away from Calais he was to be driven. He would be able to convert time into mileage with the use of a map later. Right now, Eddie tried to remain calm and composed but the white steam indicated the taxi hadn't driven far that morning. That and the blindfold suggested Marty and his friends did not want him to know where they were travelling to. The journey was interrupted by a succession of stop-starts and Eddie decided the traffic lights were impeding progress.

Reaching five hundred seconds in his mind, Eddie felt the car speed up and reach a constant speed. He decided they were leaving Calais on an open road. North or south, he wondered, or inland?

'Are we still in France?' asked Eddie. 'I came to see Louis Martin. I mean him no harm.'

'Silencieux, nous y sommes presque,' voiced someone from the front of the car.

'Marty!' replied Eddie. 'Is that you?'

The point of a needle penetrated Eddie's upper arm and he gasped before lapsing into unconsciousness.

Later, he knew not how long, Eddie woke to find himself locked in a room which had no windows. He noticed that his clothing was dishevelled, and he had been strip-searched. The only furniture was a table and the desk at which he had been placed.

The door opened and two men walked in. They gave him a glass of water. He declined a cigarette and eyed them both before acknowledging Marty when he entered the room.

'Remain seated, Marius,' ordered Marty. 'Your wish has been granted. I'm sure that you understand that the kind of operations we are engaged in demand a high level of security.'

'The blindfold was one thing. There was no need for the needle.'

'Our decision, not yours.'

'Where are we, Marty.'

'France, of course.'

A whiff of cigar smoke heralded the arrival of a large fat man who waddled into the room smoking a huge Havana cigar and dripping two gold necklaces of unequal proportion. Each of the man's chubby fingers wore a gold ring, some studded with diamonds. The cut of his suit was elegance personified, his shirt and tie were of silk, and his highly polished leather shoes were from a class that Eddie had never before experienced.

'Marius Luka!'

'Louis Martin!' replied Eddie. 'So we meet at last.'

'A friend of Adrian and more recently of Marty. A Romanian with a bank account in Bratislava, or so I'm told.'

'Correct,' replied Eddie. 'I'm sure you've checked me out otherwise you wouldn't have brought me here.'

'I like to smell the pig before I roast it,' replied Louis. 'Or to be more precise, before I do business with an individual.'

Exhaling gradually, Eddie felt relieved to hear the latter part of Louis Martin's sentence and replied, 'Likewise! What I want is a straightforward business deal, that's all. I make no apology for messing either Adrian or Marty about. I do business only with the top man and no other.'

Louis Martin nodded, blew cigar smoke into Eddie's face, and said, 'You'll take the experience of a cigar from Havana with me?'

'Thank you but I don't smoke. I'm here to do business, not exchange pleasantries.'

'Very well!' replied Louis who set aside his cigar for a moment. He leaned forward, placed both his arms on the table before him, and said in a relaxed manner, 'The arrangement is one traveller at five thousand pounds sterling a time payable in cash only and before departure. There is no discount for minors or females. That figure increases to one hundred thousand pounds if the subject is wanted by the police anywhere in the world and includes the provision of false identity papers and the safe delivery of the subject to a specified address in England. I reserve the right to cancel that arrangement if I smell a rat or am not satisfied with the personnel involved. There will be no refund and you can consider your life expectancy to be shortened if I feel our operation is threatened in any way. If you provide less than one hundred travellers per month then the arrangement between us ceases forthwith.'

'How do I pay you?'

'You don't. You will be given details of how to pay once our operation is up running. We take cash only in notes that are not serialised or in number format.'

'Used notes only?'

'Correct! Is everything understood and clear?'

'How many of you are involved in this enterprise?'

'You ask too many questions.'

'Just interested, that's all. When do we start?'

'Are you ready now?'

'A phone call away.'

'In that case, we start now and the first journey will be this weekend. Marty will contact you with the meeting point. You will have one hour to get your people there ready to cross the Channel. Bring sufficient cash with you for every traveller.'

'How do I know I can trust you?'

'You don't, but I assure you that you can. We are most unlikely to ever meet again but my contacts will provide a communication channel between us. Understood?'

'Perfectly!'

'You will be returned to Calais shortly.'

'Are you going to needle me again?'

'No, the glass of water you are drinking is laced with a sedative. You will feel groggy soon and then fall asleep. Be assured, these precautions are intended to preserve our freedom and extend the longevity of our enterprise.'

'You mean your safety. Not mine. Just one thing,'

'Go on.'

'You do not have a French accent. You are not called Louis Martin, are you?'

'I am he: the man you are looking for, but you are right, there is such human as Louis Martin. You may call me Louis and I expect you to refer to me on that basis in the months ahead.'

'Months?'

'I grant you six months. If you fail to meet my security standards, the matter between us will close. That is the main reason I choose to speak to you, Marius. So that you know me, and I know you. Now you know what I expect of you, and you know what to expect from me if things go wrong.'

'You are untouchable, aren't you?'

'So they tell me. Take him away.'

Louis stood up as two of his henchmen moved forward and took hold of Eddie by the arms. The undercover detective could not resist, felt the fatigue hit him suddenly, and melted into their arms.

An hour later, he woke up in the back of the same taxi where Marty opened the rear door and ushered him onto the Rue Descartes.

'Be here on Saturday morning, Marius. Two hours before noon. Someone will meet you with instructions for the passage across the Channel. Give them the money and follow those instructions to the letter. You can then pass the information on to your travellers and need never show up on the coastline. If you are safe from the police then I am safe and we are all safe. It's all about not getting caught by the authorities. Understood?'

'It makes sense, yes.'

'Your travellers will go to a location where they will be given a dinghy and lifejackets. They will then be directed to the coast and told how to steer and in which direction. Your people will then set off across the English Channel. Do it correctly and you will never see a dinghy or a rowing boat of any kind, but you will have provided transport for your people. You are part of the network now. Not everyone in the network knows everyone else and that's the way we intend to keep it. Who knows, one day someone will ask for you by name. Louis Martin! Now be off with you. Saturday morning!'

'Saturday morning, two hours before noon,' repeated Marius. 'I'll be here.'

The taxi drove away with Marty in the passenger seat and Marius Luka, alias Eddie Chandler, stood on the pavement dazed, tired, and now part of a serious crime gang.

Committing the registration number of the taxi to his memory, Eddie watched the vehicle drive away before thinking, an hour or more from here, that's where they took me. I could smell the sea air, so they took me to the coast, not inland. I'm no closer to identifying Louis Martin now than I was yesterday. Or am I? My leads are Adrian, Marty and a taxi. The taxi! Now I have the taxi to report to Boyd. Perhaps we can identify the gang from there, but I doubt it because they seem to have the top man closeted in a multitude of safety measures. I suppose they've de worked it out. We're not interested in the likes of Marty and Adrian. There will be hundreds of people doing the same thing. No, it's the big man himself we want and he is cocooned in a self-made safety net.

A police motor cyclist roared by with its siren blaring leaving Eddie hoping that it would pull the blue taxi in for questioning and he could arrange to follow it up at a later date.

The taxi held a true course. The police motor cyclist roared on by.

On the motorway, in England half a dozen Hell's Angels were riding their motorbikes north on the M6 from the Lancashire border into Cumbria. They thought they were being chased by the traffic cops but when a three-litre patrol car overtook them and turned into Burton Services at high speed, they all screamed in pleasure and twisted the throttle further.

'Keswick here we come!' screamed one of them.

The patrol car reduced speed and cruised to a standstill outside the services.

Bert, the driver, watched the bikers flying along the motorway and said to his partner, Lenny, 'We'll have them next time, Lenny. Now let's sort these shoplifters out.'

The two officers entered the services to be met by a shop assistant who gestured them towards a storeroom at the rear of the premises.

'There's two of them. We decided to lock them in the storeroom for you.'

'What did they take?'

'A couple of dozen prepacked sandwiches for the bus.'

'Bus?'

'Yeah! They're on a coach trip. If you wander around to the petrol pumps you'll see a single-decker coach full of people carrying flags and banners. I reckon they are university students. They're going to a demonstration somewhere. Anyway, the two we caught decided to feed everyone on the bus. They walked in, helped themselves, and then walked out. The manager caught them on the forecourt and took them back into the shop to pay for the goods. They've no money, that's why we called you.'

'I see,' replied Bert.

Traffic continued to negotiate the M6 into the Lake District as the officers made their enquiries, reported the two university students for theft, and then said, 'We could have arrested you and taken you to Kendal police station. But as you both have identification with you and the services have got their goods backs, then you will both receive a summons to appear at the local magistrate's court.'

Sheepishly, one of the students nodded and replied, 'I'm sorry. It was a stupid thing to do. It won't happen again.'

'Where are you going to?' probed Lenny.

'The Ullswater Hotel?' came the reply. 'There's a demonstration there tomorrow. It's a protest really.'

'What about? Climate change?'

'No! SARS!'

'Oh! What's that?' enquired Bert.

The two students began laughing before one of them replied, 'You'll see. It's just a day out for us. Can we go now?'

'Yes! Yes, you can. Have a nice day!'

Joining their colleagues on the coach, the students settled into the rear of the vehicle, gestured a thumbs-up sign as they left, and were soon heading north on the MT6 motorway.

'Ullswater Hotel?' queried Bert. 'What's going on there?'

'No idea!' replied Lenny. 'I've not heard anything and I've no idea what SARS is. I bet it's one of those university rag week things. Still, I'll radio an update in. Two reported for theft at Burton Service Area whilst en route to a demonstration at Ullswater Hotel. Incident closed, resuming patrol.'

'Do that,' nodded Bert. 'I'll tell the manager here what we've done. Property recovered, summons for court.'

As the traffic officers resumed their duties, half a dozen VH-60N White Hawk helicopters, escorted by a squadron of RAF Tornados, flew overheard following the motorway route into the Lake District.

The helicopters were owned by the American Secret Service but today they were occupied by ministers and delegates from Nigeria, Chad and Cameroon, as well the United States. They were all headed to Cumbria courtesy of the American flight package supported by the Nigerian leader, Adebiyi Berundi. Adebiyi was a wily old bird who had been the President of the Federal Republic of Nigeria since the last election four years ago. A good result at the security conference in the Ullswater Hotel would do much to secure his continued tenure as the head of state and help to nullify a history of recent elections that were said to be flawed by international observers. Adebiyi was at the heart of trying to defeat corruption in his country and it was no easy task. In addition to his parliamentary duties, Adebiyi was also the commander-in-chief of the Nigerian Armed Forces. When translated to English, Adebiyi meant 'Royal One', and on the day in question, he was just that as the Americans fawned over the subject and served him the best champagne money could buy.

Adebiyi looked out of the window of the helicopter and turned to one of his protection officers saying, 'Green! Everywhere is so very green. What luck they have, those that live here. They do not experience a tropical monsoon climate.'

'I've heard it rains quite a lot in the Lakes,' replied Adebiyi's colleague. 'But not like at home. Buckle up, sir. We'll soon be there.'

Abebiyi nodded, sank his champagne, and did as he was bid.

Inside one particular helicopter, officers from America's Secret Service put away their maps and briefing notes, checked on their very important passenger, and made ready for landing at the conference facility on the shores of Ullswater. They were escorting the American Secretary of

State to the conference and his duties made him the chief foreign affairs adviser to the President of the United States of America. The American Secretary of State, Nigel Vanderbilt, was the equivalent of Britain's Foreign Secretary.

Vanderbilt helped himself to another glass of water and eased his back further into the plush armchair upon which he sat. Yawning, he flicked over a page in his document folder and reminded himself of what lay ahead. His ambition was simple enough to explain but much more complex to arrange and follow through. All the Americans, Nigerians and British wanted was a way forward in the battle against terrorism in West Africa.

In the hours that followed, the helicopters landed and discharged their passengers before settling at Carlisle airport for the night. The entourage found their rooms, unpacked, enjoyed the peacefulness of the lake before an informal dinner, and readied themselves for the coming conference.

~

Chapter Fifteen
~

Dawn.
Adjildele, Lake Chad, West Africa.
On the Day of the Conference.

On the outskirts of Lake Chad, moving ever closer to the swamps, troopers from the UK's B Squadron SAS, Chad, Cameroon and Nigeria, had merged to form one formidable strike force with two simple objectives. Capture Malik and liberate any remaining hostages he had in his charge.

The President of Nigeria, Adebiyi, had signed off the military intervention and handed the operation over to Major Anderson. Dozens of interviews with the kidnapped children had led Anderson's Light Mobile Brigade to the outskirts of Ajildele where it was thought Malik may be in hiding. If Malik wasn't in the area, then where on earth could he be? That was the question on the lips of the many who wanted Boko Haram's new leader dispensed with at the earliest possible opportunity.

For the conference security team at Ullswater, the question was much easier to frame, but equally as hard to fathom. Was Malik in Chad or England?

The soldiers moved forward in their jeeps, small troop carriers, and light armoured vehicles. They knew the terrain was such that they would never make it into the swamps with their vehicles. That was the fundamental reason why Malik and his predecessors had always eluded capture over the years. They lived in the swamps where military and police vehicles found it impossible to journey.

The problem was there for all to see as the strike force drew nearer to the target area. There, in front of them, countless thin pine trees rose out of the ground like needles forming a daunting barrier to the way ahead. Here and there, dwarf trees helped masquerade the bushes and large clumps of unruly grassland that sprouted haphazardly from the ground. But the most disturbing sight was the thick fog that meandered in and out of the trees at the height of a man. The fog provided a blanket of fear, hid the unknown, and was the most dangerous part of the way ahead. Below the fog lay the swamp, deep in places and shallow in others, but always potentially lethal to those who did not know the way forward.

Gradually, quietly, the light brigade abandoned their vehicles and made their way on foot towards the edge of a swamp. If Malik's fortress was protected by the fog, the swamp, and a thousand independent unruly trees, then Anderson's men had one card to play. Surprise!

The scouts found the path described by the schoolchildren and beckoned the main body on. The children had described how they were taken to the edge of a swamp in Malik's armoured brigade of jeeps, Transit vans, and Leyland lorries. They had then been forced to walk through the swamps to a village in the centre where there were lots of tents, brick buildings, mud huts and drinking water. They had walked to the centre and then the other vehicles had re-joined them a few hours later having taken a long and circuitous journey to get there. Some of the children had remembered the man with the machete who had beaten down the hoops at the school ground. It was he who had marked the pine trees with his machete. This is how they would keep to the path, he had explained, follow the trees marked by my machete. And then they had walked on.

It had taken Anderson and his men only a short time to find the two trees that stood on either side of one of the many pathways into the swamp. Both trees had suffered a prominent slash from a machete at waist height. The thin bark of the tree had been disfigured to the point that a keen eye could see the blemish, note the deformity in the bark, and realise that this was a sign. It was the safest way into the wetlands. The markings pointed the way to Malik's secret hideaway.

Anderson gestured to one of the men beside him and said, 'Yes! Activate. Let the drones clear a path for us.'

The trooper engaged his console and launched the first of the drones. Each gained height and moved out across the swamp, above the fog, searching for the way ahead, and looking for the enemy who was unaware of the combined's advance.

On the streets of Cumbria, a young woman dressed in jeans and a duffle coat entered a telephone kiosk, dialled 999, and said, 'A bomb will explode in the newsagent shop near the Narrows, in Penrith, in fifteen minutes. You have only fifteen minutes to evacuate the shop.'

The woman left the kiosk leaving the phone hanging from its socket, still live, and a voice asking questions on the other end of the phone.

Two minutes later, an elderly gentleman wearing a dark suit set off by a white shirt and red tie, used a phone in a kiosk at Carlisle and reported that a bomb would explode in both the bus station and the railway station. He warned the authorities that they had less than fifteen minutes to close the two enterprises and evacuate the buildings.

As the clock on the Musgrave Monument in Penrith raced on towards eleven o'clock, more bomb calls were made to Cumbria Police, the Fire and Rescue Service, the Ambulance Service, and the offices of two local newspapers.

In police headquarters, all hell broke loose when dispatchers promptly reacted by diverting patrols to the various locations to deal with the reported devices.

Blaring sirens and flashing lights filled the streets as more similar telephone calls were made and acted upon by the various authorities involved.

In Penrith, Superintendent Roy Fowler lifted his phone and dialled the Operations Centre at the Ullswater Hotel.

'Are you listening to the force wireless system, Anthea?' enquired Fowler. 'It's either activists, idiots, or real-life bombers at work. What's your take on it?'

'Hoax bomb calls?' posed Anthea. 'They're time-wasters.'

'Yes! Diversionary tactics, I'd say,' agreed Fowler. 'Those two traffic men were right to report the incident at Burton Services. There's a demonstration alright, and it's down your way. I'll guess someone in London let the cat out of the bag. I hope the uniforms I sent you are enough to prevent trouble, but the reality is that someone wants us to respond to every call, move staff around the county as if they were headless chickens, and let our guard down. It's started. Tell Boyd, I'll deal with the hoax bomb calls. But we're ten minutes into a raft of telephone calls and they just keep coming. Sorry, but I can't afford to ignore them.'

'I understand,' replied Anthea who heard a muffled explosion in the background of the phone call. 'What the hell was that?'

In Penrith town centre, a bomb exploded in a litter bin near the Monument. Two pounds of Semtex secured in a plastic bait box that would normally have suited any under-car explosive device during 'the Troubles' of Northern Ireland blew the nearby shop windows out, blasted an elderly couple to the ground, destroyed the bin, and spoilt the calm of a beautiful day.

'I'll get back to you,' shouted Fowler.

The phone went dead.

On the road to Kirkstone Pass from Eamont Bridge: the B5320, a succession of coaches, vans, and private cars made their way towards the Ullswater Hotel.

A lone traveller guided his black Kawasaki 500 motorcycle into the nearside of the road and set the vehicle on its stand. He removed a shoulder bag from a pannier bag and walked a short distance to the bridge that crossed the River Eamont at Pooley Bridge.

Stumbling awkwardly down the bank, the stranger arrived at the river's edge. Wearing a long black all-in-one motorcycle suit and thigh-high waders, he took half a dozen steps before he was beneath the military-style road bridge that had been recently erected following floods in the area. He removed a device from the shoulder bag and hid it in the metal structure that was the underside of the road bridge.

The motorcyclist returned to his bike, kickstarted the machine, and headed south passing the Duke of Portland Boating House before nearing the site of the conference and a gathering of vehicles laden with demonstrators.

On televisions throughout the county, a newsflash burst across the screens announcing, *'Breaking News… Secret Security Conference at Ullswater under attack.'*

~

Chapter Sixteen

~

Ullswater,
The Conference Hotel
(continuous)

The first of the coaches arrived at the security conference and began discharging their passengers. Within minutes, more coaches had gathered on the main road close to the hotel together with minibuses, vans and several private cars.

The protestors formed up, unfurled their banners and flags, and lined up at the request of a man wearing a high vis sleeveless jacket who was using a megaphone. He was soon joined by two ladies who were also equipped with megaphones.

There was a crackle when his apparatus burst into life and the organiser began positioning the protestors into lines.

'Hurry along now,' he ordered. 'Get off the main road and into the car park where we shall form up and walk down to the conference. Quickly now. There's no time to waste.'

A uniformed police officer approached the man in charge, introduced himself as Inspector Jones and said, 'Your right to protest peacefully is understood, sir, but I must ask you to respect the fact that the hotel and grounds are private property. The car park is owned by English Heritage, and you are allowed to gather there for today only. Please confine yourself to the public highway that leads to the hotel. Once you reach the archway entrance, kindly remember that you are thereafter on private property. The long driveway to the hotel is private and you are not granted further access to the site.'

'Says who?'

'Says the owners,' replied Inspector Jones. 'What are you protesting about? Terrorism in West Africa presumably?'

'No! SARS!'

'SARS? If my memory serves me well that's a protest against the excesses of the Special Anti-Robbery Squad in Nigeria.'

'That's right. That's what the protest is about.'

'Where are you from?'

'Glasgow! Birmingham! London! And all points north, south and east. I'm chairman of the combined universities debating group.'

'Are you, indeed! I see. Did you know that SARS was disbanded about two years ago? The squad no longer exists. It came to a close at the same time the covid pandemic started. You could debate that. It would keep you all busy.'

'Not what we've been told. The Nigerian government have re-instated it. That special anti-robbery squad was notorious for cruelty against crime suspects.'

Confused and unsure, Inspector Jones replied, 'I think you'll be proved wrong.'

'Too late, pal. We've come to have our say. We're all anti-police.'

'Anti-police?'

'Oh! Don't worry, pal. I'll keep them right. They're just students who think they know it all.'

'Keep to the rules!' ordered the Inspector. 'Stay away from private property.'

The organisers ushered the protestors onto the mile-long driveway that led from the main road to the hotel's main entrance. They began chanting, 'SARS OUT! SARS OUT!'

Both the operations centre and the conference hotel sat inside an area that was surrounded by temporary heavy-duty fencing. The structure was designed as a solid inner cordon that boasted one manned opening. The gateway allowed access to emergency vehicles or vehicles linked to the hotel by employment, but the driver of every vehicle had been issued with a pass and expected to be stopped and checked before gaining entry to the site. An outer cordon also existed, and this began at the archway entrance to the hotel grounds about a mile from the highway. It was close to the location where the buses had unloaded their passengers.

Inspector Jones returned to a fleet of police personnel carriers and gestured the drivers to take up a position at the inner cordon. Quite deliberately, the carriers drove past the protestors, clearly intent on displaying a significant police presence.

Jones didn't want trouble, but he had the upper hand in numbers and was keen to let the opposition know it.

Inside the operations centre, Anthea and Boyd watched the meeting take place on CCTV.

'Looks like our efforts to keep the conference under wraps have gone askew,' suggested Boyd.

'You said it might,' replied Anthea. 'I remember you telling me that you had told the Home Secretary that we still might get a demonstration in Cumbria, albeit a smaller one than you might expect in London.'

'That's true. The difference is London has thousands of cops to call on. We've got a few hundred if we're lucky.

'Let's be thankful to the traffic department for spotting some of those coaches yesterday otherwise Fowler might not have been so keen to help.'

Boyd turned to another bank of CCTV where he studied the faces on the screen as the operators panned and zoomed into various individuals as they walked down the lane from the main road continually chanting 'SARS OUT' and waving their flags.

'SARS OUT?' queried Boyd. 'All that is over. It sounds to me like the organisers have connections in Peckham who have resurrected SARS as a means to an end.'

'Which makes me think,' offered Anthea. 'That the whole day is going to be filled with diversionary tactics until the main attack comes. I'm not sure that any of those protestors have any idea of why they have been brought here. The reality is they are being used to lull us into uncertainty, divert our focus, and allow one of their number to strike at the very heart of government.'

'Maybe not one of their number,' proposed Boyd. 'It's more likely that the students are unwittingly providing cover to a covert entry of some kind. Maybe our potential assassin has dressed up as a student, I don't know. Update all supervisors. I want the uniforms to keep order and I want the detectives to keep their eyes peeled for the Peckham crew, Malik and Zak. All the photos are on the wall beneath the clocks if anyone needs to refresh their memory. Okay?'

'Will do,' replied Anthea who addressed the wireless system once more.

'Glancing at the force computer system, Boyd said, 'Looks like a bomb explosion in Penrith. One small bomb in a litter bin but big enough to send a place like Penrith into haywire. Are we fully deployed, Anthea?'

'Our marksmen are on the rooftop of the hotel and our close protection units are as close as they can be without taking part in the conference. Uniform has the demo to look after. We have the faces to look for.'

'And the conference itself?'

'Is going ahead as planned without any problems. Ricky is taking over from me here shortly and I'll be joining the marksmen on the roof. Bannerman has the conference room locked down tight. The delegates won't even be able to hear the chanting.'

'Good! By the way, there's another one on the Cumbria screen. Bomb disposal has been called to Pooley Bridge. It's the new bridge over the river.'

Anthea swivelled her seat, tapped the relevant keyboard, and read, 'It's recorded as a suspicious incident! A motorcyclist wearing a black all in one motorcycle suit was seen to place an object amongst the metalwork underneath the road bridge. Another tactic forcing us to divert manpower away from the conference to deal with a suspect device?'

'Possibly,' replied Boyd. Any description of the bike?'

'A black Kawasaki 500 with two rear panniers.'

'Peckham!' replied Boyd. 'Coincidence or is that the motorcyclist from Peckham?'

'We might be in Cumbria,' remarked Anthea. 'But I fancy Peckham is trying to take us over today.'

Ricky French arrived and said, 'The system is configured to read and record traffic movements on the motorways into and out of Cumbria. I'll activate a search and recover program. If the motorbike entered Cumbria during the previous twenty-four hours, we should have it on camera. Let me know if you want me to go further afield. For example, if it entered the county at Carnforth Interchange in the south, I'll interrogate the Lancashire motorway camera system. I should be able to track when it entered Lancashire and just keep going backwards.'

'Reverse engineering?' suggested Boyd.

'Technology!' replied Ricky. 'It will take time but if you need me to do it, I will.'

'Hold it for now,' instructed Boyd. 'It's probably a hoax but let's see what happens at Pooley.'

'Will do.'

'Can you tell me what I had for breakfast, Ricky?'

'Not yet, but it's only a question of time.'

Anthea stepped back and leaned against the wall. She shook her head and said, 'I got a feeling this is going to be a long day whether it's computerised or not.'

'You reckon?' enquired Boyd.

'If the Peckham crew are here, along with other Boko Haram supporters from the UK, then we've got a bigger problem than we ever envisaged.'

'You could be right.'

'Oh, I'm right, Guvnor,' declared Anthea looking directly into Boyd's steel-blue eyes. 'If they've got enough balls and Semtex to set off a bomb in Penrith, what the hell are they likely to do here in the middle of nowhere?'

'Destroy us?'

'Not without a fight.'

'I think we're about to find out what their capabilities are,' voiced Boyd. 'One thing is for sure I believe we have underestimated them, and I'll have to carry the can for that. Go and do what you do best, Anthea. I'm going to check these screens for the Peckham crew.'

'Anyone in particular?'

'Kareem, Yan, Moussa, Malik and Zak! The photos are in the briefing package for the watchers. Dark-skinned Nigerians should give the game away.'

'Unless they're all wearing masks, balaclavas, and hoodies. You'll never find them in that lot. What about Ester Abara?'

'Interestingly, she has pulled out of the conference as a result of her having developed a cold,' revealed Boyd.

'An excuse, no doubt. She knows what is going to happen. That's why she isn't here,' suggested Anthea.

'Yes, precisely. The Red Alpha team has an eyeball on Ester in her London apartment. She hasn't moved from there all day.'

Anthea rattled a keyboard, pointed at the screen, and said, 'Look at the CCTV coverage of the protestors coming down the lane. Must be a few hundred of them now, and more coaches arriving at the car park. You're going to hit a thousand faces in a very short time. They've only just begun.'

Boyd breathed out, grimaced, and replied, 'I completely underestimated how well this Peckham team has managed themselves. Somehow, they've caused this. What more could go wrong?'

Anthea nodded, gestured good luck to her colleagues, and headed for the hotel with the words, 'Everything!'

On the main road, two Transit vans, each bearing the logo of a hire company, turned off the highway and stopped in the lane. They were positioned behind the protestors who were inching their way towards the hotel complex. Four men jumped out of the rear of one of the vans and joined the throng of students. Dressed in jeans, trainers, dark hoodies and black anti-covid masks, they began chanting with the rest of them.

'SARS OUT! SARS OUT!'

Five minutes into the protest and the first bottle was thrown at police lines.

There was a roar of approval from the heart of the protestors when it struck the side of a police van and disintegrated. Seconds later, a second and third bottle were thrown and landed amongst the police line.

'SARS OUT! SARS OUT!'

The police line joined arms, retreated a few steps to consolidate the linkage, and then held firm when the protestors gained speed and drew nearer to the police. No physical contact was apparent, but the opposing sides were getting closer to each other.

Inspector Jones sensed a change in the mood and ordered a detachment of his reserves to don their NATO riot helmets and equip themselves with riot shields. In a short time, flat hats and baseball caps were replaced by riot helmets. Every helmet was fitted with a strong plastic visor. The visor was designed to deflect materials thrown into the facial area. The rest of the helmet protected the skull, jawline, cheek bones and neck area.

There was a succession of clicks when the officers tightened the chin strap and prepared themselves.

'Move to the rear of the cordon,' ordered Jones. 'And stand by for deployment as required.'

In Pooley Bridge, a DAF truck bearing the insignia of the Royal Logistics Corps arrived in the village. A bomb disposal officer dressed in a heavy suit of body armour. It was known in the trade as either a bomb suit or a blast suit.

Members of the public who had seen the motorcyclist plant the device beneath the bridge stepped forward, pointed the way, and watched as the military began their operation.

In the Ullswater security conference complex, stones were thrown by the protestors, penetrated the first line of uniform police, and confirmed that the objective of some of the students was to cause problems.

Yard by yard, the protestors demonstrated their illegal intentions by nearing the archway entrance that heralded the entrance to the Ullswater hotel.

In the car park, two more buses from Glasgow arrived and discharged their passengers into the lane.

Watching the CCTV, Boyd shared with Ricky, 'My mistake! More! Look! We don't have enough to deal with the increasing numbers and it's not even midday yet.'

'When you've shot yourself in the foot, there's only one thing you can do,' suggested Ricky.

'What's that?'

'Call for reinforcements,' replied Ricky. 'I'm on it.'

Ricky made the call as Boyd bit his bottom lip and watched another assortment of vehicles arrive in the area. It was too late for another planning scenario. The game was on, and Boyd felt he was about to lose. Second place was always the first loser.

'Deploying drones,' remarked Ricky. 'You wanted close-ups. Let's see what we can find.'

Inside the conference room, tea and coffee were served and the delegates from Nigeria, America, and Great Britain, engaged in small talk before gradually getting to grips with the reason for the meeting. Peace in West Africa was on the cards in the guise of increased expenditure and more staffing concerning education, governance, and anticorruption.

The Secretary of State from America, Nigel Vanderbilt, shook hands with the Nigerian President, Adebiyi Berundi, as the British Foreign Secretary suggested they enjoyed the view from the bay window.

'Ullswater!' offered Sir Henry Fielding. 'Such a beautiful location, don't you think?'

'Absolutely,' replied Nigel. 'What do you think of it, Adebiyi?'

'I think it is a quite remarkable place that you have brought us to,' replied the Nigerian. 'The view is breathtaking. There is, however, one thing I would like to discuss with you both concerning the educational standards that we are trying to achieve in Chad, Morocco, Cameroon, and my own country.'

'How can we help?' probed Sir Henry.

'In the UK you have something called Ofsted. An organisation that visits schools and, as far I can tell, seems to check as to whether they are any good or not. Am I right?'

'Ah! Ofsted!' smiled Sir Henry. 'Or to give the organisation its official title, the Office for Standards in Education, Children's Services and Skills. What an excellent subject to debate at a conference such as this, Your Excellency.'

'Adebiyi, please, Sir Henry. Let us spend our time together in an informal manner. Tell me more about your Ofsted.'

'It is a non-ministerial department of the UK government, reporting to our parliament. Ofsted is responsible for inspecting a range of educational institutions, including state schools and some independent schools. It occurs to me that is entirely possible that such an organisation would be welcomed by your population.'

'We would need to itemise the things that matter most in our educational system so that we might set targets to achieve,' proposed Adebiyi. 'I will begin with security but would like to work towards a Nigerian style Ofsted. Does that seem feasible?'

'It certainly does,' replied Sir Henry.

The trio debated the subject, drank their coffees and tea, and then returned to the conference table where they joined the other delegates.

At the entrance to the conference room, Bannerman heard the first muffled strains of far-off chanting. He double-checked his Gloch 17 semi-automatic handgun and wondered if there was a storm gathering close by.

Boyd's mobile rang. It was Maude Black: the Home Secretary.

'I'm receiving reports from Cumbria's Chief Constable that you are insisting on more staff to protect the conference, Commander Boyd. I thought we had decided Ullswater would be a quiet place to hold such an event?'

'We did but it seems there has been a leak from central government and I'm sure you know where it came from.'

'I do indeed, Commander. I have instructed surrounding forces to respond to Cumbria's request and activate mutual aid assistance. Reinforcements from Lancashire and Northumbria are on their way.'

'Understood,' replied Boyd. 'Let's hope they arrive on time.'

'You have ground control, Commander. Don't let anyone spoil that conference. We have far too much at stake in West Africa and our interests are wide-reaching. Do whatever you have to do to enforce security. Is that understood, Mister Boyd?'

'Perfectly,' voiced Boyd. 'I thought you were attending the conference, Home Secretary?'

'I will make an appearance on our secure zoom facility later today. Sir Henry is representing our interests. I have every faith in him. You have my number, Mister Boyd. Don't hesitate to contact me if things go awry. There is much more at stake than policing, schools and educational facilities. All such things are part of a society that needs to defeat corruption. Proceed accordingly.'

'Of course,' replied Boyd.

The line went dead leaving Boyd to wonder whether he was a Commander or a Mister? Does she support us or not, thought Boyd? I'm one or the other, surely not both. Am I a friend or a foe, a useful contact, or a convenient Achilles' heel if everything goes wrong and the various governments represented here today end up with egg on their face? Is that what it means to be a Commander? Great when you're winning but a coconut shy if you lose?

'Deploying drones,' declared Ricky. 'Three up and separating. One to cover car park arrivals; one to cover the protestors in the lane, and the other to circle the edge of the lake and the hotel complex. Screens one, two and three apply.'

'Noted!' replied Boyd.

'Drone four launched,' responded Ricky. 'Lake's perimeter patrol, just in case. It's on screen four, Guvnor.'

'Got it,' from Boyd.

'SARS OUT!' SARS OUT!'

The protest march had changed into a full-blown demonstration as the mass of flag-waving, banner carrying, campaigners reached the archway entrance that petered out into the low wall that surrounded the hotel complex.

Inspector Jones radioed, 'Dog units to assume positions, please. Deploy to the rear of the public order units.'

'Roger!' replied John Reed. 'Come on, Lucy, he mouthed before engaging the radio further with, 'Short leashes only at this stage. Ten paces apart and adopt a holding pattern. No prisoners. Containment only.'

There was a raft of acknowledgements from the dog section before Reed moved towards the main entrance and took command of his team.

At the hotel, Jake Bingham, of the American Secret Service, cornered Bannerman and insisted, 'If you can't stop these people coming any further down the lane into the complex, I'm going to extricate the Secretary of State by helicopter and leave you to it.'

'We're on it,' remarked Bannerman. 'You worry too much.'

'Only because you Brits are a soft touch when it comes to demonstrations,' proposed Bingham. 'You're outnumbered and I don't like it. I'm making the helicopters ready for a quick egress. I'll tell you now, don't get in our way.'

Bannerman bit his lip and said, 'I wouldn't dream of it, and we are in control.'

'Me too,' nodded Bingham who engaged his radio frequency and ordered, 'Encircle and secure all entrance points. Team one stand by. Take close order on the Secretary of State. Eagles One, Two and Three prepare for take-off. Stand by for the critical phase. Acknowledge!'

Outside, the first Molotov cocktail winged its way through the air scattering petrol on the crowd below. It landed at the feet of Inspector Jones who kicked it away and shouted, 'Shields! Switch!'

There was a flurry of activity in the police lines when a row upon row of riot police moved swiftly from the rear ranks to the front ranks and took up a confrontational position in front of the demonstrators.

In a heartbeat, those officers now at the rear, discarded their flat caps and made for the personnel carriers where they changed into riot gear. All attempts made to placate the demonstration with a twist of friendly social policing had failed. Jones steeled himself for the coming fray.

Another Molotov cocktail glided through the atmosphere and exploded on a riot officer's shield.

'Petrol bombs from the rear of the demo,' quipped Ricky in the operations centre. 'Drone coverage shows occupants of a Transit van, which looks like a hire van, are responsible. Video running per evidence-gathering protocols.'

Assessing the CCTV footage, Boyd remarked, 'No trace of the Peckham crew. Inform Inspector Jones. He needs to target the petrol bombers if he can.'

'Will do,' replied Ricky. 'Oh no! See what I see?'

'What now?'

'One of our boys has been downed by a petrol bomb. His coverall is on fire and he's rolling on the ground trying to put the fire out.'

Boyd immediately looked at the screen and said, 'He's back on his feet but they've lost ground. The demonstrators are through.'

'Units two, three and four, advance!' ordered Jones.

As the police columns buckled under a barrage of petrol bombs, sticks, and stones, the reserves moved forward, plugged the hole in the line, and held fast.

Way behind the demonstrators, the rear doors of a black hire van opened and three men carrying holdalls leapt over the wall and into a wooded area that ran adjacent to the lane leading to the hotel.

Another barrage of missiles followed, took down officers in the line, and caused the police to retreat even further.

In the operations centre, Ricky pointed at the CCTV screens and shouted to Boyd, 'Armed intruders! Here are your men, Guvnor.'

Rushing to examine the screen, Boyd nodded, patched the transmission through to Anthea, and said, 'Three gunmen carrying holdalls. One has taken up a position in the woods running parallel to the lane. He's removed a long rifle from a holdall. The two others are moving through the woods carrying identical holdalls. Trigger alert! Trigger! Trigger! Trigger!'

'I have that,' replied Anthea engaging her binoculars. 'No sign at the moment. I can't see them. I'm scanning the area.'

'Two black Transits entered some time ago,' radioed Ricky. 'One dropped off some toxics who began hurling petrol bombs at the police. This second one sat quietly until the doors eventually opened and a trio carrying the bags came out. They're in the woods. They've separated. Stand by!'

Through the binoculars, Anthea picked up the first gunman and said, 'I have Yan in my sight. Three clicks from the archway entrance and creeping low towards us.'

'Got that,' replied Boyd now looking through his binoculars too. 'I also see Kareem and Moussa. All three are wearing dark camouflage clothing and carrying long rifles. Do you have them, Anthea?'

'One out of three only at present. Stand by!'

Ricky manipulated the controls and tried to improve the product from the drone coverage. Anthea gestured to her rooftop sniper team to spread out and concentrate on the wooded area, and Boyd radioed Bannerman with, 'Bannerman! We have a Trigger situation approximately half a mile from your location. Hold your position. We are monitoring and will engage if necessary. The subjects are Yan,

Moussa and Kareem from the Peckham team. All armed with long rifles.'

'I have that,' from Bannerman. 'No change at this location. We are locked down.'

Ricky handed Boyd a headset with the words, 'You'd better put this on, Guvnor, the Home Secretary is monitoring the CCTV and radio transmissions via a visual-audio link.'

Taking the headset in his free hand, Boyd heard the Maude Black say, 'You are authorised to shoot, Commander.'

'Get out of my head,' snapped Boyd as he threw the headset to one side. 'I need to focus.'

In the lane, the mass of protestors had broken through into the grounds. They'd breached the wall and were under the brick archway that heralded the entrance to the hotel. They were on private property, and it didn't mean anything to them. The mass separated, widened their attack, and clashed bodily with the police lines for the first time.

'Units five and six, bolster the team,' radioed Jones.

More riot police stepped forward, made a wedge in the police line, and began pushing the protestors back.

A rock whistled through the air and struck Inspector Jones in the face. He crumpled to the ground, lost radio contact, and felt the feet of the advancing mob stamp on his body as he drifted into unconsciousness.

'Advance!' screamed John Reed who snapped his leash and guided Lucy into the melee with his team to the left and right of him.

Lucy snarled, then she barked, then she bounded forward with Reed now working her in a tight semicircle until he reached Inspector Jones's body.

'Cover me!' shouted Reed standing over Jones with his feet apart.

Lucy barked and jumped at the protestors who scattered when five other dogs bared their teeth, yapped and barked, and drove the protestors back a good twenty yards.

'Recover!' screamed Reed still standing over Jones with his free hand brandishing a baton ready to strike anyone who threatened him or the injured policeman.

Lucy strained at the leash, pranced and barked, yapped at those who dared to near here, and protected two uniforms who rushed forward, grabbed Jones under the arms, and pulled him into the relative safety of the police column.

A sergeant bent down and poured the contents of a water bottle onto Jones's face.

Jones coughed, shook his head, and grabbed the bottle. He took a drink and spluttered it out when he felt his head throbbing.

'You alright, Inspector?'

'Yes! Yes! I think so. What happened?'

'You got clobbered by a brick. Reed came to the rescue. Just keep away from him for the moment. The dog is rampant and likely to bite someone's hand off.'

Groggy, Jones replied, 'I can recommend where the dog should start. Reed! John Reed! Wow! Where was I?'

'About a second or two from being trampled to death.'

In the operations centre, Ricky pointed at a screen and shouted, 'There are three gunmen in the woods. They are loading their weapons. Anthea?'

'I have them,' radioed Anthea.

'This is Bannerman,' from the conference room. 'Jake Bingham is about to bring the conference to a close. He's telling me it's all over. The Yanks must protect their man.'

Boyd stepped forward and said, 'Bannerman! Activate the last defence!'

Bannerman took two steps from his location outside the conference room. He flipped over what resembled a wall-mounted fire alarm and heard a set of armour-plated shields crash down and over the windows of the conference room. The building was impregnable. The delegates were safe even though they were now aware of the sound of chanting and violence outside on the grounds. And the smell of burning from the firebombs was wreaking havoc in the nostrils.

Bannerman turned to Jake Bingham and murmured, 'I told you not to worry. Now prepare your men at each door and tell them to relax. We're in charge and I do this for a living.'

The Head of the Secret Service detail stared at Bannerman, shook his head, and walked away.

Outside, in the woods, a suppressor was fitted to the barrel of a rifle. A finger curled around a trigger and eased the mechanism. The bullet left the rifle and sliced through the atmosphere before smashing into the hotel wall only inches from an armour-plated conference room window.

'Shots fired!' radioed Ricky. 'Where are the reinforcements that were promised?'

Coolly, calmly, Boyd responded with, 'And I have a positive sighting of Zak Zakaria walking towards the hotel wearing a heavy-looking anorak. I'm going outside. Ricky, you have control.'

'Control! Err… Guvnor! I'm a tech guy, a gizmo King. What do you want me to do?'

'Update Anthea! Watch! Listen!'

Boyd moved his Glock from a shoulder holster to the small of his back and said, 'In my life, I've made mistakes. This might be another. If I don't come back, tell Meg and the kids I will them love through eternity.'

'Guvnor! Don't journey out there! We need you here.'

'Watch out for me, Ricky!'

'Guvnor! At least take the headset.'

'No thanks! I don't want politicians telling me what to do, Ricky.'

'Take it,' pleaded Ricky. 'You're linked to Anthea, Antonia, and everyone in the operation. You just never know what might happen. Major Anderson is looking for Malik in Chad. Anthea is positioning her snipers on the rooftops. Bannerman is trying to stop the Yanks from bursting out of the conference room, and Antonia always has a card up her sleeve. Take the headset, Guvnor. You gave me control. Now that's an order.'

Shaking his head, smiling nonchalantly, Boyd snatched the headset and secured it properly saying, 'Okay! Okay! I hear you, Ricky. I'll go with your high-tech stuff for what good it'll do.'

'If it means anything to you, Guvnor. It's a journey too far. I have control. Don't go out there. That's an order too.'

Walking out of the room, Boyd ignored his colleague and made his way into the grounds of the hotel. He glanced at the beauty of Ullswater and the glory of its surrounding Fells, before walking towards Zak Zakaria who was headed straight for him with his right thumb positioned over the detonating device of a heavily laden suicide jacket.

'Boyd!' from Anthea. 'Don't do it, Boyd. It's too dangerous. He's going to blow you to kingdom come.'

'What the hell are you doing, Billy,' screamed Antonia on the radio. 'Take cover, Billy. The man is a lunatic. He's a suicide bomber for God's sake,'

~

Chapter Seventeen
~

Adjildele, Lake Chad
West Africa
(Simultaneous)

Major Anderson studied the drone coverage on his mobile phone and located a building that was guarded by four of Malik's men. They were heavily armed with guns and machetes as they casually strolled around the immediate area. Turning to a younger man who was perhaps knocking on the door of thirty, Anderson studied his colleague for a moment and said, 'Go on. Don't just stand there. what's on your mind, Tom?'

'Is that the Boko Haram headquarters?' voiced Captain Tom Adams: a tall slimly built officer who was Anderson's second in command.

'Not sure yet,' replied Major Anderson. 'It looks more to me like a cell block or a prison structure.'

'How do you make that out?'

Showing the images on his mobile phone, Anderson explained, 'In the eastern part of the village, I see a large building with an opening at the front. If you look closely, Tom, you'll see spaces where we westerners would fit a door and glass windows. But there are no glass windows and no wooden doors in this part of the world, only the swamps and the desert sands blowing in from the Sahara. There are a couple of jeeps and a few pickups parked nearby. But the building I am interested in lies in the western part of the settlement and is surrounded by armed men. It only boasts one door. Do you see it?'

Captain Adams nodded.

'The building has a wooden door but there are no openings for any windows. Just a purpose-built construction that has no open spaces in its design. Now tell me, Tom, why would you build such a place and finish it with one wooden door and no window spaces?'

'Because its contents are hidden, private, and cannot be seen by others,' suggested the captain. 'A prison cell to hold all the kidnapped people we hear about. I'd say it was where they keep all those individuals that are held for ransom.'

'Me too! Good man!' declared Anderson. 'We'll do a covert approach, Tom.'

The minutes ticked by as six SAS troopers, supported by elements of the combined strike force, slithered out of the swamp area on their bellies and surreptitiously approached one of the few brick-built structures in the village.

One of the guards fidgeted with the trigger mechanism of his Uzi submachine gun and did not feel the ice-cold steel blade that cut across his throat. Neither did his body react to the pressure exerted on the *popliteal fossa* of his lower limb when a trooper gently kicked the shallow depression at the back of the knee joint and held him as he quietly slid to the ground and bled to death en route. A pool of bright red blood spoiled the victim's shirt and jeans and soon darkened before muddying the soil.

Close by, a guard paused to light a cigarette, inhaled, and then coughed slightly when the tobacco bit into his throat. There was a stifled whimper when he drew his last breath and died at the hands of a trooper who stuck a blade into the Boko Haram's man side.

Within an instant, the guards were dispensed with.

The SAS trooper found the keys on one of the bodies and unlocked the front door of the building. Inside, they found one woman and three children who were held in captivity.

Conditions inside the makeshift prison cell were appalling. There was one low-level bunk upon which to sleep and two soiled blankets on the floor. A dirty plastic tray laden with a jug of water and a stale loaf of bread were the only items of nutrition present. One solitary candle sprouted from a plain white saucer. It was difficult to tell whether it had ever been lit or was just for show

'What is your name?' asked the SAS trooper.

'Zakaria! Yolanda Zakaria!' The woman was distraught and anxious, simultaneously weeping tears of joy and fear as she shivered uneasily in the presence of the soldiers. 'You are not Nigerian. Who are you?'

'British! Tell me, are these your children?'

'Yes! I am so pleased you found us,' she cried.

'What are they called?' probed the SAS man.

'The boys are Hassan and Kayode! My daughter is called Yetunde! Why?' she agonized.

'And your husband, where is he?'

'I don't know. They took him away from me,' replied Yolanda. 'Is he here or somewhere else?'

'What is his name?'

'Zak! Zak Zakaria! We were kidnapped from Sangari when the school was set on fire by Malik. Where is Zak? Where is my husband, Mister British man?'

'Where is Malik?'

'I do not know. We have been locked up all these days. I have not seen Malik since we were captured. My husband! Where did they take him? Is he still here? Is he still alive? Please tell me.'

The SAS trooper stepped aside and radioed Major Anderson with, 'Commander! We have the Zakaria woman and her three children. She's telling me they were kidnapped and I'm inclined to believe her. There's no sign of Malik!'

A feeling of terrific elation rippled through Anderson's body before he replied, 'Can you extract them by the same route?'

The trooper glanced outside, studied the gaunt children and their mother, and replied, 'Doubtful! These kids can hardly stand up. I don't think they've eaten properly for days'

There was a scream of pure hatred that interrupted the conversation when a handful of Malik's men suddenly emerged from the larger building, saw the bodies of their comrades littering the ground, and attacked the rescuers with a barrage of gunfire.

The SAS troopers returned fire as Malik himself came into view and ordered the rest of his Boko Haram Brigade into action.

'Contact!' radioed Anderson to his base. 'Shots fired. Engaging. Air support requested.' Turning to the rest of his strike force, Anderson shouted, 'Break cover! Advance!'

The combined forces raced from the edge of the swamps and, mostly firing from the hip, charged at the Boko Haram Brigade.

One of the terrorists took a round in the chest and fell to the ground out of the game. But others threw themselves behind the sizeable boulders that were strewn around the village like discarded marbles in an evil playing field.

The incessant sound of gunfire was broken only by the occasional hand grenade exploding near a row of Leyland army trucks. The vehicles had been lined up in the centre of the village by Malik's men when they had arrived back from their last raid. It was from this location that the self-styled Boko Haram Brigade of Lake Chad defended their military headquarters against an attack by Major Andersons's forces.

With the element of surprise firmly in Anderson's arsenal, his men had covertly sneaked into the village via a secret pathway through the swamps, blown up some of the army trucks, and were now using shoulder-fired missiles to destroy Malik's remaining vehicles. The deadliest mobile weapon that Malik's mob possessed was a convoy of pickup vans equipped with heavy machine gun platforms in the rear. When used by properly trained soldiers, such vehicles were fast-moving, easy to use, quick to deploy, and lethal in their bearing. Numbering twenty or more, the vehicles were being ripped to pieces by gunfire from Anderson's men.

Malik had other ideas and leapt onto the rear of one of the pickups. Spinning around the platform, he rattled a long salvo from a heavy machine gun at his enemy.

Anderson's troops dived for cover as the Boko Haram Brigade fought back and turned the skirmish into a blood bath.

With the village surrounded by the combined forces, and Boko Haram retaliating awesomely and frighteningly, Major Anderson breathed a sigh of relief when he heard several rotary wings invading his ears.

Two helicopter gunships came into view, hovered above the village, and blasted away at the target.

Leaping from his pickup, Malik scampered beneath it when the ground around him erupted in a ball of fire.

The helicopters changed tack, re-engaged, and scorched the earth as Malik's men scrambled into every possible hiding place that granted them some sort of reprieve. Those who stood their ground fired wildly into the air at the ground attack helicopters. Some of their bullets hit the target but the light armoured ballistic panels fitted to the gunships withstood the onslaught and held firm.

A direct hit on a boulder from one of the helicopters blew the stone into a zillion pieces that rained down on the terrorists. The ground was saturated with explosions, craters, scars, and the bodies of the fallen terrorists. In the blink of an eye, Adjildele had been turned into a battlefield where the sanctity of life had been cast aside in the name of freedom and justice.

The helicopter gunships finally withdrew, their ammunition spent and their fuel low.

Malik's men cheered at the departure, fired once more at their enemy in the sky, and then jumped for cover when Anderson's men renewed their attack.

Undeterred, by the loss of more than half of his brigade, Malik climbed onto the rear pickup platform and resumed the attack. He swung his heavy machine gun placement into a new position determined to shoot down either of the retreating helicopters. Pulling the triggers, he fired both barrels at the fleeing whirlybirds.

As the bullets winged their way through the sky towards the gunships, Major Anderson dropped to one knee, took careful aim, and fired at Malik.

The bullet penetrated Malik's skull. The Boko Haram leader fell backwards and in his final throes let the machine gun rake aimlessly into the skies above Chad.

There was a clatter when Malik's machete hit the side of the pickup as he fell from grace and died in the headquarters of his evil creation.

Malik was no more.

Anderson's men advanced at a rapid pace, mopped up the surviving Boko Haram men, and quickly secured the Zakaria family to safety.

'Commander! Sitrep, please!' rippled through the airwaves.

Anderson clicked his radio and replied, 'All secure! Taking prisoners at this location. Malik is dead. The Zakaria family are in our safekeeping. Extraction procedures are in progress. Out!'

~

Chapter Eighteen

~

Pooley Bridge,
Ullswater, Cumbria
(Simultaneous)

The Bomb Disposal Unit from Catterick Garrison had arrived, surveyed the scene, spoken to the locals, and deployed a wheelbarrow to the bridge in the belief that the apparatus might suppress the improvised explosive device and render it obsolete. The unit wasn't taking any chances with this one. On the streets of Penrith, a litter bin had been destroyed when a two-pound bomb exploded. The resultant damage to nearby shops, windows, vehicles, and street furniture was such that the decision had been made to blow up the device that had been hidden beneath Pooley Bridge. The road was closed, and the village was in lockdown. The local community had complied with a police request to stand well back from the scene. No-one argued. The news about the earlier bomb in Penrith's town centre was prolific.

From a nearby car park, the operator manipulated the switches on the machine and watched the wheelbarrow's slow progress on the screen that relayed an image to him.

Realistically, the wheelbarrow wouldn't blow anything up beneath the bridge. It was a slow-moving remotely controlled robot designed for use by British Army bomb disposal teams operating in Northern Ireland, mainland Britain, and Iraq. When correctly positioned close to its target, the operator used the robot to fire a high-pressure jet of water at any visible wires emanating from the device. Such a jet of water sought to penetrate the explosive device and disrupt the power supply. When successful, it broke the electrical circuit and rendered the device inactive. The explosive substance might still be present, but the detonation phase had been deemed inoperable.

The wheelbarrow struggled ungracefully along the tarmac, paused, swung left, and then reacted to its electronic instruction when it then turned right and approached the bridge. It was as if it were a disciplined soldier who was slow to react to the orders given. The wheelbarrow boasted prowess but little speed.

A hand remotely guided the machine into position and brought it to a standstill. The digits on the hand carefully touched the controls and edged the robot forward.

Watching closely from afar, the crowd grew restless at the lethargic manner the wheelbarrow had adopted. The seemingly lacklustre performance lacked charisma.

A village resident lifted his hand to stifle a yawn.

There was a flash of light when the bomb exploded beneath the bridge. It was followed by the sound of the explosion and then the blast wave. The locals watching saw it first, heard it second, and then lastly felt it. The flash was over in the blink of an eye; the sound invaded the village and could be heard miles away, and the blast wave was an experience not to be forgotten.

Metal twisted, contorted, and broke away from its fixture. Simultaneously, the tarmac erupted, flew into the air at tremendous speed and then crashed into the River Eamont below following the concrete, steel girders and metallic trappings into the watery depths.

The blast rippled along the tarmac on the main road from the bridge into the village.

A yawning man felt his knees wobble and momentarily lost his balance. Windows in the nearest house blew apart. A microsecond later the windows in the second storey of a hotel burst outwards and rained down on the guests below. A child's bicycle fell from its stand and hit the ground, and inside one of the pubs, the optics shook whilst a row of pint glasses rattled against the glassware.

Close to the site of the explosion, the wheelbarrow catapulted into the air before crashing down on the buckled tarmac.

The river carried debris away from the site as onlookers realised the bridge was no more. There was a gap where once there stood a bridge. The river was in full flow following the recent snowfall. Access to the main body of Ullswater had been denied due to the bomb explosion and the damage caused. The main route to the Ullswater conference had been successfully destroyed.

A convoy of police vans carrying reinforcements to the demonstration pulled up at the entrance to the village. Their passage to the Ullswater Hotel was denied. They were cut off from their colleagues. The only viable route to the hotel was to turn around and travel a more circuitous route that would easily add more than an hour to the journey.

On the grounds of the Ullswater Hotel, another petrol bomb hurtled over the heads of the leading demonstrators and landed in the police lines. A banner, folded and aimed like a spear, sailed into the police column only to be fended off by an officer's shield.

There was a roar from the mob when an officer fell. A dog barked at the line of protestors. There was the swish of a baton through the air when a demonstrator felt the harsh reaction from an officer in the line. Tempers flared. If there was a reason for the demonstration, it was lost in the melee of violence and ever-increasing chaotic hatred.

A trio of assassins readied their rifles in the wood.

Closer to the entrance to the hotel, Zak Zakaria walked towards Boyd with his finger hovering over the detonation button of an explosive device. He was wearing an oversized black nylon jacket covering a suicide belt packed with twenty kilograms of explosives. The coat of self-destruction served to annihilate the enemies of the men from the swamp. All he needed to do was press the button that would send an electronic pulse down the wire. The detonation would follow and a zillion ball bearings, nails, screws, bolts, high explosives, and other objects that served as shrapnel, would speed through the air and maximize the number of casualties.

Zak's mind was made up. No more bad dreams; no more nightmares. It was his time. His jacket was festooned with wires leading to pockets where the hidden steel projectiles shaped to fly and pierce the human body, glass, metal, and anything standing in its way, were located.

For Zak, it was the end of his journey.

For Boyd, it was the epitome of a lifetime's journey working in the world of counter-terrorism. His work had been all about preventing people from killing each other, about learning of cultures and religions whose very origins had often been different and opposed to each other from time immemorial. It was these cultures and religions, together with a never-ending appetite for sovereignty and power that, as far as Boyd was concerned, were the causes of terrorism. He'd read it all, done it all, and knew just about all there was to know about terrorists from the cradle of their birth to their last breath. If a tee-shirt was the prize for a counter-terrorist officer, then Boyd had won it and worn it like no one else.

Yet something was missing in Boyd's journey: A manual. No manual had ever been devised to teach someone how to deal with a terrorist wearing a suicide jacket other than the obvious.

'Shoot him!' pierced Boyd's headset. 'You are authorised to shoot to kill,' from the Defence Secretary.

'Follow the orders, Boyd,' from the Home Secretary. 'The safety of the Nigerian package is paramount to the nation's interests in Africa. Comply!'

'Shoot him, Guvnor!' from Ricky. 'He's going to kill you!'

But Boyd knew that a bullet in Zak's chest would not destroy the potential of the suicide vest. Furthermore, he did not consider himself to be a pawn in the global political game. Well-made suicide vests were built to absorb a bullet and render it futile. Only a carefully placed bullet in the neck would work because the bullet would enter the spinal cord and paralyse Zak's body. Instant paralysis would prevent Zak's finger from detonating the bomb.

'Zak! Stay where you are,' shouted Boyd.

There was a look of surprise on Zak's face.

'How do you know my name?'

'Stand still,' shouted Boyd.

Zak kept walking towards the hotel. Only Boyd separated the walking time bomb from the entrance to the hotel and death and destruction.

The front police line broke. A ruck developed as a particularly ugly set of demonstrators engaged in hand-to-hand fighting with the police. Pushing, shoving, punching, kicking became the norm when an officer dropped his shield and lost ground.

'More reinforcements required urgently!' radioed Inspector Jones.

'Held at Pooley Bridge. Road closed due to bomb attack,' replied Ricky from the control centre. 'Suggest give ground and regroup!'

The police lines didn't wait for the order. They ran back, ran for their lives, and retreated twenty yards before Jones called a stop and they reformed. It was the power of the man that called his comrades to stop. The power of a man recently floored, almost killed in a stampede, who now stood tall and took command.

'Stand with me and beside me,' shouted Jones. 'Do not yield another inch.'

But it was another twenty yards that the demonstrators had won; another twenty yards closer to the conference room, and a major blow to the confidence of the police.

Inside the conference room, the delegates were becoming anxious. They were worried about the growing noise from outside now clear in their ears.

Nigel Vanderbilt looked alarmingly at his Secret Service man and said, 'Find out what's going on. It sounds like the Brits are losing it.'

The Nigerian President, Adebiyi Berundi, nodded his head and added, 'I do not like what I hear. I wish we had stayed in London close to my embassy. Are we in danger, Sir Henry?'

Britain's Foreign Secretary clasped both men on their shoulders and said, 'Of course not, my dear friends. It's just the light atmosphere of the Lake District. The sound carries so much easier through the thin air than it does in London. I'll order more coffee and we'll continue our discussion.'

'Why are the steel shutters covering the windows?' enquired Adebiyi. 'Colleagues on my negotiating team are somewhat concerned as to the issue. Are we under attack?'

'Not at all,' replied Sir Henry.

'It's just that the UK has so many vested interests in Nigeria that the last thing we want is casualties of any kind,' replied the Nigerian President. 'The noise from the demonstration, that you told us would never happen because of our location, plus the metal shutters, suggest to me that you cannot ensure our safety. If that is the case, I believe I would be correct in assuming that you cannot ensure any of the promises that you have made during the conference.'

'I assure you, your Excellency,' replied Sir Henry. 'All is well. Now then, coffee or would you prefer a tea?'

Nigel Vanderbilt leaned across to Sir Henry and whispered, 'You're a Goddamned liar, Fielding! Get that Bannerman in here. It's time we got out.'

'You're not in any danger,' offered Sir Henry. 'We politicians always tell the truth as well you know.'

In the woods, another suppressor was fitted to a barrel. A finger curled around the trigger. A shot was fired and rifled through the air before slamming into a steel shutter.

The sound of metal against metal resonated through the conference room.

On the tarmac close to the hotel, Boyd faced Zak and said, 'Why are you here, Zak?'

'What?'

'Oh, yes, I know who you are, Zak. You're from Sangari in Chad, aren't you? I know all about you. I know you are a good man. I want to talk to you about your life in Chad, Zak.'

Confused, Zak thrust his right hand forward, held his thumb above the detonating button, and screamed, 'Keep back! Keep away! I am going to kill you all.'

'Why?'

'Because!'

'Because what? You are not a killer, Zak. You are of the Kanuri tribe. You are renowned for the peace you bring to others. You are farmers who tend the land and produce rice and go fishing in the Lake so that you may feed your people.'

'I am trained to kill, and I will kill.'

'No, you won't,' pleaded Boyd. 'You are a good man, Zak.'

'Who told you I was Kanuri? How do you know who I am?'

'It is my job to know such things, Zak. I asked about you. My friends told me.'

'Friends? What friends? You are not from Chad.'

'The policeman on the train told me that you saved his life. His trousers were caught up in the railway carriage, Zak. You released him and saved his life otherwise he would have bounced along for miles and died on the railway line. You're not a killer, Zak. You saved a man's life.'

The man from Lake Chad stepped forward. A tear formed in his eye and his face grew fragile in its being when he replied, 'You are wrong. I am here to kill. They took me to the Sahara and taught me how to kill.'

'Shoot to kill,' ordered the Defence Secretary in Boyd's headset. 'He's going to detonate that bomb any second.'

'Agreed!' from the Home Secretary. 'Comply, Commander Boyd. We don't negotiate with terrorists. Eliminate him.'

'No! I'm going to talk to him,' replied Boyd.

'Who are you talking to?' from Zak.

'Dear God! No! What are you playing at?' from Maude Black, the Home Secretary.

'I have operational control,' declared Boyd. 'And I will not relinquish it unless one of you is stood beside me making the decisions instead of me. I can see the man. I can reach out and touch him. I'm talking to him. Listen to me or get out of my head.'

There was no reply from the politicians.

Boyd flicked a button on his radio system and said, 'I'm talking on the wireless system, Zak. I'm talking to my friends about you. Who took you to the Sahara and taught you how to kill others, Zak?'

Zak did not reply. He merely looked straight ahead at Boyd.

'You need to know that I'm talking to my friends on my wireless system.' Boyd indicated his headset and continued, 'I'm asking my friends a question, Zak. Why would a trained assassin try to save a policeman from falling from a moving train whilst he was on the way to kill scores of American, Nigerian, and British politicians at a conference? It doesn't make sense. I'm not convinced you are a terrorist. Z

'Can you answer my question, Zak?'

Zak was shaking, his hand unsteady on the button he was holding. His finger was less than an inch from the trigger.

'Did you hear that, Zak?'

Zak nodded and felt a tear roll down his cheek. He began to wobble from side to side, more tears slid down his cheek and he squinted his eyes.

'You're not a killer until you press that button. If you do that you will be killed instantly, Zak. You'll never see your family again.'

'Yolanda!' from the mouth of a bemused terrorist.

'Target acquired,' rippled across the wireless network.

On the hotel rooftop, a trigger was gently squeezed, and a bullet began its journey through the spiral twists of a rifled barrel. The bullet flew through the air and penetrated the terrorist's skull directly above the nose.

'Target down,' across the network from Anthea. 'One Tango down in the woods. I confirm Target Moussa is down.'

Moussa fell backwards into the wood dropping his rifle at his feet and then rolling onto his side. He was dead before he hit the ground.

There was another movement in the woods when Kareem hopped over the wall and took cover behind the demonstrators.

'Sniper team! Report contacts!' from Anthea.

There was no reply. Yan and Kareem were unseen.

On the tarmac, Boyd continued, 'Your memory, Zak! I want your memories. Tell me about home and Yolanda, and your children, Zak. How many kids have you? What are their names? You love them, don't you, Zak?'

The suicide bomber did not reply. His face was a picture of confusion and tearful desperation. He took another step forward, waved the trigger button from side to side, and said, 'I have to do it. I swore I would do it. Get out of my way.'

'Tell me about the Kanuri, Zak. Peace-loving, aren't they?'

Zak remained silent.

'Why are you here, Zak?'

From the hotel rooftop, DS Janice Burns transmitted, 'Contact! Tango Two! Yan. Acquiring!'

'Why are you here, Zak?' resumed Boyd.

In the woods, Yan steadied his weapon on the dry-stone wall and fired two shots in quick succession. Both bullets rattled into the same window shutter that had been targeted previously. The shutter creaked and then fell from its fixture exposing the glass window looking into the conference room.

Bannerman shouted to the security team, 'I'll cover the window from outside. Get everyone down on the floor.'

Rushing outside Bannerman glanced at the broken shutter covering the window, realised they were not fit for purpose, and then swivelled around to study the oncoming mass of demonstrators. What he saw frightened him. Bannerman began to run full pelt towards the rioters.

From the hotel roof, the Detective Sergeant radioed, 'Target acquired. Stand by!' Janice took a shot and followed with, 'Target down. Tango Two Yan is down.'

Yan fell back against a tree and then slumped forward over the dry-stone wall. His rifle fell to the ground, rolled down a slope, and clattered onto the tarmac.

A demonstrator heard the clatter, glanced over his shoulder at the fallen weapon, and yelled, 'Gun! 'A cop with a gun!'

Despite the number of shots made by the trio from Peckham, it was the first time the protestors had seen a weapon. Suppressors on rifles had negated the sound of the shots fired, but now panic ensued and the demonstrators dropped their banners and flags and separated.

Total mayhem penetrated the demonstration when the word 'Gun' spread like wildfire. Any thoughts of entering the conference facility died when the knowledge that a cop had a gun rippled through the mass.

They ran to the left, to the right, and then raced towards the car park where the vans and minibuses were parked. They had mistaken a terrorist's weapon for a cop's gun. Hundreds of people sprinted to get out of the way.

It was a cop with a gun. He'd dropped the gun. Why did he have a gun? Was the cop going to shoot them? How many more cops had guns aimed at them?

Glancing across at Boyd and Yak, Bannerman kept on running into the mass pushing people out of his way and determined to get through the war zone alive.

Oblivious to the events taking place, Boyd and Zak played their game. One wanted to stop an assassination attempt; the other was determined to carry out his orders.

'Who sent you here?' from Boyd.

'Malik!'

'All of you?' voiced Boyd sensing a change in Zak's disposition.

'No! The others drowned in the sea.'

'Why did Malik send you?'

'To kill people at the conference and stop the Anglo-Nigerian agreement taking place. Malik does not want western education in Africa.'

'He's Boko Haram, isn't he? Boko Haram means Western education is forbidden.'

'They want their Islamic state as well. You are trying to help me, I know,' said Zak. 'But step away. I don't want to kill you. It's the others I must kill, or else. I know where the conference hotel is. That's where I'm headed. Get out of my way.'

'You said you must kill or else, Zak. Or else what?'

'Good Mister Policeman, step away. I'm going to press the trigger now.'

'I'll tell you what,' said Boyd. 'Malik kidnapped your children from school and then took Yolanda from your home in Sangari, didn't he? I know, Zak. I know why you are here.'

'Malik will kill my wife and children if I don't kill myself and those people at the conference. I'm going to save the lives of my wife and my children. They are more important than politicians in a conference room. Get out of my way.'

Zak tried to sidestep Boyd and took another few steps forward in the process, but Boyd matched him.

'I have a friend out there, Zak. He's on the end of the phone. I'm waiting for a call from him.'

'Your people are going to kill me. Look at them. Abe told me I am wanted for murder. I didn't push that cop off the train I tried to save him.'

'I know, they told you lies, Zak, I met the policeman. He's alive thanks to you, Zak. I've already told you. Weren't you listening or are you lost and confused? You saved him because you loosened his trousers from the stanchion on the train and he fell away otherwise he might have been dragged along for miles and broken his back. Thank you, Zak. You're not a true killer, Zak. You are a proxy bomber.'

'A what?'

'A proxy bomber! It means someone is forcing you to do something because they've kidnapped your family. I know, I'm right, aren't I, Zak? Now take your finger off the button and let go of the trigger, Zak.'

Bannerman was still sprinting through the crowd and approaching the woods. The crowd was dispersing, now panic-stricken at the thought of police coming at them with guns. It was pandemonium on the banks of Ullswater.

'No trace of Kareem,' from Anthea to the sniper team on the radio network.

'I'm not going to kill you, Zak,' continued Boyd. 'I believe you, Zak. I believe what you told me. Malik made you do this. You've been forced into it.'

Bannerman was almost within reach of Kareem.

Kareem was holding a mobile phone. He was tapping the screen. He was making a call.

'It's no good,' wept Zak. 'They told me if I didn't do it, they could remotely active the bomb.'

'Remotely activate? How?' probed Boyd.

'With a mobile phone,' replied Zak.

Kareem's fingers tapped the screen. He looked up.

Bannerman drew his pistol whilst still on the run.

Kareem's mouth dropped open. His finger rose to hit the last number.

Bannerman fired twice shooting Kareem dead.

The mobile phone fell to the ground, the number incomplete.

Bannerman pointed his pistol at the mobile and fired two shots into the screen. The mobile exploded. The signal had gone. The device was safe.

"Tango Three Kareem is down,' radioed Bannerman. A mobile phone remote activation is denied. Boyd! Boyd! Did you get that?'

'Permission!' rattled over the radio network. 'Permission to speak. It's Major Anderson in Chad.'

'Patching you through,' from Ricky. 'Stand by! Guvnor! I've got Chad on the line!'

'I'm listening,' replied Boyd!

'Boyd!' from Anderson. 'Are you there, Boyd?'

'Go ahead,' replied Boyd.

'It's Anderson in Adjildele. Malik is dead. Zak's family has been rescued.'

'What are their names?' shouted Boyd.

'Yolanda Zakaria! The boys are Hassan and Kayode! His daughter is called Yetunde! I repeat, Malik is dead. Zak's wife and kids were kidnapped by Malik and the Boko Haram men from the swamp. He's a proxy bomb, Boyd. It's a proxy bomb attack.'

'Got that,' replied Boyd. 'Did you hear that, Zak? Hassan, Kayode, Yetunde and Yolanda are all safe. Did you hear that, Zak?'

'I needn't kill anyone.'

'That's right. It's all over, Zak.'

Zak wobbled, lost his balance with the shock of it all, and fell into Boyd's arms, weeping, confused, distraught and exhausted.

'It's over, Zak. Just don't move. Stand still and I'll help you take off that vest. Now just put the trigger down and we'll get you out of the vest.'

Dropping to his knees, Zak handed Boyd the detonating trigger as Bannerman appeared at Boyd's side and said, 'Here, let me help you. Easy now, Zak. Lie still! Don't move! This is going to take some time but easy does it, okay?'

'Okay! Yeah! I'm okay. We're all okay.'

'Commander Boyd! Sitrep!' from Maude Black.

'Incident closed,' replied Boyd. 'All secure!'

'Thank the Lord,' replied the Home Secretary. 'Well done!'

'I'm not impressed,' from Butler: The Defence Secretary. 'Boyd refused to obey a lawful order from Her Majesty's Government. What you perceive to be good police work is incorrect. The Commander was told to shoot the man. He failed to obey the order.'

Boyd snapped, 'I swore allegiance to the crown, not the government of the day. Now if there's nothing else, I've work to do before I go home to see my wife and kids.'

Boyd tore the headset off and threw it to the ground where the last transmission was loud enough to be heard, 'Goddamn you Boyd! Goddamn you for your bloody insolence.'

Maude intervened with, 'The matter concerning the conduct of Commander Boyd is closed with the thanks of myself and Her Majesty's Government. Butler, you are relieved from your post.'

'What! You can't do that to me,' replied Butler.

In Butler's office in Whitehall, the door opened and Detective Inspector Joe Harkness walked in and said, 'But I can. Dennis Butler, I am arresting you on suspicion of committing offences under the Official Secrets Act. You do not have to say anything. But, it may harm your defence if you do not mention when questioned something which you later rely on in court. Anything you do say may be given in evidence.'

'What?' replied a stunned and confused Butler.

'You heard me,' replied Joe Harkness. 'You're under arrest and I will tell you now that my colleagues are at an apartment in South London arresting Ester Abara for offences under the same act. The game's up, Mr Butler.' Turning to colleagues behind him, Harkness declared, 'Take him away.'

Within minutes Ester Abara and Dennis Butler were in custody, Zak Zakaria was secure, the suicide vest was removed from his body and made safe, and a sense of calm descended once again on Lake Ullswater.

~

Chapter Nineteen
~

France
One week later.

The taxi was headed out on the A16. It was the popular coast road from Calais to Dunkirk. In the rear of the taxi, a wealthy man gazed nonchalantly out of the window as the world passed by. He smoked a huge Havana cigar whilst dripping two gold necklaces of unequal proportion from his oversized neck. Each of the man's chubby fingers wore a gold ring, some of them were studded with precious diamonds of unknown value. The cut of his suit was elegance personified, his shirt and tie were of silk and his leather shoes were highly polished. The man oozed power as he sat comfortably in the rear of the vehicle.

The taxi bypassed Dunkirk and then headed towards the sea following the road to Bray-Dunes. The commune was situated in the Nord department in northern France, Close to the Belgian border, Bray-Dunes was the northernmost commune and the northernmost point in all of France.

A mobile phone rang and the cigar-smoking passenger answered with, 'My darling, I will be home very shortly. I have a surprise for you.' The conversation continued and the man reached inside his suit jacket and removed a velvet box containing a diamond necklace. He opened the box, appreciated the expensive jewellery and said, 'You're going to love it. See you soon.'

Smiling happily, gloriously independent, secure and a constant enigma, Louis Martin pocketed the necklace and then clung to the roof strap when a thirty two-ton articulated wagon emerged at speed from a side road and ploughed into the side of the taxi.

The taxi overturned.

The wagon stopped, reversed, and drove once again into the taxi pushing it towards the cliffs and the sea.

There was one long constant scream from Louis Martin when the taxi careered over the edge of the cliff and splashed down into the roaring waves that were the English Channel.

The man who had made millions from illegal trafficking was no more. He died in the sea that had been his office and place of work for over a decade.

The man who was driving the articulated wagon braked hard, stopped, and then placed the vehicle into first gear. He released the clutch and as the vehicle slowly gathered speed and headed for the cliffs, he jumped from the vehicle.

The wagon plunged into the English Channel.

The man turned his back and walked away. A Citroen car drew up almost immediately. The back door opened, and the wagon driver jumped in. The Citroen drove away leaving a clear road.

It was the end of the Louis Martin regime.

In the office of the Special Crime Unit in London, Boyd reflected on the mistakes he had made, the foolish hero he had become, and the whereabouts of the one who had got away scot-free. The unit had failed to identify the rider of the black Kawasaki motorcycle who had laid down the bomb at Pooley Bridge. The bomber was still at large It was a reminder that out there, on the streets of England, a terrorist walked free and unknown. There was still work to be done and evil to defeat.

In N'Djamena, Roger Buckley strolled casually to his office for another day's work as Britain's lone MI6 officer in Chad. Today, he was a happy spy because recent news had congratulated him on a job well done with regards to Zak Zakaria.

Roger reflected on Sangari, Lake Chad, and the misty swamps that dominated that part of the country. The mist rose from the depths of the swamp and gradually spread its restless blind tentacles to create a silent white blanket. The spirit of the mist wanted no more than to govern the downtrodden everglades in which it had been born. The spectre was a dull grey colour, to begin with, but once the haze was established a silvery-white mist fully emerged from the swamp and concealed the precarious pathways that crisscrossed the savannah.

It was such a dangerous forbidding place but the lake was dying now, retreating into itself for no apparent reason other than a plethora of explanations offered by the scientific community.

Elsewhere, a man walked with his newly arrived wife and children by a lake in Cumbria.

The water splashed when the first flat stone of the day skimmed across the surface before gradually sinking to the bottom of the lake.

A child bent down and copied his father. Then two more children mimicked their father and tried to skim stones across the lake.

The man held the woman's hand and looked into her eyes saying, 'Yolanda, we're safe now. This is our new home. It's beautiful. They call it Ullswater. We're going to be safe now.'

She smiled. They kissed and were happy in the knowledge that the Zakaria family were together once more, safe from the ravages of war, terrorism, and the evils of the men from the swamps.

~

The End.
Until the next time... *Paul Anthony*

~

Author's Notes
~
Boko Haram

Sometimes fiction can run close to fact.

Boko Haram is a terrorist organization based in northeastern Nigeria. It is also active in Chad, Niger, and northern Cameroon. Founded by Mohammed Yusuf in 2002, Boko Haram was led by Abubakar Shekau from 2009 until he died in 2021. In 2016, the group split, resulting in the emergence of a hostile faction known as the Islamic State's West Africa Province. (Referred to in this book as ISWAP).

When the group was first formed, its main goal was to 'purify' Islam in northern Nigeria and overthrow the Nigerian government. The group formerly aligned itself with the Islamic State of Iraq and the Levant and is famous for its brutality. Since 2009, Boko Haram has killed tens of thousands of people in frequent attacks against the police, armed forces and civilians. It has resulted in the deaths of more than 300,000 children and displaced 2.3 million individuals from their homes. Between 2012 and 2018, the Global Terrorism Index showed Boko Haram to be the deadliest terror group in the world.

After its founding in 2002, Boko Haram's increasing radicalisation led to the suppression operation by the Nigerian military and the killing of its leader Mohammed Yusuf in July 2009. Its unexpected resurgence, following a mass prison break in September 2010 in Bauchi, was accompanied by increasingly sophisticated attacks, initially against soft targets, but progressing in 2011 to include suicide bombings of police buildings and the United Nations office in Abuja. The government's establishment of a state of emergency at the beginning of 2012, extended in the following year to cover the entire northeast of Nigeria, led to an increase in both security force cases of abuse and militant attacks.

Of the 2.3 million people displaced by the conflict since May 2013, at least 250,000 left Nigeria and fled to Cameroon, Chad or Niger. Boko Haram killed over 6,600 people in 2014. The group has carried out massacres including the killing by fire of 59 schoolboys in February 2014 and mass abductions including the kidnapping of 276 schoolgirls in Chibok, Borno State, Nigeria, in April 2014. Corruption in the security services and human rights abuses committed by them have hampered efforts to counter the unrest.

In mid-2014, the militants gained control of swaths of territory in and around their home state of Borno, estimated at 50,000 square kilometres (20,000 square miles) in January 2015, but did not capture the state capital, Maiduguri, where the group was originally based. On 7 March 2015, Boko Haram's leader Abubakar Shekau pledged allegiance to the Islamic State of Iraq and the Levant. According to the BBC, due to internal disputes between the two groups, hundreds of terrorists left Boko Haram and formed 'Islamic State's West Africa Province'.

In September 2015, the Director of Information at the Defence Headquarters of Nigeria announced that all Boko Haram camps had been destroyed but attacks from the group continue. In 2019, the president of Nigeria, Muhammadu Buhari claimed that Boko Haram was 'technically defeated'. However, attacks by Boko Haram have escalated and it still poses a major threat as of 2022.

The name 'Boko Haram' is usually translated as 'Western education is forbidden'. Haram is from the Arabic meaning 'forbidden'; and the Hausa word Boko means 'fake' which is used to refer to secular Western education. In a 2009 statement, they denounced that translation as the work of the 'infidel media', claiming the true translation is 'Western Civilization is forbidden', and that they are not 'opposed to formal education coming from the West' but 'believe in the supremacy of Islamic culture (not education)'.

Some analysts have emphasized economic causes as a factor in Boko Haram's success. Wealth in Nigeria is concentrated amongst members of a small political elite, mainly in the Christian south of the country. Nigeria is Africa's biggest economy, but 60% of its population of approximately 175 million live on less than one American dollar a day.

In 2018, the first UK-Nigeria security and defence partnership came about.

The National Security Advisors of the United Kingdom and Nigeria hosted the inaugural dialogue in support of a Security and Defence Partnership which took place between 31 January and 2 February 2022, in London. Defence Staff Talks and a cross-government forum on Human Rights took place in parallel.

The Governments of both countries affirmed their commitment to deepen the partnership in the face of complex and evolving global threats that do not respect international borders including terrorism, conflict, human trafficking, serious and organised crimes, drug trafficking, cyber-crime and piracy. The United Kingdom and Nigeria agree on the importance of police reform in Nigeria. In this regard, Nigeria affirms its commitment to implement the Police Act 2020 which includes provisions to strengthen human rights measures and accountability and responsive e policing.

The two countries are on a journey to bring peace and stability to the area.

~

Printed in Great Britain
by Amazon